A DEADLY AFFAIR

The Agatha Christie Collection

The Man in the Brown Suit
The Secret of Chimneys
The Seven Dials Mystery
The Mysterious Mr. Quin
The Sittaford Mystery
Parker Pyne Investigates
Why Didn't They Ask Evans?
Murder Is Easy
The Regatta Mystery and Other Stories
And Then There Were None
Towards Zero
Death Comes as the End
Sparkling Cyanide
The Witness for the Prosecution and Other Stories
Crooked House
Three Blind Mice and Other Stories
They Came to Baghdad
Destination Unknown
Ordeal by Innocence
Double Sin and Other Stories
The Pale Horse
Star over Bethlehem: Poems and Holiday Stories
Endless Night
Passenger to Frankfurt
The Golden Ball and Other Stories
The Mousetrap and Other Plays
The Harlequin Tea Set

The Hercule Poirot Mysteries

The Mysterious Affair at Styles
The Murder on the Links
Poirot Investigates
The Murder of Roger Ackroyd
The Big Four
The Mystery of the Blue Train
Peril at End House
Lord Edgware Dies
Murder on the Orient Express
Three Act Tragedy
Death in the Clouds
The A.B.C. Murders
Murder in Mesopotamia
Cards on the Table
Murder in the Mews and Other Stories
Dumb Witness
Death on the Nile
Appointment with Death
Hercule Poirot's Christmas
Sad Cypress
One, Two, Buckle My Shoe
Evil Under the Sun
Five Little Pigs
The Hollow
The Labors of Hercules
Taken at the Flood
The Under Dog and Other Stories
Mrs. McGinty's Dead
After the Funeral
Hickory Dickory Dock
Dead Man's Folly
Cat Among the Pigeons
The Clocks
Third Girl
Hallowe'en Party
Elephants Can Remember
Curtain: Poirot's Last Case

The Miss Marple Mysteries

The Murder at the Vicarage
The Body in the Library
The Moving Finger
A Murder Is Announced
They Do It with Mirrors
A Pocket Full of Rye
4:50 from Paddington
The Mirror Crack'd
A Caribbean Mystery
At Bertram's Hotel
Nemesis
Sleeping Murder
Miss Marple: The Complete Short Story Collection

The Tommy and Tuppence Mysteries

The Secret Adversary
Partners in Crime
N or M?
By the Pricking of My Thumbs
Postern of Fate

AGATHA CHRISTIE

A DEADLY AFFAIR

UNEXPECTED LOVE STORIES FROM THE QUEEN OF MYSTERY

WILLIAM MORROW
An Imprint of HarperCollins*Publishers*

The text in this collection was previously published in a different format.
Pages 259–263 constitute an extension of the copyright page.

HarperCollins books may be purchased for educational, business, or sales promotional use. For information, please email the Special Markets Department at SPsales@harpercollins.com.

FIRST EDITION

Designed by Diahann Sturge

Library of Congress Cataloging-in-Publication Data has been applied for.

ISBN 978-0-06-314234-3

21 22 23 24 25 26 LSC 10 9 8 7 6 5 4 3 2 1

Contents

The King of Clubs	1
The Face of Helen	22
Death on the Nile	45
Death by Drowning	63
The Double Clue	88
Finessing the King/ The Gentleman Dressed in Newspaper	101
Fruitful Sunday	120
Wasps' Nest	133
The Case of the Caretaker	145
The Man in the Mist	161
The Case of the Rich Woman	182
Magnolia Blossom	201
The Love Detectives	224
Affairs of the Heart: Agatha's Early Courtships	251
Bibliography	259

The King of Clubs

I

"Truth," I observed, laying aside the *Daily Newsmonger,* "is stranger than fiction!"

The remark was not, perhaps, an original one. It appeared to incense my friend. Tilting his egg-shaped head on one side, the little man carefully flicked an imaginary fleck of dust from his carefully creased trousers, and observed: "How profound! What a thinker is my friend Hastings!"

Without displaying any annoyance at this quite uncalled-for gibe, I tapped the sheet I had laid aside.

"You've read this morning's paper?"

"I have. And after reading it, I folded it anew symmetrically. I did not cast it on the floor as you have done, with your so lamentable absence of order and method."

(That is the worst of Poirot. Order and Method are his gods. He goes so far as to attribute all his success to them.)

"Then you saw the account of the murder of Henry Reedburn, the impresario? It was that which prompted my remark. Not only is truth stranger than fiction—it is more dramatic. Think of that solid middle-class English family, the Oglanders. Father and mother, son and daughter, typical of thousands of families all over this country. The men of the family go to the city every day; the women look after the house. Their lives are perfectly peaceful, and utterly monotonous. Last night they were sitting in their neat suburban drawing room at Daisymead, Streatham, playing bridge. Suddenly, without any warning, the French window bursts open, and a woman staggers into the room. Her grey satin frock is marked with a crimson stain. She utters one word, "Murder!" before she sinks to the ground insensible. It is possible that they recognize her from her pictures as Valerie Saintclair, the famous dancer who has lately taken London by storm!"

"Is this your eloquence, or that of the *Daily Newsmonger?*" inquired Poirot.

"The *Daily Newsmonger* was in a hurry to go to press, and contented itself with bare facts. But the dramatic possibilities of the story struck me at once."

Poirot nodded thoughtfully. "Wherever there is human nature, there is drama. *But*—it is not always just where you think it is. Remember that. Still, I too am interested in the case, since it is likely that I shall be connected with it."

"Indeed?"

"Yes. A gentleman rang me up this morning, and made an appointment with me on behalf of Prince Paul of Maurania."

"But what has that to do with it?"

"You do not read your pretty little English scandal-papers. The ones with the funny stories, and 'a little mouse has heard—' or 'a little bird would like to know—' See here."

I followed his short stubby finger along the paragraph: "—whether the foreign prince and the famous dancer are *really* affinities! And if the lady likes her new diamond ring!"

"And now to resume your so dramatic narrative," said Poirot. "Mademoiselle Saintclair had just fainted on the drawing room carpet at Daisymead, you remember."

I shrugged. "As a result of Mademoiselle's first murmured words when she came round, the two male Oglanders stepped out, one to fetch a doctor to attend to the lady, who was evidently suffering terribly from shock, and the other to the police station—whence after telling his story, he accompanied the police to Mon Désir, Mr. Reedburn's magnificent villa, which is situated at no great distance from Daisymead. There they found the great man, who by the way suffers from a somewhat unsavoury reputation, lying in the library with the back of his head cracked open like an eggshell."

"I have cramped your style," said Poirot kindly. "Forgive me, I pray . . . Ah, here is M. le Prince!"

Our distinguished visitor was announced under the title of Count Feodor. He was a strange-looking youth, tall, eager, with a weak chin, the famous Mauranberg mouth, and the dark fiery eyes of a fanatic.

"M. Poirot?"

My friend bowed.

"Monsieur, I am in terrible trouble, greater than I can well express—"

Poirot waved his hand. "I comprehend your anxiety. Mademoiselle Saintclair is a very dear friend, is it not so?"

The prince replied simply: "I hope to make her my wife."

Poirot sat up in his chair, and his eyes opened.

The prince continued: "I should not be the first of my family to make a morganatic marriage. My brother Alexander has also defied the Emperor. We are living now in more enlightened days, free from the old caste-prejudice. Besides, Mademoiselle Saintclair, in actual fact, is quite my equal in rank. You have heard hints as to her history?"

"There are many romantic stories of her origin—not an uncommon thing with famous dancers. I have heard that she is the daughter of an Irish charwoman, also the story which makes her mother a Russian grand duchess."

"The first story is, of course, nonsense," said the young man. "But the second is true. Valerie, though bound to secrecy, has let me guess as much. Besides, she proves it unconsciously in a thousand ways. I believe in heredity, M. Poirot."

"I too believe in heredity," said Poirot thoughtfully. "I have seen some strange things in connection with it—*moi qui vous parle* . . . But to business, M. le Prince. What do you want of me? What do you fear? I may speak freely, may I not? Is there anything to connect Mademoiselle Saintclair with the crime? She knew Reedburn of course?"

"Yes. He professed to be in love with her."

"And she?"

"She would have nothing to say to him."

Poirot looked at him keenly. "Had she any reason to fear him?"

The young man hesitated. "There was an incident. You know Zara, the clairvoyant?"

"No."

"She is wonderful. You should consult her some time. Valerie and I went to see her last week. She read the cards for us. She spoke to Valerie of trouble—of gathering clouds; then she turned up the last card—the covering card, they call it. It was the king of clubs. She said to Valerie: 'Beware. There is a man who holds you in his power. You fear him—you are in great danger through him. You know whom I mean?' Valerie was white to the lips. She nodded and said: 'Yes, yes, I know.' Shortly afterwards we left. Zara's last words to Valerie were: 'Beware of the king of clubs. Danger threatens you!' I questioned Valerie. She would tell me nothing—assured me that all was well. But now, after last night, I am more sure than ever that in the king of clubs Valerie saw Reedburn, and that he was the man she feared."

The Prince paused abruptly. "Now you understand my agitation when I opened the paper this morning. Supposing Valerie, in a fit of madness—oh, it is impossible!"

Poirot rose from his seat, and patted the young man kindly on the shoulder. "Do not distress yourself, I beg of you. Leave it in my hands."

"You will go to Streatham? I gather she is still there, at Daisymead—prostrated by the shock."

"I will go at once."

"I have arranged matters—through the embassy. You will be allowed access everywhere."

"Then we will depart—Hastings, you will accompany me? Au revoir, M. le Prince."

II

Mon Désir was an exceptionally fine villa, thoroughly modern and comfortable. A short carriage-drive led up to it from the road, and beautiful gardens extended behind the house for some acres.

On mentioning Prince Paul's name, the butler who answered the door at once took us to the scene of the tragedy. The library was a magnificent room, running from back to front of the whole building, with a window at either end, one giving on the front carriage-drive, and the other on the garden. It was in the recess of the latter that the body had lain. It had been removed not long before, the police having concluded their examination.

"That is annoying," I murmured to Poirot. "Who knows what clues they may have destroyed?"

My little friend smiled. "Eh—Eh! How often must I tell you that clues come from *within?* In the little grey cells of the brain lies the solution of every mystery."

He turned to the butler. "I suppose, except for the removal of the body, the room has not been touched?"

"No, sir. It's just as it was when the police came up last night."

"These curtains, now. I see they pull right across the window recess. They are the same in the other window. Were they drawn last night?"

"Yes, sir, I draw them every night."

"Then Reedburn must have drawn them back himself?"

"I suppose so, sir."

"Did you know your master expected a visitor last night?"

"He did not say so, sir. But he gave orders he was not to be disturbed after dinner. You see, sir, there is a door leading out of the library on to the terrace at the side of the house. He could have admitted anyone that way."

"Was he in the habit of doing that?"

The butler coughed discreetly. "I believe so, sir."

Poirot strode to the door in question. It was unlocked. He stepped through it on to the terrace which joined the drive on the right; on the left it led up to a red brick wall.

"The fruit garden, sir. There is a door leading into it farther along, but it was always locked at six o'clock."

Poirot nodded, and reentered the library, the butler following.

"Did you hear nothing of last night's events?"

"Well, sir, we heard voices in the library, a little before nine. But that wasn't unusual, especially being a lady's voice. But of course, once we were all in the servants' hall, right the other side, we didn't hear anything at all. And then, about eleven o'clock, the police came."

"How many voices did you hear?"

"I couldn't say, sir. I only noticed the lady's."

"Ah!"

"I beg pardon, sir, but Dr. Ryan is still in the house, if you would care to see him."

We jumped at the suggestion, and in a few minutes the doctor, a cheery, middle-aged man, joined us, and gave Poirot all the information he required. Reedburn had been lying near the window, his head by the marble window seat. There were two wounds, one between the eyes, and the other, the fatal one, on the back of the head.

"He was lying on his back?"

"Yes. There is the mark." He pointed to a small dark stain on the floor.

"Could not the blow on the back of the head have been caused by his striking the floor?"

"Impossible. Whatever the weapon was, it penetrated some distance into the skull."

Poirot looked thoughtfully in front of him. In the embrasure of each window was a carved marble seat, the arms being fashioned in the form of a lion's head. A light came into Poirot's eyes. "Supposing he had fallen backwards on this projecting lion's head, and slipped from there to the ground. Would not that cause a wound such as you describe?"

"Yes, it would. But the angle at which he was lying makes that theory impossible. And besides there could not fail to be traces of blood on the marble of the seat."

"Unless they were washed away?"

The doctor shrugged his shoulders. "That is hardly likely. It would be to no one's advantage to give an accident the appearance of murder."

"Quite so," acquiesced Poirot. "Could either of the blows have been struck by a woman, do you think?"

"Oh, quite out of the question, I should say. You are thinking of Mademoiselle Saintclair, I suppose?"

"I think of no one in particular until I am sure," said Poirot gently.

He turned his attention to the open French window, and the doctor continued:

"It is through here that Mademoiselle Saintclair fled. You can just catch a glimpse of Daisymead between the trees. Of course, there are many houses nearer to the front of the house on the road, but as it happens, Daisymead, though some distance away, is the only house visible this side."

"Thank you for your amiability, Doctor," said Poirot. "Come, Hastings, we will follow the footsteps of Mademoiselle."

III

Poirot led the way down through the garden, out through an iron gate, across a short stretch of green and in through the garden gate of Daisymead, which was an unpretentious little house in about half an acre of ground. There was a small flight of steps leading up to a French window. Poirot nodded in their direction.

"That is the way Mademoiselle Saintclair went. For us, who have not her urgency to plead, it will be better to go round to the front door."

A maid admitted us and took us into the drawing room, then went in search of Mrs. Oglander. The room had evidently not been touched since the night before. The ashes were still in the grate, and the bridge table was still in the centre of the room, with a dummy exposed, and the hands thrown down. The place was somewhat overloaded with gimcrack ornaments, and a good many family portraits of surpassing ugliness adorned the walls.

Poirot gazed at them more leniently than I did, and straightened one or two that were hanging a shade askew. "*La famille,* it is a strong tie, is it not? Sentiment, it takes the place of beauty."

I agreed, my eyes being fixed on a family group comprising a gentleman with whiskers, a lady with a high "front" of hair, a solid, thick-set boy, and two little girls tied up with a good many unnecessary bows of ribbon. I took this to be the Oglander family in earlier days, and studied it with interest.

The door opened, and a young woman came in. Her dark hair was neatly arranged, and she wore a drab-coloured sportscoat and a tweed skirt.

She looked at us inquiringly. Poirot stepped forward. "Miss Oglander? I regret to derange you—especially after all you have been through. The whole affair must have been most disturbing."

"It has been rather upsetting," admitted the young lady cautiously. I began to think that the elements of drama were wasted on Miss Oglander, that her lack of imagination rose superior to any tragedy. I was confirmed in this belief as she continued: "I must apologize for the state this room is in. Servants get so foolishly excited."

"It was here that you were sitting last night, *n'est-ce pas?*"

"Yes, we were playing bridge after supper, when—"

"Excuse me—how long had you been playing?"

"Well—" Miss Oglander considered. "I really can't say. I suppose it must have been about ten o'clock. We had had several rubbers, I know."

"And you yourself were sitting—where?"

"Facing the window. I was playing with my mother and had gone one no trump. Suddenly, without any warning, the window burst open, and Miss Saintclair staggered into the room."

"You recognized her?"

"I had a vague idea her face was familiar."

"She is still here, is she not?"

"Yes, but she refuses to see anyone. She is still quite prostrated."

"I think she will see me. Will you tell her that I am here at the express request of Prince Paul of Maurania?"

I fancied that the mention of a royal prince rather shook Miss Oglander's imperturbable calm. But she left the room on her errand without any further remark, and returned almost immediately to say that Mademoiselle Saintclair would see us in her room.

We followed her upstairs, and into a fair-sized light bedroom. On a couch by the window a woman was lying who turned her head as we entered. The contrast between the two women struck me at once, the more so as in actual features and colouring they were not unalike—but oh, the difference! Not a look, not a gesture of Valerie Saintclair's but expressed drama. She seemed to exhale an atmosphere of romance. A scarlet flannel dressing gown covered her feet—a homely garment in all conscience; but the charm of her personality invested it with an exotic flavour, and it seemed an Eastern robe of glowing colour.

Her large dark eyes fastened themselves on Poirot.

"You come from Paul?" Her voice matched her appearance—it was full and languid.

"Yes, mademoiselle. I am here to serve him—and you."

"What do you want to know?"

"Everything that happened last night. *But everything!*"

She smiled rather wearily.

"Do you think I should lie? I am not stupid. I see well enough that there can be no concealment. He held a secret of mine, that man who is dead. He threatened me with it.

For Paul's sake, I endeavoured to make terms with him. I could not risk losing Paul . . . Now that he is dead, I am safe. But for all that, I did not kill him."

Poirot shook his head with a smile. "It is not necessary to tell me that, mademoiselle. Now recount to me what happened last night."

"I offered him money. He appeared to be willing to treat with me. He appointed last night at nine o'clock. I was to go to Mon Désir. I knew the place; I had been there before. I was to go round to the side door into the library, so that the servants should not see me."

"Excuse me, mademoiselle, but were you not afraid to trust yourself alone there at night?"

Was it my fancy, or was there a momentary pause before she answered?

"Perhaps I was. But you see, there was no one I could ask to go with me. And I was desperate. Reedburn admitted me to the library. Oh, that man! I am glad he is dead! He played with me, as a cat does with a mouse. He taunted me. I begged and implored him on my knees. I offered him every jewel I have. All in vain! Then he named his own terms. Perhaps you can guess what they were. I refused. I told him what I thought of him. I raved at him. He remained calmly smiling. And then, as I fell to silence at last, there was a sound—from behind the curtain in the window . . . He heard it too. He strode to the curtains and flung them wide apart. There was a man there, hiding—a dreadful-looking man, a sort of tramp. He struck at Mr. Reedburn—then he struck again, and he went down. The tramp clutched at me with his bloodstained hand. I tore myself free, slipped through the window, and ran for my life. Then I perceived the lights in this house, and made for them. The blinds were up, and I saw some people playing bridge. I almost fell into the room. I just managed to gasp out 'Murder!' and then everything went black—"

"Thank you, mademoiselle. It must have been a great shock to your nervous system. As to this tramp, could you describe him? Do you remember what he was wearing?"

"No—it was all so quick. But I should know the man anywhere. His face is burnt in on my brain."

"Just one more question, mademoiselle. The curtains of the *other* window, the one giving on the drive, were they drawn?"

For the first time a puzzled expression crept over the dancer's face. She seemed to be trying to remember.

"Eh bien, mademoiselle?"

"I think—I am almost sure—yes, quite sure! They were *not* drawn."

"That is curious, since the other ones were. No matter. It is, I dare say, of no great importance. You are remaining here long, mademoiselle?"

"The doctor thinks I shall be fit to return to town to-morrow." She looked round the room. Miss Oglander had gone out. "These people, they are very kind—but they are not of my world. I shock them! And to me—well, I am not fond of the *bourgeoisie!*"

A faint note of bitterness underlay her words.

Poirot nodded. "I understand. I hope I have not fatigued you unduly with my questions?"

"Not at all, monsieur. I am only too anxious Paul should know all as soon as possible."

"Then I will wish you good day, mademoiselle."

As Poirot was leaving the room, he paused, and pounced on a pair of patent-leather slippers. "Yours, mademoiselle?"

"Yes, monsieur. They have just been cleaned and brought up."

"Ah!" said Poirot, as we descended the stairs. "It seems that the domestics are not too excited to clean shoes, though they forget a grate. Well, *mon ami,* at first there appeared to be one or two points of interest, but I fear, I very much fear, that we must regard the case as finished. It all seems straightforward enough."

"And the murderer?"

"Hercule Poirot does not hunt down tramps," replied my friend grandiloquently.

IV

Miss Oglander met us in the hall. "If you will wait in the drawing room a minute, Mamma would like to speak to you."

The room was still untouched, and Poirot idly gathered up the cards, shuffling them with his tiny, fastidiously groomed hands.

"Do you know what I think, my friend?"

"No?" I said eagerly.

"I think that Miss Oglander made a mistake in going one no trump. She should have gone three spades."

"Poirot! You are the limit."

"*Mon Dieu,* I cannot always be talking blood and thunder!"

Suddenly he stiffened: "Hastings—*Hastings*. See! The king of clubs is missing from the pack!"

"Zara!" I cried.

"Eh?" He did not seem to understand my allusion. Mechanically he stacked the cards and put them away in their cases. His face was very grave.

"Hastings," he said at last, "I, Hercule Poirot, have come near to making a big mistake—a very big mistake."

I gazed at him, impressed, but utterly uncomprehending.

"We must begin again, Hastings. Yes, we must begin again. But this time we shall not err."

He was interrupted by the entrance of a handsome middle-aged lady. She carried some household books in her hand. Poirot bowed to her.

"Do I understand, sir, that you are a friend of—er—Miss Saintclair's?"

"I come from a friend of hers, madame."

"Oh, I see. I thought perhaps—"

Poirot suddenly waved brusquely at the window.

"Your blinds were not pulled down last night?"

"No—I suppose that is why Miss Saintclair saw the light so plainly."

"There was moonlight last night. I wonder that you did not see Mademoiselle Saintclair from your seat here facing the windows?"

"I suppose we were engrossed with our game. Nothing like this has ever happened before to us."

"I can quite believe that, madame. And I will put your mind at rest. Mademoiselle Saintclair is leaving tomorrow."

"Oh!" The good lady's face cleared.

"And I will wish you good morning, madame."

A servant was cleaning the steps as we went out of the front door. Poirot addressed her.

"Was it you who cleaned the shoes of the young lady upstairs?"

The maid shook her head. "No, sir. I don't think they've been cleaned."

"Who cleaned them, then?" I inquired of Poirot, as we walked down the road.

"Nobody. They did not need cleaning."

"I grant that walking on the road or path on a fine night would not soil them. But surely after going through the long grass of the garden, they would have been soiled and stained."

"Yes," said Poirot with a curious smile. "In that case, I agree, they would have been stained."

"But—"

"Have patience a little half hour, my friend. We are going back to Mon Désir."

V

The butler looked surprised at our reappearance, but offered no objection to our returning to the library.

"Hi, that's the wrong window, Poirot," I cried as he made for the one overlooking the carriage-drive.

"I think not, my friend. See here." He pointed to the marble lion's head. On it was a faint discoloured smear. He shifted his finger and pointed to a similar stain on the polished floor.

"Someone struck Reedburn a blow with his clenched fist between the eyes. He fell backward on this projecting bit of marble, then slipped to the floor. Afterwards, he was dragged across the floor to the other window, and laid there instead, but not quite at the same angle, as the Doctor's evidence told us."

"But why? It seems utterly unnecessary."

"On the contrary, it was essential. Also, it is the key to the murderer's identity—though, by the way, he had no intention of killing Reedburn, and so it is hardly permissible to call him a murderer. He must be a very strong man!"

"Because of having dragged the body across the floor?"

"Not altogether. It has been an interesting case. I nearly made an imbecile of myself, though."

"Do you mean to say it is over, that you know everything?"

"Yes."

A remembrance smote me. "No," I cried. "There is one thing you do *not* know!"

"And that?"

"You do not know where the missing king of clubs is!"

"Eh? Oh, that is droll! That is very droll, my friend."

"Why?"

"Because it is in my pocket!" He drew it forth with a flourish.

"Oh!" I said, rather crestfallen. "Where did you find it? Here?"

"There was nothing sensational about it. It had simply not been taken out with the other cards. It was in the box."

"H'm! All the same, it gave you an idea, didn't it?"

"Yes, my friend. I present my respects to His Majesty."

"And to Madame Zara!"

"Ah, yes—to the lady also."

"Well, what are we going to do now?"

"We are going to return to town. But I must have a few words with a certain lady at Daisymead first."

The same little maid opened the door to us.

"They're all at lunch now, sir—unless it's Miss Saintclair you want to see, and she's resting."

"It will do if I can see Mrs. Oglander for a few minutes. Will you tell her?"

We were led into the drawing room to wait. I had a glimpse of the family in the dining room as we passed, now reinforced by the presence of two heavy, solid-looking men, one with a moustache, the other with a beard also.

In a few minutes Mrs. Oglander came into the room, looking inquiringly at Poirot, who bowed.

"Madame, we, in our country, have a great tenderness, a great respect for the mother. The *mère de famille,* she is everything!"

Mrs. Oglander looked rather astonished at this opening.

"It is for that reason that I have come—to allay a mother's anxiety. The murderer of Mr. Reedburn will not be discovered. Have no fear. I, Hercule Poirot, tell you so. I am right, am I not? Or is it a wife that I must reassure?"

There was a moment's pause. Mrs. Oglander seemed searching Poirot with her eyes. At last she said quietly: "I don't know how you know—but yes, you are right."

Poirot nodded gravely. "That is all, madame. But do not be uneasy. Your English policemen have not the eyes of Hercule Poirot." He tapped the family portrait on the wall with his fingernail.

"You had another daughter once. She is dead, madame?"

Again there was a pause, as she searched him with her eyes. Then she answered: "Yes, she is dead."

"Ah!" said Poirot briskly. "Well, we must return to town. You permit that I return the king of clubs to the pack? It was your only slip. You understand, to have played bridge for an hour or so, with only fifty-one cards—well, no one who knows anything of the game would credit it for a minute! *Bonjour!*"

"And now, my friend," said Poirot as we stepped towards the station, "you see it all!"

"I see nothing! Who killed Reedburn?"

"John Oglander, Junior. I was not quite sure if it was the father or the son, but I fixed on the son as being the stronger and younger of the two. It had to be one of them, because of the window."

"Why?"

"There were four exits from the library—two doors, two windows; but evidently only one would do. Three exits gave on the front, directly or indirectly. The tragedy had to occur in the back window in order to make it appear that Valerie Saintclair came to Daisymead by chance. Really, of course, she fainted, and John Oglander carried her across over his shoulders. That is why I said he must be a strong man."

"Did they go there together, then?"

"Yes. You remember Valerie's hesitation when I asked her if she was not afraid to go alone? John Oglander went with her—which didn't improve Reedburn's temper, I fancy. They quarrelled, and it was probably some insult levelled at Valerie that made Oglander hit him. The rest, you know."

"But why the bridge?"

"Bridge presupposes four players. A simple thing like that carries a lot of conviction. Who would have supposed that there had been only three people in that room all the evening?"

I was still puzzled.

"There's one thing I don't understand. What have the Oglanders to do with the dancer Valerie Saintclair?"

"Ah, that I wonder you did not see. And yet you looked long enough at that picture on the wall—longer than I did. Mrs. Oglander's other daughter may be dead to her family, but the world knows her as Valerie Saintclair!"

"What?"

"Did you not see the resemblance the moment you saw the two sisters together?"

"No," I confessed. "I only thought how extraordinarily dissimilar they were."

"That is because your mind is so open to external romantic impressions, my dear Hastings. The features are almost identical. So is the colouring. The interesting thing is that Valerie is ashamed of her family, and her family is ashamed of her. Nevertheless, in a moment of peril, she turned to her brother for help, and when things went wrong, they all hung together in a remarkable way. Family strength is a marvellous thing. They can all act, that family. That is where Valerie gets her histrionic talent from. I, like Prince Paul, believe in heredity! They deceived *me!* But for a lucky accident, and test question to Mrs. Oglander by which I got her to contradict her daughter's account of how they were sitting, the Oglander family would have put a defeat on Hercule Poirot."

"What shall you tell the Prince?"

"That Valerie could not possibly have committed the crime, and that I doubt if that tramp will ever be found. Also, to convey my compliments to Zara. A curious coincidence, that! I think I shall call this little affair the Adventure of the King of Clubs. What do you think, my friend?"

The Face of Helen

Mr. Satterthwaite was at the Opera and sat alone in his big box on the first tier. Outside the door was a printed card bearing his name. An appreciator and a connoisseur of all the arts, Mr. Satterthwaite was especially fond of good music, and was a regular subscriber to Covent Garden every year, reserving a box for Tuesdays and Fridays throughout the season.

But it was not often that he sat in it alone. He was a gregarious little gentleman, and he liked filling his box with the élite of the great world to which he belonged, and also with the aristocracy of the artistic world in which he was equally at home. He was alone tonight because a Countess had disappointed him. The Countess, besides being a beautiful and celebrated woman, was also a good mother. Her children had been attacked by that common and distressing disease, the mumps, and the Countess remained at home in tearful confabulation with exquisitely starched nurses. Her husband, who had supplied her with the aforementioned children and a title, but who was otherwise a complete nonentity, had seized at the chance to escape. Nothing bored him more than music.

So Mr. Satterthwaite sat alone. *Cavalleria Rusticana* and

Pagliacci were being given that night, and since the first had never appealed to him, he arrived just after the curtain went down, on Santuzza's death agony, in time to glance round the house with practised eyes, before everyone streamed out, bent on paying visits or fighting for coffee or lemonade. Mr. Satterthwaite adjusted his opera glasses, looked round the house, marked down his prey and sallied forth with a well mapped out plan of campaign ahead of him. A plan, however, which he did not put into execution, for just outside his box he cannoned into a tall dark man, and recognized him with a pleasurable thrill of excitement.

"Mr. Quin," cried Mr. Satterthwaite.

He seized his friend warmly by the hand, clutching him as though he feared any minute to see him vanish into thin air.

"You must share my box," said Mr. Satterthwaite determinedly. "You are not with a party?"

"No, I am sitting by myself in the stalls," responded Mr. Quin with a smile.

"Then, that is settled," said Mr. Satterthwaite with a sigh of relief.

His manner was almost comic, had there been anyone to observe it.

"You are very kind," said Mr. Quin.

"Not at all. It is a pleasure. I didn't know you were fond of music?"

"There are reasons why I am attracted to—*Pagliacci*."

"Ah! of course," said Mr. Satterthwaite, nodding sapiently, though, if put to it, he would have found it hard to explain just why he had used that expression. "Of course, you would be."

They went back to the box at the first summons of the bell, and leaning over the front of it, they watched the people returning to the stalls.

"That's a beautiful head," observed Mr. Satterthwaite suddenly.

He indicated with his glasses a spot immediately beneath them in the stalls circle. A girl sat there whose face they could not see—only the pure gold of her hair that fitted with the closeness of a cap till it merged into the white neck.

"A Greek head," said Mr. Satterthwaite reverently. "Pure Greek." He sighed happily. "It's a remarkable thing when you come to think of it—how very few people have hair that *fits* them. It's more noticeable now that everyone is shingled."

"You are so observant," said Mr. Quin.

"I see things," admitted Mr. Satterthwaite. "I do see things. For instance, I picked out that head at once. We must have a look at her face sooner or later. But it won't match, I'm sure. That would be a chance in a thousand."

Almost as the words left his lips, the lights flickered and went down, the sharp rap of the conductor's baton was heard, and the opera began. A new tenor, said to be a second Caruso, was singing that night. He had been referred to by the newspapers as a Jugo Slav, a Czech, an Albanian, a Magyar, and a Bulgarian, with a beautiful impartiality. He had given an extraordinary concert at the Albert Hall, a programme of the folk songs of his native hills, with a specially tuned orchestra. They were in strange half-tones and the would-be musical had pronounced them "too marvellous." Real musicians had reserved judgment, realizing that the ear had to be specially trained and attuned before any criticism was possible. It was quite a relief to some people to find this evening that Yoaschbim could sing in ordinary Italian with all the traditional sobs and quivers.

The curtain went down on the first act and applause burst out vociferously. Mr. Satterthwaite turned to Mr. Quin. He realized that the latter was waiting for him to pronounce judgment, and plumed himself a little. After all, he *knew.* As a critic he was well-nigh infallible.

Very slowly he nodded his head.

"It is the real thing," he said.

"You think so?"

"As fine a voice as Caruso's. People will not recognize that it is so at first, for his technique is not yet perfect. There are ragged edges, a lack of certainty in the attack. But the voice is there—magnificent."

"I went to his concert at the Albert Hall," said Mr. Quin.

"Did you? I could not go."

"He made a wonderful hit with a Shepherd's Song."

"I read about it," said Mr. Satterthwaite. "The refrain ends each time with a high note—a kind of cry. A note midway between A and B flat. Very curious."

Yoaschbim had taken three calls, bowing and smiling. The lights went up and the people began to file out. Mr. Satterthwaite leant over to watch the girl with the golden head. She rose, adjusted her scarf, and turned.

Mr. Satterthwaite caught his breath. There were, he knew, such faces in the world—faces that made history.

The girl moved to the gangway, her companion, a

young man, beside her. And Mr. Satterthwaite noticed how every man in the vicinity looked—and continued to look covertly.

"Beauty!" said Mr. Satterthwaite to himself. "There is such a thing. Not charm, nor attraction, nor magnetism, nor any of the things we talk about so glibly—just sheer beauty. The shape of a face, the line of an eyebrow, the curve of a jaw. He quoted softly under his breath: *"The face that launched a thousand ships."* And for the first time he realized the meaning of those words.

He glanced across at Mr. Quin, who was watching him in what seemed such perfect comprehension that Mr. Satterthwaite felt there was no need for words.

"I've always wondered," he said simply, "what such women were really like."

"You mean?"

"The Helens, the Cleopatras, the Mary Stuarts."

Mr. Quin nodded thoughtfully.

"If we go out," he suggested, "we may—see."

They went out together, and their quest was successful. The pair they were in search of were seated on a lounge halfway up the staircase. For the first time, Mr. Satterthwaite noted the girl's companion, a dark young man, not handsome, but with a suggestion of restless fire about him. A face full of strange angles; jutting cheek-bones, a forceful, slightly crooked jaw, deep-set eyes that were curiously light under the dark, overhanging brows.

"An interesting face," said Mr. Satterthwaite to himself. "A real face. It means something."

The young man was leaning forward talking earnestly. The girl was listening. Neither of them belonged to Mr.

Satterthwaite's world. He took them to be of the "Arty" class. The girl wore a rather shapeless garment of cheap green silk. Her shoes were of soiled, white satin. The young man wore his evening clothes with an air of being uncomfortable in them.

The two men passed and repassed several times. The fourth time they did so, the couple had been joined by a third—a fair young man with a suggestion of the clerk about him. With his coming a certain tension had set in. The newcomer was fidgetting with his tie and seemed ill at ease, the girl's beautiful face was turned gravely up towards him, and her companion was scowling furiously.

"The usual story," said Mr. Quin very softly, as they passed.

"Yes," said Mr. Satterthwaite with a sigh. "It's inevitable, I suppose. The snarling of two dogs over a bone. It always has been, it always will be. And yet, one could wish for something different. Beauty—" he stopped. Beauty, to Mr. Satterthwaite, meant something very wonderful. He found it difficult to speak of it. He looked at Mr. Quin, who nodded his head gravely in understanding.

They went back to their seats for the second act.

At the close of the performance, Mr. Satterthwaite turned eagerly to his friend.

"It is a wet night. My car is here. You must allow me to drive you—er—somewhere."

The last word was Mr. Satterthwaite's delicacy coming into play. "To drive you home" would, he felt, have savoured of curiosity. Mr. Quin had always been singularly reticent. It was extraordinary how little Mr. Satterthwaite knew about him.

"But perhaps," continued the little man, "you have your own car waiting?"

"No," said Mr. Quin, "I have no car waiting."

"Then—"

But Mr. Quin shook his head.

"You are most kind," he said, "but I prefer to go my own way. Besides," he said with a rather curious smile, "if anything should—happen, it will be for you to act. Good-night, and thank you. Once again we have seen the drama together."

He had gone so quickly that Mr. Satterthwaite had no time to protest, but he was left with a faint uneasiness stirring in his mind. To what drama did Mr. Quin refer? *Pagliacci* or another?

Masters, Mr. Satterthwaite's chauffeur, was in the habit of waiting in a side street. His master disliked the long delay while the cars drew up in turn before the Opera house. Now, as on previous occasions, he walked rapidly round the corner and along the street towards where he knew he should find Masters awaiting him. Just in front of him were a girl and a man, and even as he recognized them, another man joined them.

It all broke out in a minute. A man's voice, angrily uplifted. Another man's voice in injured protest. And then the scuffle. Blows, angry breathing, more blows, the form of a policeman appearing majestically from nowhere—and in another minute Mr. Satterthwaite was beside the girl where she shrank back against the wall.

"Allow me," he said. "You must not stay here."

He took her by the arm and marshalled her swiftly down the street. Once she looked back.

"Oughtn't I—?" she began uncertainly.

Mr. Satterthwaite shook his head.

"It would be very unpleasant for you to be mixed up in it. You would probably be asked to go along to the police station with them. I am sure neither of your—friends would wish that."

He stopped.

"This is my car. If you will allow me to do so, I shall have much pleasure in driving you home."

The girl looked at him searchingly. The staid respectability of Mr. Satterthwaite impressed her favourably. She bent her head.

"Thank you," she said, and got into the car, the door of which Masters was holding open.

In reply to a question from Mr. Satterthwaite, she gave an address in Chelsea, and he got in beside her.

The girl was upset and not in the mood for talking, and Mr. Satterthwaite was too tactful to intrude upon her thoughts. Presently, however, she turned to him and spoke of her own accord.

"I wish," she said pettishly, "people wouldn't be so silly."

"It is a nuisance," agreed Mr. Satterthwaite.

His matter-of-fact manner put her at her ease, and she went on as though feeling the need of confiding in someone.

"It wasn't as though—I mean, well, it was like this. Mr. Eastney and I have been friends for a long time—ever since I came to London. He's taken no end of trouble about my voice, and got me some very good introductions, and he's been more kind to me than I can say. He's absolutely music mad. It was very good of him to take me tonight. I'm sure he can't really afford it. And then Mr. Burns came up and spoke to us—quite nicely, I'm sure, and Phil (Mr. Eastney) got sulky about it. I don't know why he should. It's a free country, I'm sure. And Mr. Burns is always pleasant, and good-tempered. Then just as we were walking to the Tube, he came up and joined us, and he hadn't so much as said two words before Philip flew out at him like a madman. And—Oh! I don't like it."

"Don't you?" asked Mr. Satterthwaite very softly.

She blushed, but very little. There was none of the conscious siren about her. A certain measure of pleasurable excitement in being fought for there must be—that was only nature, but Mr. Satterthwaite decided that a worried perplexity lay uppermost, and he had the clue to it in another moment when she observed inconsequently:

"I do hope he hasn't hurt him."

"Now which is 'him?' " thought Mr. Satterthwaite, smiling to himself in the darkness.

He backed his own judgment and said:

"You hope Mr.—er—Eastney hasn't hurt Mr. Burns?"

She nodded.

"Yes, that's what I said. It seems so dreadful. I wish I knew."

The car was drawing up.

"Are you on the telephone?" he asked.

"Yes."

"If you like, I will find out exactly what has happened, and then telephone to you."

The girl's face brightened.

"Oh, that would be very kind of you. Are you sure it's not too much bother?"

"Not in the least."

She thanked him again and gave him her telephone number, adding with a touch of shyness: "My name is Gillian West."

As he was driven through the night, bound on his errand, a curious smile came to Mr. Satterthwaite's lips.

He thought: "So that is all it is . . . '*The shape of a face, the curve of a jaw!*' "

But he fulfilled his promise.

The following Sunday afternoon Mr. Satterthwaite went to Kew Gardens to admire the rhododendrons. Very long ago (incredibly long ago, it seemed to Mr. Satterthwaite) he had driven down to Kew Gardens with a certain young lady to see the bluebells. Mr. Satterthwaite had arranged very carefully beforehand in his own mind exactly what he was going to say, and the precise words he would use in asking the young lady for her hand in marriage. He was just conning them over in his mind, and responding to her raptures about the bluebells a little absentmindedly, when the shock came. The young lady stopped exclaiming at the bluebells and suddenly confided in Mr. Satterthwaite (as a true friend) her love for another. Mr. Satterthwaite put away the little set speech he had prepared, and hastily rummaged for sympathy and friendship in the bottom drawer of his mind.

Such was Mr. Satterthwaite's romance—a rather tepid early Victorian one, but it had left him with a romantic attachment to Kew Gardens, and he would often go there to see the bluebells, or, if he had been abroad later than usual, the rhododendrons, and would sigh to himself, and feel rather sentimental, and really enjoy himself very much indeed in an old-fashioned, romantic way.

This particular afternoon he was strolling back past the tea houses when he recognized a couple sitting at one of the small tables on the grass. They were Gillian West and the fair young man, and at that same moment they recognized him. He saw the girl flush and speak eagerly to her companion. In another minute he was shaking hands with them both in his correct, rather prim fashion, and had accepted the shy invitation proffered him to have tea with them.

"I can't tell you, sir," said Mr. Burns, "how grateful I am to you for looking after Gillian the other night. She told me all about it."

"Yes, indeed," said the girl. "It was ever so kind of you."

Mr. Satterthwaite felt pleased and interested in the pair. Their naïveté and sincerity touched him. Also, it was to him a peep into a world with which he was not well acquainted. These people were of a class unknown to him.

In his little dried-up way, Mr. Satterthwaite could be very sympathetic. Very soon he was hearing all about his new friends. He noted that Mr. Burns had become Charlie, and he was not unprepared for the statement that the two were engaged.

"As a matter of fact," said Mr. Burns with refreshing candour, "it just happened this afternoon, didn't it, Gil?"

Burns was a clerk in a shipping firm. He was making a fair salary, had a little money of his own, and the two proposed to be married quite soon.

Mr. Satterthwaite listened, and nodded, and congratulated.

"An ordinary young man," he thought to himself, "a very ordinary young man. Nice, straightforward young chap, plenty to say for himself, good opinion of himself without being conceited, nice-looking without being unduly handsome. Nothing remarkable about him and will never set the Thames on fire. And the girl loves him. . . ."

Aloud he said: "And Mr. Eastney—"

He purposely broke off, but he had said enough to produce an effect for which he was not unprepared. Charlie Burns's face darkened, and Gillian looked troubled. More than troubled, he thought. She looked afraid.

"I don't like it," she said in a low voice. Her words were addressed to Mr. Satterthwaite, as though she knew by instinct that he would understand a feeling incomprehensible to her lover. "You see—he's done a lot for me. He's encouraged me to take up singing, and—and helped me with it. But I've known all the time that my voice wasn't really good—not first class. Of course, I've had engagements—"

She stopped.

"You've had a bit of trouble too," said Burns. "A girl wants someone to look after her. Gillian's had a lot of unpleasantness, Mr. Satterthwaite. Altogether she's had a lot of unpleasantness. She's a good-looker, as you can see, and—well, that often leads to trouble for a girl."

Between them, Mr. Satterthwaite became enlightened as to various happenings which were vaguely classed by Burns under the heading of "unpleasantness." A young man who had shot himself, the extraordinary conduct of a Bank Manager (who was a married man!), a violent stranger (who must have been balmy!), the wild behaviour of an elderly artist. A trail of violence and tragedy that Gillian West had left in her wake, recited in the commonplace tones of Charles Burns. "And it's my opinion," he ended, "that this fellow Eastney is a bit cracked. Gillian would have had trouble with him if I hadn't turned up to look after her."

His laugh sounded a little fatuous to Mr. Satterthwaite, and no responsive smile came to the girl's face. She was looking earnestly at Mr. Satterthwaite.

"Phil's all right," she said slowly. "He cares for me, I know, and I care for him like a friend—but—but not anything more. I don't know how he'll take the news about Charlie, I'm sure. He—I'm so afraid he'll be—"

She stopped, inarticulate in face of the dangers she vaguely sensed.

"If I can help you in any way," said Mr. Satterthwaite warmly, "pray command me."

He fancied Charlie Burns looked vaguely resentful, but Gillian said at once: "Thank you."

Mr. Satterthwaite left his new friends after having promised to take tea with Gillian on the following Thursday.

When Thursday came, Mr. Satterthwaite felt a little thrill of pleasurable anticipation. He thought: "I'm an old man—but not too old to be thrilled by a face. A face . . ." Then he shook his head with a sense of foreboding.

Gillian was alone. Charlie Burns was to come in later. She looked much happier, Mr. Satterthwaite thought, as though a load had been lifted from her mind. Indeed, she frankly admitted as much.

"I dreaded telling Phil about Charles. It was silly of me. I ought to have known Phil better. He was upset, of course, but no one could have been sweeter. Really sweet he was.

Look what he sent me this morning—a wedding present. Isn't it magnificent?"

It was indeed rather magnificent for a young man in Philip Eastney's circumstances. A four-valve wireless set, of the latest type.

"We both love music so much, you see," explained the girl. "Phil said that when I was listening to a concert on this, I should always think of him a little. And I'm sure I shall. Because we have been such friends."

"You must be proud of your friend," said Mr. Satterthwaite gently. "He seems to have taken the blow like a true sportsman."

Gillian nodded. He saw the quick tears come into her eyes.

"He asked me to do one thing for him. Tonight is the anniversary of the day we first met. He asked me if I would stay at home quietly this evening and listen to the wireless programme—not to go out with Charlie anywhere. I said, of course I would, and that I was very touched, and that I would think of him with a lot of gratitude and affection."

Mr. Satterthwaite nodded, but he was puzzled. He was seldom at fault in his delineation of character, and he would have judged Philip Eastney quite incapable of such a sentimental request. The young man must be of a more banal order than he supposed. Gillian evidently thought the idea quite in keeping with her rejected lover's character. Mr. Satterthwaite was a little—just a little—disappointed. He was sentimental himself, and knew it, but he expected better things of the rest of the world. Besides sentiment belonged to his age. It had no part to play in the modern world.

He asked Gillian to sing and she complied. He told her her voice was charming, but he knew quite well in his own mind that it was distinctly second class. Any success that could have come to her in the profession she had adopted would have been won by her face, not her voice.

He was not particularly anxious to see young Burns again, so presently he rose to go. It was at that moment that his attention was attracted by an ornament on the mantelpiece which stood out among the other rather gimcrack objects like a jewel on a dust heap.

It was a curving beaker of thin green glass, long-stemmed and graceful, and poised on the edge of it was what looked like a gigantic soap bubble, a ball of iridescent glass. Gillian noticed his absorption.

"That's an extra wedding present from Phil. It's rather pretty, I think. He works in a sort of glass factory."

"It is a beautiful thing," said Mr. Satterthwaite reverently. "The glass blowers of Murano might have been proud of that."

He went away with his interest in Philip Eastney strangely stimulated. An extraordinarily interesting young man. And yet the girl with the wonderful face preferred Charlie Burns. What a strange and inscrutable universe!

It had just occurred to Mr. Satterthwaite that, owing to the remarkable beauty of Gillian West, his evening with Mr. Quin had somehow missed fire. As a rule, every meeting with that mysterious individual had resulted in some strange and unforeseen happening. It was with the hope of perhaps running against the man of mystery that Mr. Satterthwaite bent his steps towards the *Arlecchino* Restaurant where once, in the days gone by, he had met Mr. Quin, and which Mr. Quin had said he often frequented.

Mr. Satterthwaite went from room to room at the *Arlecchino,* looking hopefully about him, but there was no sign of Mr. Quin's dark, smiling face. There was, however, somebody else. Sitting at a small table alone was Philip Eastney.

The place was crowded and Mr. Satterthwaite took his seat opposite the young man. He felt a sudden strange sense of exultation, as though he were caught up and made part of a shimmering pattern of events. He was in this thing—whatever it was. He knew now what Mr. Quin had meant that evening at the Opera. There was a drama going on, and in it was a part, an important part, for Mr. Satterthwaite. He must not fail to take his cue and speak his lines.

He sat down opposite Philip Eastney with the sense of accomplishing the inevitable. It was easy enough to get into conversation. Eastney seemed anxious to talk. Mr. Satterthwaite was, as always, an encouraging and sympathetic listener. They talked of the war, of explosives, of poison gases. Eastney had a lot to say about these last, for during the greater part of the war he had been engaged in their manufacture. Mr. Satterthwaite found him really interesting.

There was one gas, Eastney said, that had never been tried. The Armistice had come too soon. Great things had been hoped for it. One whiff of it was deadly. He warmed to animation as he spoke.

Having broken the ice, Mr. Satterthwaite gently turned the conversation to music. Eastney's thin face lit up. He spoke with the passion and abandon of the real music lover.

They discussed Yoaschbim, and the young man was enthusiastic. Both he and Mr. Satterthwaite agreed that nothing on earth could surpass a really fine tenor voice. Eastney as a boy had heard Caruso and he had never forgotten it.

"Do you know that he could sing to a wine glass and shatter it?" he demanded.

"I always thought that was a fable," said Mr. Satterthwaite smiling.

"No, it's gospel truth, I believe. The thing's quite possible. It's a question of resonance."

He went off into technical details. His face was flushed and his eyes shone. The subject seemed to fascinate him, and Mr. Satterthwaite noted that he seemed to have a thorough grasp of what he was talking about. The elder man realized that he was talking to an exceptional brain, a brain that might almost be described as that of a genius. Brilliant, erratic, undecided as yet as to the true channel to give it outlet, but undoubtedly genius.

And he thought of Charlie Burns and wondered at Gillian West.

It was with quite a start that he realized how late it was getting, and he called for his bill. Eastney looked slightly apologetic.

"I'm ashamed of myself—running on so," he said. "But it was a lucky chance sent you along here tonight. I—I needed someone to talk to this evening."

He ended his speech with a curious little laugh. His eyes were still blazing with some subdued excitement. Yet there was something tragic about him.

"It has been quite a pleasure," said Mr. Satterthwaite.

"Our conversation has been most interesting and instructive to me."

He then made his funny, courteous little bow and passed out of the restaurant. The night was a warm one and as he walked slowly down the street a very odd fancy came to him. He had the feeling that he was not alone—that someone was walking by his side. In vain he told himself that the idea was a delusion—it persisted. Someone was walking beside him down that dark, quiet street, someone whom he could not see. He wondered what it was that brought the figure of Mr. Quin so clearly before his mind. He felt exactly as though Mr. Quin were there walking beside him, and yet he had only to use his eyes to assure himself that it was not so, that he was alone.

But the thought of Mr. Quin persisted, and with it came something else: a need, an urgency of some kind, an oppressive foreboding of calamity. There was something he must do—and do quickly. There was something very wrong, and it lay in his hands to put it right.

So strong was the feeling that Mr. Satterthwaite forebore to fight against it. Instead, he shut his eyes and tried to bring that mental image of Mr. Quin nearer. If he could only have asked Mr. Quin—but even as the thought flashed through his mind he knew it was wrong. It was never any use asking Mr. Quin anything. "The threads are all in your hands"—that was the kind of thing Mr. Quin would say.

The threads. Threads of what? He analysed his own feeling and impressions carefully. That presentiment of danger, now. Whom did it threaten?

At once a picture rose up before his eyes, the picture of Gillian West sitting alone listening to the wireless.

Mr. Satterthwaite flung a penny to a passing newspaper boy, and snatched at a paper. He turned at once to the London Radio programme. Yoaschbim was broadcasting tonight, he noted with interest. He was singing "Salve Dimora," from Faust and, afterwards, a selection of his folk songs. "The Shepherd's Song," "The Fish," "The Little Deer," etc.

Mr. Satterthwaite crumpled the paper together. The knowledge of what Gillian was listening to seemed to make the picture of her clearer. Sitting there alone . . .

An odd request, that, of Philip Eastney's. Not like the man, not like him at all. There was no sentimentality in Eastney. He was a man of violent feeling, a dangerous man, perhaps—

Again his thought brought up with a jerk. A dangerous man—that meant something. *"The threads are all in your hands."* That meeting with Philip Eastney tonight—rather odd. A lucky chance, Eastney had said. Was it chance? Or was it part of that interwoven design of which Mr. Satterthwaite had once or twice been conscious this evening?

He cast his mind back. There must be *something* in Eastney's conversation, some clue there. There must, or else why this strange feeling of urgency? What had he talked about? Singing, war work, Caruso.

Caruso—Mr. Satterthwaite's thoughts went off at a tangent. Yoaschbim's voice was very nearly equal to that of Caruso. Gillian would be sitting listening to it now as it rang out true and powerful, echoing round the room, setting glasses ringing—

He caught his breath. Glasses ringing! Caruso, singing to a wine glass and the wine glass breaking. Yoachbim singing in the London studio and in a room over a mile away the crash and tinkle of glass—not a wine glass, a thin, green, glass beaker. A crystal soap bubble falling, a soap bubble that perhaps was not empty . . .

It was at that moment that Mr. Satterthwaite, as judged by passers-by, suddenly went mad. He tore open the newspaper once more, took a brief glance at the wireless announcements and then began to run for his life down the quiet street. At the end of it he found a crawling taxi, and jumping into it, he yelled an address to the driver and the information that it was life or death to get there quickly. The driver, judging him mentally afflicted but rich, did his utmost.

Mr. Satterthwaite lay back, his head a jumble of fragmentary thoughts, forgotten bits of science learned at school, phrases used by Eastney that night. Resonance—natural periods—if the period of the force coincides with the natural period—there was something about a suspension bridge, soldiers marching over it and the swing of their stride being the same as the period of the bridge. Eastney had studied the subject. Eastney knew. And Eastney was a genius.

At 10:45 Yoaschbim was to broadcast. It was that now. Yes, but the Faust had to come first. It was the "Shepherd's Song," with the great shout after the refrain that would—that would—do what?

His mind went whirling round again. Tones, overtones, half-tones. He didn't know much about these things—but Eastney knew. Pray heaven he would be in time!

The taxi stopped. Mr. Satterthwaite flung himself out and raced up the stone stairs to a second floor like a young athlete. The door of the flat was ajar. He pushed it open and the great tenor voice welcomed him. The words of the "Shepherd's Song" were familiar to him in a less unconventional setting.

"Shepherd, see they horse's flowing main—"

He was in time then. He burst open the sitting-room door. Gillian was sitting there in a tall chair by the fireplace.

"Bayra Mischa's daughter is to wed today:
To the wedding I must haste away."

She must have thought him mad. He clutched at her, crying out something incomprehensible, and half pulled, half dragged her out till they stood upon the stairway.

"To the wedding I must haste away—
Ya-ha!"

A wonderful high note, full-throated, powerful, hit full in the middle, a note any singer might be proud of. And with it another sound, the faint tinkle of broken glass.

A stray cat darted past them and in through the flat door. Gillian made a movement, but Mr. Satterthwaite held her back, speaking incoherently.

"No, no—it's deadly: no smell, nothing to warn you. A mere whiff, and it's all over. Nobody knows quite how deadly it would be. It's unlike anything that's ever been tried before."

He was repeating the things that Philip Eastney had told him over the table at dinner.

Gillian stared at him uncomprehendingly.

Philip Eastney drew out his watch and looked at it. It was just half-past eleven. For the past three-quarters of an hour he had been pacing up and down the Embankment. He looked out over the Thames and then turned—to look into the face of his dinner companion.

"That's odd," he said, and laughed. "We seem fated to run into each other tonight."

"If you call it Fate," said Mr. Satterthwaite.

Philip Eastney looked at him more attentively and his own expression changed.

"Yes?" he said quietly.

Mr. Satterthwaite went straight to the point.

"I have just come from Miss West's flat."

"Yes?"

The same voice, with the same deadly quiet.

"We have—taken a dead cat out of it."

There was silence, then Eastney said:

"Who are you?"

Mr. Satterthwaite spoke for some time. He recited the whole history of events.

"So you see, I was in time," he ended up. He paused and added quite gently:

"Have you anything—to say?"

He expected something, some outburst, some wild justification. But nothing came.

"No," said Philip Eastney quietly, and turned on his heel and walked away, Mr. Satterthwaite looked after him till his figure was swallowed up in the gloom. In spite of himself, he had a strange fellow feeling for Eastney, the feeling of an artist for another artist, of a sentimentalist for a real lover, of a plain man for a genius.

At last he roused himself with a start and began to walk in the same direction as Eastney. A fog was beginning to come up. Presently he met a policeman who looked at him suspiciously.

"Did you hear a kind of splash just now?" asked the policeman.

"No," said Mr. Satterthwaite.

The policeman was peering out over the river.

"Another of these suicides, I expect," he grunted disconsolately. "They will do it."

"I suppose," said Mr. Satterthwaite, "that they have their reasons."

"Money, mostly," said the policeman. "Sometimes it's a woman," he said, as he prepared to move away. "It's not always their fault, but some women cause a lot of trouble."

"Some women," agreed Mr. Satterthwaite softly.

When the policeman had gone on, he sat down on a seat with the fog coming up all around him, and thought about Helen of Troy, and wondered if she were a nice, ordinary woman, blessed or cursed with a wonderful face.

Death on the Nile

Lady Grayle was nervous. From the moment of coming on board the S.S. *Fayoum* she complained of everything. She did not like her cabin. She could bear the morning sun, but not the afternoon sun. Pamela Grayle, her niece, obligingly gave up her cabin on the other side. Lady Grayle accepted it grudgingly.

She snapped at Miss MacNaughton, her nurse, for having given her the wrong scarf and for having packed her little pillow instead of leaving it out. She snapped at her husband, Sir George, for having just bought her the wrong string of beads. It was lapis she wanted, not carnelian. George was a fool!

Sir George said anxiously, "Sorry, me dear, sorry. I'll go back and change 'em. Plenty of time."

She did not snap at Basil West, her husband's private secretary, because nobody ever snapped at Basil. His smile disarmed you before you began.

But the worst of it fell assuredly to the dragoman—an imposing and richly dressed personage whom nothing could disturb.

When Lady Grayle caught sight of a stranger in a basket

chair and realized that he was a fellow passenger, the vials of her wrath were poured out like water.

"They told me distinctly at the office that we were the only passengers! It was the end of the season and there was no one else going!"

"That right lady," said Mohammed calmly. "Just you and party and one gentleman, that's all."

"But I was told that there would be only ourselves."

"That quite right, lady."

"It's not all right! It was a lie! What is that man doing here?"

"He come later, lady. After you take tickets. He only decide to come this morning."

"It's an absolute swindle!"

"That's all right, lady, him very quiet gentleman, very nice, very quiet."

"You're a fool! You know nothing about it. Miss MacNaughton, where are you? Oh, there you are. I've repeatedly asked you to stay near me. I might feel faint. Help me to my cabin and give me an aspirin, and don't let Mohammed come near me. He keeps on saying 'That's right, lady,' till I feel I could scream."

Miss McNaughton proffered an arm without a word.

She was a tall woman of about thirty-five, handsome in a quiet, dark way. She settled Lady Grayle in the cabin, propped her up with cushions, administered an aspirin and listened to the thin flow of complaint.

Lady Grayle was forty-eight. She had suffered since she was sixteen from the complaint of having too much money. She had married that impoverished baronet, Sir George Grayle, ten years before.

She was a big woman, not bad looking as regarded features, but her face was fretful and lined, and the lavish makeup she applied only accentuated the blemishes of time and temper. Her hair had been in turn platinum-blonde and henna-red, and was looking tired in consequence. She was overdressed and wore too much jewellery.

"Tell Sir George," she finished, while the silent Miss MacNaughton waited with an expressionless face—"tell Sir George that he *must* get that man off the boat! I *must* have privacy. All I've gone through lately—" She shut her eyes.

"Yes, Lady Grayle," said Miss MacNaughton, and left the cabin.

The offending last-minute passenger was still sitting in the deck chair. He had his back to Luxor and was staring out across the Nile to where the distant hills showed golden above a line of dark green.

Miss MacNaughton gave him a swift, appraising glance as she passed.

She found Sir George in the lounge. He was holding a string of beads in his hand and looking at it doubtfully.

"Tell me, Miss MacNaughton, do you think these will be all right?"

Miss MacNaughton gave a swift glance at the lapis.

"Very nice indeed," she said.

"You think Lady Grayle will be pleased—eh?"

"Oh no, I shouldn't say that, Sir George. You see, nothing *would* please her. That's the real truth of it. By the way, she sent me with a message to you. She wants you to get rid of this extra passenger."

Sir George's jaw dropped. "How can I? What could I say to the fellow?"

"Of course you can't." Elsie MacNaughton's voice was brisk and kindly. "Just say there was nothing to be done."

She added encouragingly, "It will be all right."

"You think it will, eh?" His face was ludicrously pathetic.

Elsie MacNaughton's voice was still kinder as she said: "You really must not take these things to heart, Sir George. It's just health, you know. Don't take it seriously."

"You think she's really bad, nurse?"

A shadow crossed the nurse's face. There was something odd in her voice as she answered: "Yes, I—I don't quite like her condition. But please don't worry, Sir George. You mustn't. You really mustn't." She gave him a friendly smile and went out.

Pamela came in, very languid and cool in her white.

"Hallo, Nunks."

"Hallo, Pam, my dear."

"What have you got there? Oh, nice!"

"Well, I'm so glad you think so. Do you think your aunt will think so, too?"

"She's incapable of liking anything. I can't think why you married the woman, Nunks."

Sir George was silent. A confused panorama of unsuccessful racing, pressing creditors and a handsome if domineering woman rose before his mental vision.

"Poor old dear," said Pamela. "I suppose you had to do it. But she does give us both rather hell, doesn't she?"

"Since she's been ill—" began Sir George.

Pamela interrupted him.

"She's not ill! Not really. She can always do anything she wants to. Why, while you were up at Assouan she was as merry as a—a cricket. I bet you Miss MacNaughton knows she's a fraud."

"I don't know what we'd do without Miss MacNaughton," said Sir George with a sigh.

"She's an efficient creature," admitted Pamela. "I don't exactly dote on her as you do, though, Nunks. Oh, you do! Don't contradict. You think she's wonderful. So she is, in a way. But she's a dark horse. I never know what she's thinking. Still, she manages the old cat quite well."

"Look here, Pam, you mustn't speak of your aunt like that. Dash it all, she's very good to you."

"Yes, she pays all our bills, doesn't she? It's a hell of a life, though."

Sir George passed on to a less painful subject. "What are we to do about this fellow who's coming on the trip? Your aunt wants the boat to herself."

"Well, she can't have it," said Pamela coolly. "The man's quite presentable. His name's Parker Pyne. I should think he was a civil servant out of the Records Department—if there is such a thing. Funny thing is, I seem to have heard the name somewhere. Basil!" The secretary had just entered. "Where have I seen the name Parker Pyne?"

"Front page of *The Times* Agony column," replied the young man promptly. " 'Are you happy? If not, consult Mr. Parker Pyne.' "

"Never! How frightfully amusing! Let's tell him all our troubles all the way to Cairo."

"I haven't any," said Basil West simply. "We're going to glide down the golden Nile, and see temples"—he looked quickly at Sir George, who had picked up a paper—"together."

The last word was only just breathed, but Pamela caught it. Her eyes met his.

"You're right, Basil," she said lightly. "It's good to be alive."

Sir George got up and went out. Pamela's face clouded over.

"What's the matter, my sweet?"

"My detested aunt by marriage—"

"Don't worry," said Basil quickly. "What does it matter what she gets into her head? Don't contradict her. You see," he laughed, "it's good camouflage."

The benevolent figure of Mr. Parker Pyne entered the lounge. Behind him came the picturesque figure of Mohammed, prepared to say his piece.

"Lady, gentlemans, we start now. In a few minutes we pass temples of Karnak right-hand side. I tell you story now about little boy who went to buy a roasted lamb for his father. . . ."

Mr. Parker Pyne mopped his forehead. He had just returned from a visit to the Temple of Dendera. Riding on a donkey was, he felt, an exercise ill suited to his figure. He was proceeding to remove his collar when a note propped up on the dressing table caught his attention. He opened it. It ran as follows:

Dear Sir,—I should be obliged if you should not visit the Temple of Abydos, but would remain on the boat, as I wish to consult you.

Yours truly,

Ariadne Grayle

A smile creased Mr. Parker Pyne's large, bland face. He reached for a sheet of paper and unscrewed his fountain pen.

Dear Lady Grayle (he wrote), *I am sorry to disappoint you, but I am at present on holiday and am not doing any professional business.*

He signed his name and dispatched the letter by a steward. As he completed his change of toilet, another note was brought to him.

Dear Mr. Parker Pyne,—I appreciate the fact that you are on holiday, but I am prepared to pay a fee of a hundred pounds for a consultation.
Yours truly,
Ariadne Grayle

Mr. Parker Pyne's eyebrows rose. He tapped his teeth thoughtfully with his fountain pen. He wanted to see Abydos, but a hundred pounds was a hundred pounds. And Egypt had been even more wickedly expensive than he had imagined.

Dear Lady Grayle (he wrote),*—I shall not visit the Temple of Abydos.*
Yours faithfully,
J. Parker Pyne

Mr. Parker Pyne's refusal to leave the boat was a source of great grief to Mohammed.

"Very nice temple. All my gentlemans like see that temple. I get you carriage. I get you chair and sailors carry you."

Mr. Parker Pyne refused all these tempting offers.

The others set off.

Mr. Parker Pyne waited on deck. Presently the door of Lady Grayle's cabin opened and the lady herself trailed out on deck.

"Such a hot afternoon," she observed graciously. "I see you have stayed behind, Mr. Pyne. Very wise of you. Shall we have some tea together in the lounge?"

Mr. Parker Pyne rose promptly and followed her. It cannot be denied that he was curious.

It seemed as though Lady Grayle felt some difficulty in coming to the point. She fluttered from this subject to that. But finally she spoke in an altered voice.

"Mr. Pyne, what I am about to tell you is in the strictest confidence! You do understand that, don't you?"

"Naturally."

She paused, took a deep breath. Mr. Parker Pyne waited.

"I want to know whether or not my husband is poisoning me."

Whatever Mr. Parker Pyne had expected, it was not this. He showed his astonishment plainly. "That is a very serious accusation to make, Lady Grayle."

"Well, I'm not a fool and I wasn't born yesterday. I've had my suspicions for some time. Whenever George goes away I get better. My food doesn't disagree with me and I feel a different woman. There must be some reason for that."

"What you say is very serious, Lady Grayle. You must

remember I am not a detective. I am, if you like to put it that way, a heart specialist—"

She interrupted him. "Eh—and don't you think it worries me, all this? It's not a policeman I want—I can look after myself, thank you—it's certainty I want. I've got to *know.* I'm not a wicked woman, Mr. Pyne. I act fairly by those who act fairly by me. A bargain's a bargain. I've kept my side of it. I've paid my husband's debts and I've not stinted him in money."

Mr. Parker Pyne had a fleeting pang of pity for Sir George. "And as for the girl she's had clothes and parties and this, that and the other. Common gratitude is all I ask."

"Gratitude is not a thing that can be produced to order, Lady Grayle."

"Nonsense!" said Lady Grayle. She went on: "Well, there it is! Find out the truth for me! Once I *know*—"

He looked at her curiously. "Once you know, what then, Lady Grayle?"

"That's my business." Her lips closed sharply.

Mr. Parker Pyne hesitated a minute, then he said: "You will excuse me, Lady Grayle, but I have the impression that you are not being entirely frank with me."

"That's absurd. I've told you exactly what I want you to find out."

"Yes, but not the reason *why?*"

Their eyes met. Hers fell first.

"I should think the reason was self-evident," she said.

"No, because I am in doubt upon one point."

"What is that?"

"Do you want your suspicions proved right or wrong?"

"Really, Mr. Pyne!" The lady rose to her feet, quivering with indignation.

Mr. Parker Pyne nodded his head gently. "Yes, yes," he said. "But that doesn't answer my question, you know."

"Oh!" Words seemed to fail her. She swept out of the room.

Left alone, Mr. Parker Pyne became very thoughtful. He was so deep in his own thoughts that he started perceptibly when someone came in and sat down opposite him. It was Miss MacNaughton.

"Surely you're all back very soon," said Mr. Parker Pyne.

"The others aren't back. I said I had a headache and came back alone." She hesitated. "Where is Lady Grayle?"

"I should imagine lying down in her cabin."

"Oh, then that's all right. I don't want her to know I've come back."

"You didn't come on her account then?"

Miss MacNaughton shook her head. "No, I came back to see you."

Mr. Parker Pyne was surprised. He would have said offhand that Miss MacNaughton was eminently capable of looking after troubles herself without seeking outside advice. It seemed that he was wrong.

"I've watched you since we all came on board. I think you're a person of wide experience and good judgement. And I want advice very badly."

"And yet—excuse me, Miss MacNaughton—but you're not the type that usually seeks advice. I should say that you were a person who was quite content to rely on her own judgement."

"Normally, yes. But I am in a very peculiar position."

She hesitated a moment. "I do not usually talk about my cases. But in this instance I think it is necessary. Mr. Pyne, when I left England with Lady Grayle, she was a straightforward case. In plain language, there was nothing the matter with her. That's not quite true, perhaps. Too much leisure and too much money do produce a definite pathological condition. Having a few floors to scrub every day and five or six children to look after would have made Lady Grayle a perfectly healthy and a much happier woman."

Mr. Parker Pyne nodded.

"As a hospital nurse, one sees a lot of these nervous cases. Lady Grayle *enjoyed* her bad health. It was my part not to minimize her sufferings, to be as tactful as I could—and to enjoy the trip myself as much as possible."

"Very sensible," said Mr. Parker Pyne.

"But Mr. Pyne, things are not as they were. The suffering that Lady Grayle complains of now is real and not imagined."

"You mean?"

"I have come to suspect that Lady Grayle is being poisoned."

"Since when have you suspected this?"

"For the past three weeks."

"Do you suspect—any particular person?"

Her eyes dropped. For the first time her voice lacked sincerity. "No."

"I put it to you, Miss MacNaughton, that you do suspect one particular person, and that that person is Sir George Grayle."

"Oh, no, no, I can't believe it of him! He is so pathetic, so childlike. He couldn't be a cold-blooded poisoner." Her voice had an anguished note in it.

"And yet you have noticed that whenever Sir George is absent his wife is better and that her periods of illness correspond with his return."

She did not answer.

"What poison do you suspect? Arsenic?"

"Something of that kind. Arsenic or antimony."

"And what steps have you taken?"

"I have done my utmost to supervise what Lady Grayle eats and drinks."

Mr. Parker Pyne nodded. "Do you think Lady Grayle has any suspicion herself?" he asked casually.

"Oh, no, I'm sure she hasn't."

"There you are wrong," said Mr. Parker Pyne. "Lady Grayle *does* suspect."

Miss MacNaughton showed her astonishment.

"Lady Grayle is more capable of keeping a secret than you imagine," said Mr. Parker Pyne. "She is a woman who knows how to keep her own counsel very well."

"That surprises me very much," said Miss MacNaughton slowly.

"I should like to ask you one more question, Miss MacNaughton. Do you think Lady Grayle likes you?"

"I've never thought about it."

They were interrupted. Mohammed came in, his face beaming, his robes flowing behind him.

"Lady, she hear you come back; she ask for you. She say why you not come to her?"

Elsie MacNaughton rose hurriedly. Mr. Parker Pyne rose also.

"Would a consultation early tomorrow morning suit you?" he asked.

"Yes, that would be the best time. Lady Grayle sleeps late. In the meantime, I shall be very careful."

"I think Lady Grayle will be careful too."

Miss MacNaughton disappeared.

Mr. Parker Pyne did not see Lady Grayle till just before dinner. She was sitting smoking a cigarette and burning what seemed to be a letter. She took no notice at all of him, by which he gathered that she was still offended.

After dinner he played bridge with Sir George, Pamela and Basil. Everyone seemed a little distrait, and the bridge game broke up early.

It was some hours later when Mr. Parker Pyne was roused. It was Mohammed who came to him.

"Old lady, she very ill. Nurse, she very frightened. I try to get doctor."

Mr. Parker Pyne hurried on some clothes. He arrived at the doorway of Lady Grayle's cabin at the same time as Basil West. Sir George and Pamela were inside. Elsie MacNaughton was working desperately over her patient. As Mr. Parker Pyne arrived, a final convulsion seized the poor lady. Her arched body writhed and stiffened. Then she fell back on her pillows.

Mr. Parker Pyne drew Pamela gently outside.

"How awful!" the girl was half-sobbing. "How awful! Is she, is she—?"

"Dead? Yes, I am afraid it is all over."

He put her into Basil's keeping. Sir George came out of the cabin, looking dazed.

"I never thought she was really ill," he was muttering. "Never thought it for a moment."

Mr. Parker Pyne pushed past him and entered the cabin.

Elsie MacNaughton's face was white and drawn. "They have sent for a doctor?" she asked.

"Yes." Then he said: "Strychnine?"

"Yes. Those convulsions are unmistakable. Oh, I can't believe it!" She sank into a chair, weeping. He patted her shoulder.

Then an idea seemed to strike him. He left the cabin hurriedly and went to the lounge. There was a little scrap of paper left unburnt in an ashtray. Just a few words were distinguishable:

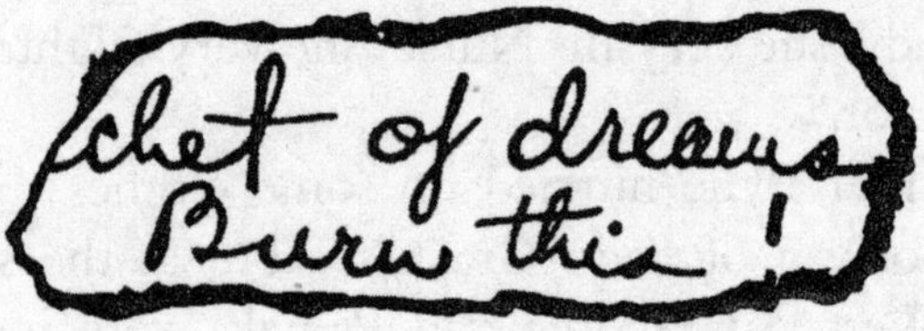

"Now, that's interesting," said Mr. Parker Pyne.

Mr. Parker Pyne sat in the room of a prominent Cairo official. "So that's the evidence," he said thoughtfully.

"Yes, pretty complete. Man must have been a damned fool."

"I shouldn't call Sir George a brainy man."

"All the same!" The other recapitulated: "Lady Grayle

wants a cup of Bovril. The nurse makes it for her. Then she must have sherry in it. Sir George produces the sherry. Two hours later, Lady Grayle dies with unmistakable signs of strychnine poisoning. A packet of strychnine is found in Sir George's cabin and another packet actually in the pocket of his dinner jacket."

"Very thorough," said Mr. Parker Pyne. "Where did the strychnine come from, by the way?"

"There's a little doubt over that. The nurse had some—in case Lady Grayle's heart troubled her—but she's contradicted herself once or twice. First she said her supply was intact, and now she says it isn't."

"Very unlike her not to be sure," was Mr. Parker Pyne's comment.

"They were in it together, in my opinion. They've got a weakness for each other, those two."

"Possibly; but if Miss MacNaughton had been planning murder, she'd have done it a good deal better. She's an efficient young woman."

"Well, there it is. In my opinion, Sir George is in for it. He hasn't a dog's chance."

"Well, well," said Mr. Parker Pyne, "I must see what I can do."

He sought out the pretty niece.

Pamela was white and indignant. "Nunks never did such a thing—never—never—never!"

"Then who did?" said Mr. Parker Pyne placidly.

Pamela came nearer. "Do you know what I think? *She did it herself.* She's been frightfully queer lately. She used to imagine things."

"What things?"

"Queer things. Basil, for instance. She was always hinting that Basil was in love with her. And Basil and I are—we are—"

"I realize that," said Mr. Parker Pyne, smiling.

"All that about Basil was pure imagination. I think she had a down on poor little Nunks, and I think she made up that story and told it to you, and then put the strychnine in his cabin and in his pocket and poisoned herself. People have done things like that, haven't they?"

"They have," admitted Mr. Parker Pyne. "But I don't think that Lady Grayle did. She wasn't, if you'll allow me to say so, the type."

"But the delusions?"

"Yes, I'd like to ask Mr. West about that."

He found the young man in his room. Basil answered his questions readily enough.

"I don't want to sound fatuous, but she took a fancy to me. That's why I daren't let her know about me and Pamela. She'd have had Sir George fire me."

"You think Miss Grayle's theory a likely one?"

"Well, it's possible, I suppose." The young man was doubtful.

"But not good enough," said Mr. Parker Pyne quietly. "No, we must find something better." He became lost in meditation for a minute or two. "A confession would be best," he said briskly. He unscrewed his fountain pen and produced a sheet of paper. "Just write it out, will you?"

Basil West stared at him in amazement. "Me? What on earth do you mean?"

"My dear young man"—Mr. Parker Pyne sounded almost paternal—"I know all about it. How you made love to the good lady. How she had scruples. How you fell in love with the pretty, penniless niece. How you arranged your plot. Slow poisoning. It might pass for natural death from gastroenteritis—if not, it would be laid to Sir George's doing, since you were careful to let the attacks coincide with his presence.

"Then your discovery that the lady was suspicious and had talked to me about the matter. Quick action! You abstracted some strychnine from Miss MacNaughton's store. Planted some of it in Sir George's cabin, and some in his pocket, and put sufficient into a cachet which you enclosed with a note to the lady, telling her it was a 'cachet of dreams.'

"A romantic idea. She'd take it as soon as the nurse had left her, and no one would know anything about it. But you made one mistake, my young man. It is useless asking a lady to burn letters. They never do. I've got all that pretty correspondence, including the one about the cachet."

Basil West had turned green. All his good looks had vanished. He looked like a trapped rat.

"Damn you," he snarled. "So you know all about it. You damned interfering Nosey Parker."

Mr. Parker Pyne was saved from physical violence by the appearance of the witnesses he had thoughtfully arranged to have listening outside the half-closed door.

Mr. Parker Pyne was again discussing the case with his friend the high official.

"And I hadn't a shred of evidence! Only an almost indecipherable fragment, with *'Burn this!'* on it. I deduced the whole story and tried it on him. It worked. I'd stumbled on the truth. The letters did it. Lady Grayle had burned every scrap he wrote, but *he didn't know that.*

"She was really a very unusual woman. I was puzzled when she came to me. What she wanted was for me to tell her that her husband was poisoning her. In that case, she meant to go off with young West. But she wanted to act fairly. Curious character."

"That poor little girl is going to suffer," said the other.

"She'll get over it," said Mr. Parker Pyne callously. "She's young. I'm anxious that Sir George should get a little enjoyment before it's too late. He's been treated like a worm for ten years. Now, Elsie MacNaughton will be very kind to him."

He beamed. Then he sighed. "I am thinking of going incognito to Greece. I really *must* have a holiday!"

Death by Drowning

Sir Henry Clithering, Ex-Commissioner of Scotland Yard, was staying with his friends the Bantrys at their place near the little village of St. Mary Mead.

On Saturday morning, coming down to breakfast at the pleasant guestly hour of ten-fifteen, he almost collided with his hostess, Mrs. Bantry, in the doorway of the breakfast room. She was rushing from the room, evidently in a condition of some excitement and distress.

Colonel Bantry was sitting at the table, his face rather redder than usual.

" 'Morning, Clithering," he said. "Nice day. Help yourself."

Sir Henry obeyed. As he took his seat, a plate of kidneys and bacon in front of him, his host went on:

"Dolly's a bit upset this morning."

"Yes—er—I rather thought so," said Sir Henry mildly.

He wondered a little. His hostess was of a placid disposition, little given to moods or excitement. As far as Sir Henry knew, she felt keenly on one subject only—gardening.

"Yes," said Colonel Bantry. "Bit of news we got this morning upset her. Girl in the village—Emmott's daughter—Emmott who keeps the Blue Boar."

"Oh, yes, of course."

"Ye-es," said Colonel Bantry ruminatively. "Pretty girl. Got herself into trouble. Usual story. I've been arguing with Dolly about that. Foolish of me. Women never see sense. Dolly was all up in arms for the girl—you know what women are—men are brutes—all the rest of it, etcetera. But it's not so simple as all that—not in these days. Girls know what they're about. Fellow who seduces a girl's not necessarily a villain. Fifty-fifty as often as not. I rather liked young Sandford myself. A young ass rather than a Don Juan, I should have said."

"It is this man Sandford who got the girl into trouble?"

"So it seems. Of course I don't know anything personally," said the Colonel cautiously. "It's all gossip and chat. You know what this place is! As I say, I *know* nothing. And I'm not like Dolly—leaping to conclusions, flinging accusations all over the place. Damn it all, one ought to be careful in what one says. You know—inquest and all that."

"Inquest?"

Colonel Bantry stared.

"Yes. Didn't I tell you? Girl drowned herself. That's what all the pother's about."

"That's a nasty business," said Sir Henry.

"Of course it is. Don't like to think of it myself. Poor pretty little devil. Her father's a hard man by all accounts. I suppose she just felt she couldn't face the music."

He paused.

"That's what's upset Dolly so."

"Where did she drown herself?"

"In the river. Just below the mill it runs pretty fast. There's a footpath and a bridge across. They think she threw herself off that. Well, well, it doesn't bear thinking about."

And with a portentous rustle, Colonel Bantry opened his newspaper and proceeded to distract his mind from painful matters by an absorption in the newest iniquities of the government.

Sir Henry was only mildly interested by the village tragedy. After breakfast, he established himself on a comfortable chair on the lawn, tilted his hat over his eyes and contemplated life from a peaceful angle.

It was about half past eleven when a neat parlourmaid tripped across the lawn.

"If you please, sir, Miss Marple has called, and would like to see you."

"Miss Marple?"

Sir Henry sat up and straightened his hat. The name surprised him. He remembered Miss Marple very well—her gentle quiet old-maidish ways, her amazing penetration. He remembered a dozen unsolved and hypothetical cases—and how in each case this typical "old maid of the village" had leaped unerringly to the right solution of the mystery. Sir Henry had a very deep respect for Miss Marple. He wondered what had brought her to see him.

Miss Marple was sitting in the drawing room—very upright as always, a gaily coloured marketing basket of foreign extraction beside her. Her cheeks were rather pink and she seemed flustered.

"Sir Henry—I am so glad. So fortunate to find you. I just happened to hear that you were staying down here . . . I do hope you will forgive me. . . ."

"This is a great pleasure," said Sir Henry, taking her hand. "I'm afraid Mrs. Bantry's out."

"Yes," said Miss Marple. "I saw her talking to Footit, the butcher, as I passed. Henry Footit was run over yesterday—that was his dog. One of those smooth-haired fox terriers, rather stout and quarrelsome, that butchers always seem to have."

"Yes," said Sir Henry helpfully.

"I was glad to get here when she wasn't at home," continued Miss Marple. "Because it was you I wanted to see. About this sad affair."

"Henry Footit?" asked Sir Henry, slightly bewildered.

Miss Marple threw him a reproachful glance.

"No, no. Rose Emmott, of course. You've heard?"

Sir Henry nodded.

"Bantry was telling me. Very sad."

He was a little puzzled. He could not conceive why Miss Marple should want to see him about Rose Emmott.

Miss Marple sat down again. Sir Henry also sat. When the old lady spoke her manner had changed. It was grave, and had a certain dignity.

"You may remember, Sir Henry, that on one or two occasions we played what was really a pleasant kind of game. Propounding mysteries and giving solutions. You were kind enough to say that I—that I did not do too badly."

"You beat us all," said Sir Henry warmly. "You displayed an absolute genius for getting to the truth. And you always instanced, I remember, some village parallel which had supplied you with the clue."

He smiled as he spoke, but Miss Marple did not smile. She remained very grave.

"What you said has emboldened me to come to you now. I feel that if I say something to you—at least you will not laugh at me."

He realized suddenly that she was in deadly earnest.

"Certainly, I will not laugh," he said gently.

"Sir Henry—this girl—Rose Emmott. She did not drown herself—*she was murdered* . . . And I know who murdered her."

Sir Henry was silent with sheer astonishment for quite three seconds. Miss Marple's voice had been perfectly quiet and unexcited. She might have been making the most ordinary statement in the world for all the emotion she showed.

"This is a very serious statement to make, Miss Marple," said Sir Henry when he had recovered his breath.

She nodded her head gently several times.

"I know—I know—that is why I have come to you."

"But, my dear lady, I am not the person to come to. I am merely a private individual nowadays. If you have knowledge of the kind you claim, you must go to the police."

"I don't think I can do that," said Miss Marple.

"But why not?"

"Because, you see, I haven't got any—what you call *knowledge.*"

"You mean it's only a guess on your part?"

"You can call it that, if you like, but it's not really that at all. I *know.* I'm in a position to know; but if I gave my reasons for knowing to Inspector Drewitt—well, he'd simply laugh. And really, I don't know that I'd blame him. It's very difficult to understand what you might call specialized knowledge."

"Such as?" suggested Sir Henry.

Miss Marple smiled a little.

"If I were to tell you that I know because of a man called Peasegood leaving turnips instead of carrots when he came round with a cart and sold vegetables to my niece several years ago—"

She stopped eloquently.

"A very appropriate name for the trade," murmured Sir Henry. "You mean that you are simply judging from the facts in a parallel case."

"I know human nature," said Miss Marple. "It's impossible not to know human nature living in a village all these years. The question is, do you believe me, or don't you?"

She looked at him very straight. The pink flush had heightened on her cheeks. Her eyes met his steadily without wavering.

Sir Henry was a man with a very vast experience of life. He made his decisions quickly without beating about the bush. Unlikely and fantastic as Miss Marple's statement might seem, he was instantly aware that he accepted it.

"I *do* believe you, Miss Marple. But I do not see what you want me to do in the matter, or why you have come to me."

"I have thought and thought about it," said Miss Marple. "As I said, it would be useless going to the police without any facts. I have no facts. What I would ask you to do is to interest yourself in the matter—Inspector Drewitt would be most flattered, I am sure. And, of course, if the matter went farther, Colonel Melchett, the Chief Constable, I am sure, would be wax in your hands."

She looked at him appealingly.

"And what data are you going to give me to work upon?"

"I thought," said Miss Marple, "of writing a name—*the* name—on a piece of paper and giving it to you. Then if, on investigation, you decided that the—the *person*—is not involved in any way—well, I shall have been quite wrong."

She paused and then added with a slight shiver. "It would be so dreadful—so very dreadful—if an innocent person were to be hanged."

"What on earth—" cried Sir Henry, startled.

She turned a distressed face upon him.

"I may be wrong about that—though I don't think so. Inspector Drewitt, you see, is really an intelligent man. But a mediocre amount of intelligence is sometimes most dangerous. It does not take one far enough."

Sir Henry looked at her curiously.

Fumbling a little, Miss Marple opened a small reticule, took out a little notebook, tore out a leaf, carefully wrote a name on it and folding it in two, handed it to Sir Henry.

He opened it and read the name. It conveyed nothing to him, but his eyebrows lifted a little. He looked across at Miss Marple and tucked the piece of paper in his pocket.

"Well, well," he said. "Rather an extraordinary business, this. I've never done anything like it before. But I'm going to back my judgment—of *you,* Miss Marple."

Sir Henry was sitting in a room with Colonel Melchett, the Chief Constable of the county, and Inspector Drewitt.

The Chief Constable was a little man of aggressively military demeanour. The Inspector was big and broad and eminently sensible.

"I really do feel I'm butting in," said Sir Henry with his pleasant smile. "I can't really tell you why I'm doing it." (Strict truth this!)

"My dear fellow, we're charmed. It's a great compliment."

"Honoured, Sir Henry," said the Inspector.

The Chief Constable was thinking: "Bored to death, poor fellow, at the Bantrys. The old man abusing the government and the old woman babbling on about bulbs."

The Inspector was thinking: "Pity we're not up against a real teaser. One of the best brains in England, I've heard it said. Pity it's all such plain sailing."

Aloud, the Chief Constable said:

"I'm afraid it's all very sordid and straightforward. First idea was that the girl had pitched herself in. She was in the family way, you understand. However, our doctor, Haydock, is a careful fellow. He noticed the bruises on each arm—upper arm. Caused before death. Just where a fellow would have taken her by the arms and flung her in."

"Would that require much strength?"

"I think not. There would be no struggle—the girl would be taken unawares. It's a footbridge of slippery wood. Easiest thing in the world to pitch her over—there's no handrail that side."

"You know for a fact that the tragedy occurred there?"

"Yes. We've got a boy—Jimmy Brown—aged twelve. He was in the woods on the other side. He heard a kind of scream from the bridge and a splash. It was dusk you know—difficult to see anything. Presently he saw something white floating down in the water and he ran and got help. They got her out, but it was too late to revive her."

Sir Henry nodded.

"The boy saw no one on the bridge?"

"No. But, as I tell you, it was dusk, and there's mist always hanging about there. I'm going to question him as to whether he saw anyone about just afterwards or just before. You see he naturally assumed that the girl had thrown herself over. Everybody did to start with."

"Still, we've got the note," said Inspector Drewitt. He turned to Sir Henry.

"Note in the dead girl's pocket, sir. Written with a kind of artist's pencil it was, and all of a sop though the paper was we managed to read it."

"And what did it say?"

"It was from young Sandford. 'All right,' that's how it ran. 'I'll meet you at the bridge at eight thirty.—R.S.' Well, it was near as might be to eight thirty—a few minutes after—when Jimmy Brown heard the cry and the splash."

"I don't know whether you've met Sandford at all?" went on Colonel Melchett. "He's been down here about a month. One of these modern day young architects who build peculiar houses. He's doing a house for Allington. God knows what it's going to be like—full of new-fangled stuff, I suppose. Glass dinner table and surgical chairs made of steel and webbing. Well, that's neither here nor there, but it shows the kind of chap Sandford is. Bolshie, you know—no morals."

"Seduction," said Sir Henry mildly, "is quite an old-established crime though it does not, of course, date back so far as murder."

Colonel Melchett stared.

"Oh! yes," he said. "Quite. Quite."

"Well, Sir Henry," said Drewitt, "there it is—an ugly business, but plain. This young Sandford gets the girl into trouble. Then he's all for clearing off back to London. He's got a girl there—nice young lady—he's engaged to be married to her. Well, naturally this business, if she gets to hear of it, may cook his goose good and proper. He meets Rose at the bridge—it's a misty evening, no one about—he catches her by the shoulders and pitches her in. A proper young swine—and deserves what's coming to him. That's my opinion."

Sir Henry was silent for a minute or two. He perceived a strong undercurrent of local prejudice. A new-fangled architect was not likely to be popular in the conservative village of St. Mary Mead.

"There is no doubt, I suppose, that this man, Sandford, was actually the father of the coming child?" he asked.

"He's the father all right," said Drewitt. "Rose Emmott let out as much to her father. She thought he'd marry her. Marry her! Not he!"

"Dear me," thought Sir Henry. "I seem to be back in mid-Victorian melodrama. Unsuspecting girl, the villain from London, the stern father, the betrayal—we only need the faithful village lover. Yes, I think it's time I asked about him."

And aloud he said:

"Hadn't the girl a young man of her own down here?"

"You mean Joe Ellis?" said the Inspector. "Good fellow Joe. Carpentering's his trade. Ah! If she'd stuck to Joe—"

Colonel Melchett nodded approval.

"Stick to your own class," he snapped.

"How did Joe Ellis take this affair?" asked Sir Henry.

"Nobody knew how he was taking it," said the Inspector. "He's a quiet fellow, is Joe. Close. Anything Rose did was right in his eyes. She had him on a string all right. Just hoped she'd come back to him someday—that was his attitude, I reckon."

"I'd like to see him," said Sir Henry.

"Oh! We're going to look him up," said Colonel Melchett. "We're not neglecting any line. I thought myself we'd see Emmott first, then Sandford, and then we can go on and see Ellis. That suits you, Clithering?"

Sir Henry said it would suit him admirably.

They found Tom Emmott at the Blue Boar. He was a big burly man of middle-age with a shifty eye and a truculent jaw.

"Glad to see you, gentlemen—good morning, Colonel. Come in here and we can be private. Can I offer you anything, gentlemen? No? It's as you please. You've come about this business of my poor girl. Ah! She was a good girl, Rose was. Always was a good girl—till this bloody swine—beg pardon, but that's what he is—till he came along. Promised her marriage, he did. But I'll have the law on him. Drove her to it, he did. Murdering swine. Bringing disgrace on all of us. My poor girl."

"Your daughter distinctly told you that Mr. Sandford was responsible for her condition?" asked Melchett crisply.

"She did. In this very room she did."

"And what did you say to her?" asked Sir Henry.

"Say to her?" The man seemed momentarily taken aback.

"Yes. You didn't, for example, threaten to turn her out of the house."

"I was a bit upset—that's only natural. I'm sure you'll

agree that's only natural. But, of course, I didn't turn her out of the house. I wouldn't do such a thing." He assumed virtuous indignation. "No. What's the law for—that's what I say. What's the law for? He'd got to do the right by her. And if he didn't, by God, he'd got to pay."

He brought down his fist on the table.

"What time did you last see your daughter?" asked Melchett.

"Yesterday—teatime."

"What was her manner then?"

"Well, much as usual. I didn't notice anything. If I'd known—"

"But you didn't know," said the Inspector drily.

They took their leave.

"Emmott hardly creates a favourable impression," said Sir Henry thoughtfully.

"Bit of a blackguard," said Melchett. "He'd have bled Sandford all right if he'd had the chance."

Their next call was on the architect. Rex Sandford was very unlike the picture Sir Henry had unconsciously formed of him. He was a tall young man, very fair and very thin. His eyes were blue and dreamy, his hair was untidy and rather too long. His speech was a little too ladylike.

Colonel Melchett introduced himself and his companions. Then passing straight to the object of his visit, he invited the architect to make a statement as to his movements on the previous evening.

"You understand," he said warningly. "I have no power to compel a statement from you and any statement you make may be used in evidence against you. I want the position to be quite clear to you."

"I—I don't understand," said Sandford.

"You understand that the girl Rose Emmott was drowned last night?"

"I know. Oh! it's too, too distressing. Really, I haven't slept a wink. I've been incapable of any work today. I feel responsible—terribly responsible."

He ran his hands through his hair, making it untidier still.

"I never meant any harm," he said piteously. "I never thought. I never dreamt she'd take it that way."

He sat down at a table and buried his face in his hands.

"Do I understand you to say, Mr. Sandford, that you refuse to make a statement as to where you were last night at eight thirty?"

"No, no—certainly not. I was out. I went for a walk."

"You went to meet Miss Emmott?"

"No. I went by myself. Through the woods. A long way."

"Then how do you account for this note, sir, which was found in the dead girl's pocket?"

And Inspector Drewitt read it unemotionally aloud.

"Now, sir," he finished. "Do you deny that you wrote that?"

"No—no. You're right. I did write it. Rose asked me to meet her. She insisted. I didn't know what to do. So I wrote that note."

"Ah, that's better," said the Inspector.

"But I didn't go!" Sandford's voice rose high and excited. "I didn't go! I felt it would be much better not. I was returning to town tomorrow. I felt it would be better not—not to meet. I intended to write from London and—and make—some arrangement."

"You are aware, sir, that this girl was going to have a child, and that she had named you as its father?"

Sandford groaned, but did not answer.

"Was that statement true, sir?"

Sandford buried his face deeper.

"I suppose so," he said in a muffled voice.

"Ah!" Inspector Drewitt could not disguise the satisfaction. "Now about this 'walk' of yours. Is there anyone who saw you last night?"

"I don't know. I don't think so. As far as I can remember, I didn't meet anybody."

"That's a pity."

"What do you mean?" Sandford stared wildly at him. "What does it matter whether I was out for a walk or not? What difference does that make to Rose drowning herself?"

"Ah!" said the Inspector. "But you see, *she didn't.* She was thrown in deliberately, Mr. Sandford."

"She was—" It took him a minute or two to take in all the horror of it. "My God! Then—"

He dropped into a chair.

Colonel Melchett made a move to depart.

"You understand, Sandford," he said. "You are on no account to leave this house."

The three men left together. The Inspector and the Chief Constable exchanged glances.

"That's enough, I think, sir," said the Inspector.

"Yes. Get a warrant made out and arrest him."

"Excuse me," said Sir Henry, "I've forgotten my gloves."

He reentered the house rapidly. Sandford was sitting just as they had left him, staring dazedly in front of him.

"I have come back," said Sir Henry, "to tell you that I personally, am anxious to do all I can to assist you. The motive of my interest in you I am not at liberty to reveal. But I am going to ask you, if you will, to tell me as briefly as possible exactly what passed between you and this girl Rose."

"She was very pretty," said Sandford. "Very pretty and very alluring. And—and she made a dead set at me. Before God, that's true. She wouldn't let me alone. And it was lonely down here, and nobody liked me much, and—and, as I say she was amazingly pretty and she seemed to know her way about and all that—" His voice died away. He looked up. "And then this happened. She wanted me to marry her. I didn't know what to do. I'm engaged to a girl in London. If she ever gets to hear of this—and she will, of course—well, it's all up. She won't understand. How could she? And I'm a rotter, of course. As I say, I didn't know what to do. I avoided seeing Rose again. I thought I'd get back to town—see my lawyer—make arrangements about money and so forth, for her. God, what a fool I've been! And it's all so clear—the case against me. But they've made a mistake. She *must* have done it herself."

"Did she ever threaten to take her life?"

Sandford shook his head.

"Never. I shouldn't have said she was that sort."

"What about a man called Joe Ellis?"

"The carpenter fellow? Good old village stock. Dull fellow—but crazy about Rose."

"He might have been jealous?" suggested Sir Henry.

"I suppose he was a bit—but he's the bovine kind. He'd suffer in silence."

"Well," said Sir Henry. "I must be going."

He rejoined the others.

"You know, Melchett," he said, "I feel we ought to have a look at this other fellow—Ellis—before we do anything drastic. Pity if you made an arrest that turned out to be a mistake. After all, jealousy is a pretty good motive for murder—and a pretty common one, too."

"That's true enough," said the Inspector. "But Joe Ellis isn't that kind. He wouldn't hurt a fly. Why, nobody's ever seen him out of temper. Still, I agree we'd better just ask him where he was last night. He'll be at home now. He lodges with Mrs. Bartlett—very decent soul—a widow, she takes in a bit of washing."

The little cottage to which they bent their footsteps was spotlessly clean and neat. A big stout woman of middle-age opened the door to them. She had a pleasant face and blue eyes.

"Good morning, Mrs. Bartlett," said the Inspector. "Is Joe Ellis here?"

"Came back not ten minutes ago," said Mrs. Bartlett. "Step inside, will you, please, sirs."

Wiping her hands on her apron she led them into a tiny front parlour with stuffed birds, china dogs, a sofa and several useless pieces of furniture.

She hurriedly arranged seats for them, picked up a whatnot bodily to make further room and went out calling:

"Joe, there's three gentlemen want to see you."

A voice from the back kitchen replied:

"I'll be there when I've cleaned myself."

Mrs. Bartlett smiled.

"Come in, Mrs. Bartlett," said Colonel Melchett. "Sit down."

"Oh, no, sir, I couldn't think of it."

Mrs. Bartlett was shocked at the idea.

"You find Joe Ellis a good lodger?" inquired Melchett in a seemingly careless tone.

"Couldn't have a better, sir. A real steady young fellow. Never touches a drop of drink. Takes a pride in his work. And always kind and helpful about the house. He put up those shelves for me, and he's fixed a new dresser in the kitchen. And any little thing that wants doing in the house—why, Joe does it as a matter of course, and won't hardly take thanks for it. Ah! there aren't many young fellows like Joe, sir."

"Some girl will be lucky someday," said Melchett carelessly. "He was rather sweet on that poor girl, Rose Emmott, wasn't he?"

Mrs. Bartlett sighed.

"It made me tired, it did. Him worshipping the ground she trod on and her not caring a snap of the fingers for him."

"Where does Joe spend his evenings, Mrs. Bartlett?"

"Here, sir, usually. He does some odd piece of work in the evenings, sometimes, and he's trying to learn bookkeeping by correspondence."

"Ah! really. Was he in yesterday evening?"

"Yes, sir."

"You're sure, Mrs. Bartlett?" said Sir Henry sharply.

She turned to him.

"Quite sure, sir."

"He didn't go out, for instance, somewhere about eight to eight thirty?"

"Oh, no." Mrs. Barlett laughed. "He was fixing the kitchen dresser for me nearly all the evening, and I was helping him."

Sir Henry looked at her smiling assured face and felt his first pang of doubt.

A moment later Ellis himself entered the room.

He was a tall broad-shouldered young man, very good-looking in a rustic way. He had shy, blue eyes and a good-tempered smile. Altogether an amiable young giant.

Melchett opened the conversation. Mrs. Bartlett withdrew to the kitchen.

"We are investigating the death of Rose Emmott. You knew her, Ellis."

"Yes." He hesitated, then muttered, "Hoped to marry her one day. Poor lass."

"You have heard of what her condition was?"

"Yes." A spark of anger showed in his eyes. "Let her down, he did. But 'twere for the best. She wouldn't have been happy married to him. I reckoned she'd come to me when this happened. I'd have looked after her."

"In spite of—"

"'Tweren't her fault. He led her astray with fine promises and all. Oh! she told me about it. She'd no call to drown herself. He weren't worth it."

"Where were you, Ellis, last night at eight thirty?"

Was it Sir Henry's fancy, or was there really a shade of constraint in the ready—almost too ready—reply.

"I was here. Fixing up a contraption in the kitchen for Mrs. B. You ask her. She'll tell you."

"He was too quick with that," thought Sir Henry. "He's a slow-thinking man. That popped out so pat that I suspect he'd got it ready beforehand."

Then he told himself that it was imagination. He was

imagining things—yes, even imagining an apprehensive glint in those blue eyes.

A few more questions and answers and they left. Sir Henry made an excuse to go to the kitchen. Mrs. Bartlett was busy at the stove. She looked up with a pleasant smile. A new dresser was fixed against the wall. It was not quite finished. Some tools lay about and some pieces of wood.

"That's what Ellis was at work on last night?" said Sir Henry.

"Yes, sir, it's a nice bit of work, isn't it? He's a very clever carpenter, Joe is."

No apprehensive gleam in her eye—no embarrassment.

But Ellis—had he imagined it? No, there *had* been something.

"I must tackle him," thought Sir Henry.

Turning to leave the kitchen, he collided with a perambulator.

"Not woken the baby up, I hope," he said.

Mrs. Bartlett's laugh rang out.

"Oh, no, sir. I've no children—more's the pity. That's what I take the laundry on, sir."

"Oh! I see—"

He paused then said on an impulse:

"Mrs. Bartlett. You knew Rose Emmott. Tell me what you really thought of her."

She looked at him curiously.

"Well, sir, I thought she was flighty. But she's dead—and I don't like to speak ill of the dead."

"But I have a reason—a very good reason for asking."

He spoke persuasively.

She seemed to consider, studying him attentively. Finally she made up her mind.

"She was a bad lot, sir," she said quietly. "I wouldn't say so before Joe. She took *him* in good and proper. That kind can—more's the pity. You know how it is, sir."

Yes, Sir Henry knew. The Joe Ellises of the world were peculiarly vulnerable. They trusted blindly. But for that very cause the shock of discovery might be greater.

He left the cottage baffled and perplexed. He was up against a blank wall. Joe Ellis had been working indoors all yesterday evening. Mrs. Bartlett had actually been there watching him. Could one possibly get round that? There was nothing to set against it—except possibly that suspicious readiness in replying on Joe Ellis's part—that suggestion of having a story pat.

"Well," said Melchett, "that seems to make the matter quite clear, eh?"

"It does, sir," agreed the Inspector. "Sandford's our man. Not a leg to stand upon. The thing's as plain as daylight. It's my opinion as the girl and her father were out to—well—practically blackmail him. He's no money to speak of—he didn't want the matter to get to his young lady's ears. He was desperate and he acted accordingly. What do you say, sir?" he added, addressing Sir Henry deferentially.

"It seems so," admitted Sir Henry. "And yet—I can hardly picture Sandford committing any violent action."

But he knew as he spoke that that objection was hardly valid. The meekest animal, when cornered, is capable of amazing actions.

"I should like to see the boy, though," he said suddenly. "The one who heard the cry."

Jimmy Brown proved to be an intelligent lad, rather small for his age, with a sharp, rather cunning face. He was eager to be questioned and was rather disappointed when checked in his dramatic tale of what he had heard on the fatal night.

"You were on the other side of the bridge, I understand," said Sir Henry. "Across the river from the village. Did you see anyone on that side as you came over the bridge?"

"There was someone walking up in the woods. Mr. Sandford, I think it was, the architecting gentleman who's building the queer house."

The three men exchanged glances.

"That was about ten minutes or so before you heard the cry?"

The boy nodded.

"Did you see anyone else—on the village side of the river?"

"A man came along the path that side. Going slow and whistling he was. Might have been Joe Ellis."

"You couldn't possibly have seen who it was," said the Inspector sharply. "What with the mist and its being dusk."

"It's on account of the whistle," said the boy. "Joe Ellis always whistles the same tune—'I wanner be happy'—it's the only tune he knows."

He spoke with the scorn of the modernist for the old-fashioned.

"Anyone might whistle a tune," said Melchett. "Was he going towards the bridge?"

"No. Other way—to village."

"I don't think we need concern ourselves with this unknown man," said Melchett. "You heard the cry and the splash and a few minutes later you saw the body floating downstream and you ran for help, going back to the bridge, crossing it, and making straight for the village. You didn't see anyone near the bridge as you ran for help?"

"I think as there were two men with a wheelbarrow on the river path; but they were some way away and I couldn't tell if they were going or coming and Mr. Giles's place was nearest—so I ran there."

"You did well, my boy," said Melchett. "You acted very creditably and with presence of mind. You're a scout, aren't you?"

"Yes, sir."

"Very good. Very good indeed."

Sir Henry was silent—thinking. He took a slip of paper from his pocket, looked at it, shook his head. It didn't seem possible—and yet—

He decided to pay a call on Miss Marple.

She received him in her pretty, slightly overcrowded old-style drawing room.

"I've come to report progress," said Sir Henry. "I'm afraid that from our point of view things aren't going well. They are going to arrest Sandford. And I must say I think they are justified."

"You have found nothing in—what shall I say—support of my theory, then?" She looked perplexed—anxious. "Perhaps I have been wrong—quite wrong. You have such wide experience—you would surely detect it if it were so."

"For one thing," said Sir Henry, "I can hardly believe it. And for another we are up against an unbreakable alibi. Joe Ellis was fixing shelves in the kitchen all the evening and Mrs. Bartlett was watching him do it."

Miss Marple leaned forward, taking in a quick breath.

"But that can't be so," she said. "It was Friday night."

"Friday night?"

"Yes—Friday night. On Friday evenings Mrs. Bartlett takes the laundry she has done round to the different people."

Sir Henry leaned back in his chair. He remembered the boy Jimmy's story of the whistling man and—yes—it would all fit in.

He rose, taking Miss Marple warmly by the hand.

"I think I see my way," he said. "At least I can try. . . ."

Five minutes later he was back at Mrs. Bartlett's cottage and facing Joe Ellis in the little parlour among the china dogs.

"You lied to us, Ellis, about last night," he said crisply. "You were not in the kitchen here fixing the dresser between eight and eight thirty. You were seen walking along the path by the river towards the bridge a few minutes before Rose Emmott was murdered."

The man gasped.

"She weren't murdered—she weren't. I had naught to do with it. She threw herself in, she did. She was desperate like. I wouldn't have harmed a hair on her head, I wouldn't."

"Then why did you lie as to where you were?" asked Sir Henry keenly.

The man's eyes shifted and lowered uncomfortably.

"I was scared. Mrs. B. saw me around there and when we heard just afterwards what had happened—well, she thought it might look bad for me. I fixed I'd say I was working here, and she agreed to back me up. She's a rare one, she is. She's always been good to me."

Without a word Sir Henry left the room and walked into the kitchen. Mrs. Bartlett was washing up at the sink.

"Mrs. Bartlett," he said, "I know everything. I think you'd better confess—that is, unless you want Joe Ellis hanged for something he didn't do . . . No. I see you don't want that. I'll tell you what happened. You were out taking the laundry home. You came across Rose Emmott. You thought she'd given Joe the chuck and was taking up with this stranger. Now she was in trouble—Joe was prepared to come to the rescue—marry her if need be, and if she'd have him. He's lived in your house for four years. You've fallen in love with him. You want him for yourself. You hated this girl—you couldn't bear that this worthless little slut should take your man from you. You're a strong woman, Mrs. Bartlett. You caught the girl by the shoulders and shoved her over into the stream. A few minutes later you met Joe Ellis. The boy Jimmy saw you together in the distance—but in the darkness and the mist he assumed the perambulator was a wheelbarrow and two men wheeling it. You persuaded Joe that he might be suspected and you concocted what was supposed to be an alibi for him, but which was really an alibi for *you*. Now then, I'm right, am I not?"

He held his breath. He had staked all on this throw.

She stood before him rubbing her hands on her apron, slowly making up her mind.

"It's just as you say, sir," she said at last, in her quiet subdued voice (a dangerous voice, Sir Henry suddenly felt it to be). "I don't know what came over me. Shameless—that's what she was. It just came over me—she shan't take Joe from me. I haven't had a happy life, sir. My husband, he was a poor lot—an invalid and cross-grained. I nursed and looked after him true. And then Joe came here to lodge. I'm not such an old woman, sir, in spite of my grey hair. I'm just forty, sir. Joe's one in a thousand. I'd have done anything for him—anything at all. He was like a little child, sir, so gentle and believing. He was mine, sir, to look after and see to. And this—this—" She swallowed—checked her emotion. Even at this moment she was a strong woman. She stood up straight and looked at Sir Henry curiously. "I'm ready to come, sir. I never thought anyone would find out. I don't know how you knew, sir—I don't, I'm sure."

Sir Henry shook his head gently.

"It was not I who knew," he said—and he thought of the piece of paper still reposing in his pocket with the words on it written in neat old-fashioned handwriting.

> "Mrs. Bartlett, with whom Joe Ellis lodges at 2 Mill Cottages."

Miss Marple had been right again.

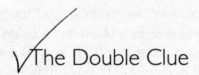

The Double Clue

But above everything—no publicity," said Mr. Marcus Hardman for perhaps the fourteenth time.

The word *publicity* occurred throughout his conversation with the regularity of a leitmotif. Mr. Hardman was a small man, delicately plump, with exquisitely manicured hands and a plaintive tenor voice. In his way, he was somewhat of a celebrity and the fashionable life was his profession. He was rich, but not remarkably so, and he spent his money zealously in the pursuit of social pleasure. His hobby was collecting. He had the collector's soul. Old lace, old fans, antique jewellery—nothing crude or modern for Marcus Hardman.

Poirot and I, obeying an urgent summons, had arrived to find the little man writhing in an agony of indecision. Under the circumstances, to call in the police was abhorrent to him. On the other hand, not to call them in was to acquiesce in the loss of some of the gems of his collection. He hit upon Poirot as a compromise.

"My rubies, Monsieur Poirot, and the emerald necklace said to have belonged to Catherine de' Medici. Oh, the emerald necklace!"

"If you will recount to me the circumstances of their disappearance?" suggested Poirot gently.

"I am endeavouring to do so. Yesterday afternoon I had a little tea party—quite an informal affair, some half a dozen people or so. I have given one or two of them during the season, and though perhaps I should not say so, they have been quite a success. Some good music—Nacora, the pianist, and Katherine Bird, the Australian contralto—in the big studio. Well, early in the afternoon, I was showing my guests my collection of medieval jewels. I keep them in the small wall safe over there. It is arranged like a cabinet inside, with coloured velvet background, to display the stones. Afterwards we inspected the fans—in the case on the wall. Then we all went to the studio for music. It was not until after everyone had gone that I discovered the safe rifled! I must have failed to shut it properly, and someone had seized the opportunity to denude it of its contents. The rubies, Monsieur Poirot, the emerald necklace—the collection of a lifetime! What would I not give to recover them! But there must be no publicity! You fully understand that, do you not, Monsieur Poirot? My own guests, my personal friends! It would be a horrible scandal!"

"Who was the last person to leave this room when you went to the studio?"

"Mr. Johnston. You may know him? The South African millionaire. He has just rented the Abbotburys' house in Park Lane. He lingered behind a few moments, I remember. But surely, oh, surely it could not be he!"

"Did any of your guests return to this room during the afternoon on any pretext?"

"I was prepared for that question, Monsieur Poirot. Three of them did so. Countess Vera Rossakoff, Mr. Bernard Parker, and Lady Runcorn."

"Let us hear about them."

"The Countess Rossakoff is a very charming Russian lady, a member of the old régime. She has recently come to this country. She had bade me good-bye, and I was therefore somewhat surprised to find her in this room apparently gazing in rapture at my cabinet of fans. You know, Monsieur Poirot, the more I think of it, the more suspicious it seems to me. Don't you agree?"

"Extremely suspicious; but let us hear about the others."

"Well, Parker simply came here to fetch a case of miniatures that I was anxious to show to Lady Runcorn."

"And Lady Runcorn herself?"

"As I daresay you know, Lady Runcorn is a middle-aged woman of considerable force of character who devotes most of her time to various charitable committees. She simply returned to fetch a handbag she had laid down somewhere."

"*Bien,* monsieur. So we have four possible suspects. The Russian countess, the English *grande dame,* the South African millionaire, and Mr. Bernard Parker. Who *is* Mr. Parker, by the way?"

The question appeared to embarrass Mr. Hardman considerably.

"He is—er—he is a young fellow. Well, in fact, a young fellow I know."

"I had already deduced as much," replied Poirot gravely. "What does he do, this Mr. Parker?"

"He is a young man about town—not, perhaps, quite in the swim, if I may so express myself."

"How did he come to be a friend of yours, may I ask?"

"Well—er—on one or two occasions he has—performed certain little commissions for me."

"Continue, monsieur," said Poirot.

Hardman looked piteously at him. Evidently the last thing he wanted to do was to continue. But as Poirot maintained an inexorable silence, he capitulated.

"You see, Monsieur Poirot—it is well-known that I am interested in antique jewels. Sometimes there is a family heirloom to be disposed of—which, mind you, would never be sold in the open market or to a dealer. But a private sale to me is a very different matter. Parker arranges the details of such things, he is in touch with both sides, and thus any little embarrassment is avoided. He brings anything of that kind to my notice. For instance, the Countess Rossakoff has brought some family jewels with her from Russia. She is anxious to sell them. Bernard Parker was to have arranged the transaction."

"I see," said Poirot thoughtfully. "And you trust him implicitly?"

"I have had no reason to do otherwise."

"Mr. Hardman, of these four people, which do you yourself suspect?"

"Oh, Monsieur Poirot, what a question! They are my friends, as I told you. I suspect none of them—or all of them, whichever way you like to put it."

"I do not agree. You suspect one of those four. It is not Countess Rossakoff. It is not Mr. Parker. Is it Lady Runcorn or Mr. Johnston?"

"You drive me into a corner, Monsieur Poirot, you do indeed. I am most anxious to have no scandal. Lady Runcorn belongs to one of the oldest families in England; but it is true, it is most unfortunately true, that her aunt, Lady Caroline, suffered from a most melancholy affliction. It was understood, of course, by all her friends, and her maid returned the teaspoons, or whatever it was, as promptly as possible. You see my predicament!"

"So Lady Runcorn had an aunt who was a kleptomaniac? Very interesting. You permit that I examine the safe?"

Mr. Hardman assenting, Poirot pushed back the door of the safe and examined the interior. The empty velvet-lined shelves gaped at us.

"Even now the door does not shut properly," murmured Poirot, as he swung it to and fro. "I wonder why? Ah, what have we here? A glove, caught in the hinge. A man's glove."

He held it out to Mr. Hardman.

"That's not one of my gloves," the latter declared.

"Aha! Something more!" Poirot bent deftly and picked up a small object from the floor of the safe. It was a flat cigarette case made of black moiré.

"My cigarette case!" cried Mr. Hardman.

"Yours? Surely not, monsieur. Those are not your initials."

He pointed to an entwined monogram of two letters executed in platinum.

Hardman took it in his hand.

"You are right," he declared. "It is very like mine, but the initials are different. A '*B*' and a '*P*.' Good heavens—Parker!"

"It would seem so," said Poirot. "A somewhat careless young man—especially if the glove is his also. That would be a double clue, would it not?"

"Bernard Parker!" murmured Hardman. "What a relief! Well, Monsieur Poirot, I leave it to you to recover the jewels. Place the matter in the hands of the police if you think fit—that is, if you are quite sure that it is he who is guilty."

"See you, my friend," said Poirot to me, as we left the house together, "he has one law for the titled, and another law for the plain, this Mr. Hardman. Me, I have not yet been ennobled, so I am on the side of the plain. I have sympathy for this young man. The whole thing was a little curious, was it not? There was Hardman suspecting Lady Runcorn; there was I, suspecting the Countess and Johnston; and all the time, the obscure Mr. Parker was our man."

"Why did you suspect the other two?"

"*Parbleu!* It is such a simple thing to be a Russian refugee or a South African millionaire. Any woman can call herself a Russian countess; anyone can buy a house in Park Lane and call himself a South African millionaire. Who is going to contradict them? But I observe that we are passing through Bury Street. Our careless young friend lives here. Let us, as you say, strike while the iron is in the fire."

Mr. Bernard Parker was at home. We found him reclining on some cushions, clad in an amazing dressing gown of purple and orange. I have seldom taken a greater dislike to anyone than I did to this particular young man with his white, effeminate face and affected lisping speech.

"Good morning, monsieur," said Poirot briskly. "I come from Mr. Hardman. Yesterday, at the party, somebody has stolen all his jewels. Permit me to ask you, monsieur—is this your glove?"

Mr. Parker's mental processes did not seem very rapid. He stared at the glove, as though gathering his wits together.

"Where did you find it?" he asked at last.

"Is it your glove, monsieur?"

Mr. Parker appeared to make up his mind.

"No, it isn't," he declared.

"And this cigarette case, is that yours?"

"Certainly not. I always carry a silver one."

"Very well, monsieur. I go to put matters in the hands of the police."

"Oh, I say, I wouldn't do that if I were you," cried Mr. Parker in some concern. "Beastly unsympathetic people, the police. Wait a bit. I'll go round and see old Hardman. Look here—oh, stop a minute."

But Poirot beat a determined retreat.

"We have given him something to think about, have we not?" he chuckled. "Tomorrow we will observe what has occurred."

But we were destined to have a reminder of the Hardman case that afternoon. Without the least warning the door flew open, and a whirlwind in human form invaded our privacy, bringing with her a swirl of sables (it was as cold as only an English June day can be) and a hat rampant with slaughtered ospreys. Countess Vera Rossakoff was a somewhat disturbing personality.

"You are Monsieur Poirot? What is this that you have done? You accuse that poor boy! It is infamous. It is scandalous. I know him. He is a chicken, a lamb—never would he steal. He has done everything for me. Will I stand by and see him martyred and butchered?"

"Tell me, madame, is this his cigarette case?" Poirot held out the black moiré case.

The Countess paused for a moment while she inspected it.

"Yes, it is his. I know it well. What of it? Did you find

it in the room? We were all there; he dropped it then, I suppose. Ah, you policemen, you are worse than the Red Guards—"

"And is this his glove?"

"How should I know? One glove is like another. Do not try to stop me—he must be set free. His character must be cleared. You shall do it. I will sell my jewels and give you much money."

"Madame—"

"It is agreed, then? No, no, do not argue. The poor boy! He came to me, the tears in his eyes. 'I will save you,' I said. 'I will go to this man—this ogre, this monster! Leave it to Vera.' Now it is settled, I go."

With as little ceremony as she had come, she swept from the room, leaving an overpowering perfume of an exotic nature behind her.

"What a woman!" I exclaimed. "And what furs!"

"Ah, yes, *they* were genuine enough. Could a spurious countess have real furs? My little joke, Hastings . . . No, she is truly Russian, I fancy. Well, well, so Master Bernard went bleating to her."

"The cigarette case is his. I wonder if the glove is also—"

With a smile Poirot drew from his pocket a second glove and placed it by the first. There was no doubt of their being a pair.

"Where did you get the second one, Poirot?"

"It was thrown down with a stick on the table in the hall in Bury Street. Truly, a very careless young man, Monsieur Parker. Well, well, *mon ami*—we must be thorough. Just for the form of the thing, I will make a little visit to Park Lane."

Needless to say, I accompanied my friend. Johnston was out, but we saw his private secretary. It transpired that Johnston had only recently arrived from South Africa. He had never been in England before.

"He is interested in precious stones, is he not?" hazarded Poirot.

"Gold mining is nearer the mark," laughed the secretary.

Poirot came away from the interview thoughtful. Late that evening, to my utter surprise, I found him earnestly studying a Russian grammar.

"Good heavens, Poirot!" I cried. "Are you learning Russian in order to converse with the Countess in her own language?"

"She certainly would not listen to my English, my friend!"

"But surely, Poirot, well-born Russians invariably speak French?"

"You are a mine of information, Hastings! I will cease puzzling over the intricacies of the Russian alphabet."

He threw the book from him with a dramatic gesture. I was not entirely satisfied. There was a twinkle in his eye which I knew of old. It was an invariable sign that Hercule Poirot was pleased with himself.

"Perhaps," I said sapiently, "you doubt her being really a Russian. You are going to test her?"

"Ah, no, no, she is Russian all right."

"Well, then—"

"If you really want to distinguish yourself over this case, Hastings, I recommend *First Steps in Russian* as an invaluable aid."

Then he laughed and would say no more. I picked up the

book from the floor and dipped into it curiously, but could make neither head nor tail of Poirot's remarks.

The following morning brought us no news of any kind, but that did not seem to worry my little friend. At breakfast, he announced his intention of calling upon Mr. Hardman early in the day. We found the elderly social butterfly at home, and seemingly a little calmer than on the previous day.

"Well, Monsieur Poirot, any news?" he demanded eagerly.

Poirot handed him a slip of paper.

"That is the person who took the jewels, monsieur. Shall I put matters in the hands of the police? Or would you prefer me to recover the jewels without bringing the police into the matter?"

Mr. Hardman was staring at the paper. At last he found his voice.

"Most astonishing. I should infinitely prefer to have no scandal in the matter. I give you *carte blanche,* Monsieur Poirot. I am sure you will be discreet."

Our next procedure was to hail a taxi, which Poirot ordered to drive to the Carlton. There he inquired for Countess Rossakoff. In a few minutes we were ushered up into the lady's suite. She came to meet us with outstretched hands, arrayed in a marvellous negligée of barbaric design.

"Monsieur Poirot!" she cried. "You have succeeded? You have cleared that poor infant?"

"Madame la Comtesse, your friend Mr. Parker is perfectly safe from arrest."

"Ah, but you are the clever little man! Superb! And so quickly too."

"On the other hand, I have promised Mr. Hardman that the jewels shall be returned to him today."

"So?"

"Therefore, madame, I should be extremely obliged if you would place them in my hands without delay. I am sorry to hurry you, but I am keeping a taxi—in case it should be necessary for me to go on to Scotland Yard; and we Belgians, madame, we practise the thrift."

The Countess had lighted a cigarette. For some seconds she sat perfectly still, blowing smoke rings, and gazing steadily at Poirot. Then she burst into a laugh, and rose. She went across to the bureau, opened a drawer, and took out a black silk handbag. She tossed it lightly to Poirot. Her tone, when she spoke, was perfectly light and unmoved.

"We Russians, on the contrary, practise prodigality," she said. "And to do that, unfortunately, one must have money. You need not look inside. They are all there."

Poirot arose.

"I congratulate you, madame, on your quick intelligence and your promptitude."

"Ah! But since you were keeping your taxi waiting, what else could I do?"

"You are too amiable, madame. You are remaining long in London?"

"I am afraid no—owing to you."

"Accept my apologies."

"We shall meet again elsewhere, perhaps."

"I hope so."

"And I—do not!" exclaimed the Countess with a laugh.

"It is a great compliment that I pay you there—there are very few men in the world whom I fear. Good-bye, Monsieur Poirot."

"Good-bye, Madame la Comtesse. Ah—pardon me, I forgot! Allow me to return you your cigarette case."

And with a bow he handed to her the little black moiré case we had found in the safe. She accepted it without any change of expression—just a lifted eyebrow and a murmured: "I see!"

"What a woman!" cried Poirot enthusiastically as we descended the stairs. "*Mon Dieu, quelle femme!* Not a word of argument—of protestation, of bluff! One quick glance, and she had sized up the position correctly. I tell you, Hastings, a woman who can accept defeat like that—with a careless smile—will go far! She is dangerous, she has the nerves of steel; she—" He tripped heavily.

"If you can manage to moderate your transports and look where you're going, it might be as well," I suggested. "When did you first suspect the Countess?"

"*Mon ami,* it was the glove *and* the cigarette case—the double clue, shall we say—that worried me. Bernard Parker might easily have dropped one or the other—but hardly both. Ah, no, that would have been *too* careless! In the same way, if someone else had placed them there to incriminate Parker, one would have been sufficient—the cigarette case *or* the glove—again not both. So I was forced to the conclusion that one of the two things did *not* belong to Parker. I imagined at first that the case was his, and that the glove was not. But when I discovered the fellow to the glove, I saw that it was the other way about.

Whose, then, was the cigarette case? Clearly, it could not belong to Lady Runcorn. The initials were wrong. Mr. Johnston? Only if he were here under a false name. I interviewed his secretary, and it was apparent at once that everything was clear and above board. There was no reticence about Mr. Johnston's past. The Countess, then? She was supposed to have brought jewels with her from Russia; she had only to take the stones from their settings, and it was extremely doubtful if they could ever be identified. What could be easier for her than to pick up one of Parker's gloves from the hall that day and thrust it into the safe? But, *bien sûr,* she did not intend to drop her own cigarette case."

"But if the case was hers, why did it have *'B.P.'* on it? The Countess's initials are *V.R.*"

Poirot smiled gently upon me.

"Exactly, *mon ami;* but in the Russian alphabet, *B* is *V* and *P* is *R.*"

"Well, you couldn't expect me to guess that. I don't know Russian."

"Neither do I, Hastings. That is why I bought my little book—and urged it on your attention."

He sighed.

"A remarkable woman. I have a feeling, my friend—a very decided feeling—I shall meet her again. Where, I wonder?"

Finessing the King

It was a wet Wednesday in the offices of the International Detective Agency. Tuppence let the *Daily Leader* fall idly from her hand.

"Do you know what I've been thinking, Tommy?"

"It's impossible to say," replied her husband. "You think of so many things, and you think of them all at once."

"I think it's time we went dancing again."

Tommy picked up the *Daily Leader* hastily.

"Our advertisement looks well," he remarked, his head on one side. "Blunt's Brilliant Detectives. Do you realise, Tuppence, that you and you alone are Blunt's Brilliant Detectives? There's glory for you, as Humpty Dumpty would say."

"I was talking about dancing."

"There's a curious point that I have observed about newspapers. I wonder if you have ever noticed it. Take these three copies of the *Daily Leader*. Can you tell me how they differ one from the other?"

Tuppence took them with some curiosity.

"It seems fairly easy," she remarked witheringly. "One is today's, one is yesterday's, and one is the day before's."

"Positively scintillating, my dear Watson. But that was

not my meaning. Observe the headline, 'Daily Leader.' Compare the three—do you see any difference between them?"

"No, I don't," said Tuppence, "and what's more, I don't believe there is any."

Tommy sighed and brought the tips of his fingers together in the most approved Sherlock Holmes fashion.

"Exactly. Yet you read the papers as much—in fact, more than I do. But I have observed and you have not. If you will look at today's *Daily Leader,* you will see that in the middle of the downstroke of the D is a small white dot, and there is another in the L of the same word. But in yesterday's paper the white dot is not in DAILY at all. There are two white dots in the L of LEADER. That of the day before again has two dots in the D of DAILY. In fact, the dot, or dots, are in a different position every day."

"Why?" asked Tuppence.

"That's a journalistic secret."

"Meaning you don't know, and can't guess."

"I will merely say this—the practice is common to all newspapers."

"Aren't you clever?" said Tuppence. "Especially at drawing red herrings across the track. Let's go back to what we were talking about before."

"What were we talking about?"

"The Three Arts Ball."

Tommy groaned.

"No, no, Tuppence. Not the Three Arts Ball. I'm not young enough. I assure you I'm not young enough."

"When I was a nice young girl," said Tuppence, "I was brought up to believe that men—especially husbands—

were dissipated beings, fond of drinking and dancing and staying up late at night. It took an exceptionally beautiful and clever wife to keep them at home. Another illusion gone! All the wives I know are hankering to go out and dance, and weeping because their husbands will wear bedroom slippers and go to bed at half past nine. And you do dance so nicely, Tommy dear."

"Gently with the butter, Tuppence."

"As a matter of fact," said Tuppence, "it's not purely for pleasure that I want to go. I'm intrigued by this advertisement."

She picked up the *Daily Leader* again and read it out.

"I should go three hearts. 12 tricks. Ace of Spades. Necessary to finesse the King."

"Rather an expensive way of learning bridge," was Tommy's comment.

"Don't be an ass. That's nothing to do with bridge. You see, I was lunching with a girl yesterday at the Ace of Spades. It's a queer little underground den in Chelsea, and she told me that it's quite the fashion at these big shows to trundle round there in the course of the evening for bacon and eggs and Welsh rarebits—Bohemian sort of stuff. It's got screened-off booths all around it. Pretty hot place, I should say."

"And your idea is—?"

"Three hearts stands for the Three Arts Ball, tomorrow night, 12 tricks is twelve o'clock, and the Ace of Spades is the Ace of Spades."

"And what about its being necessary to finesse the King?"

"Well, that's what I thought we'd find out."

"I shouldn't wonder if you weren't right, Tuppence," said

Tommy magnanimously. "But I don't quite see why you want to butt in upon other people's love affairs."

"I shan't butt in. What I'm proposing is an interesting experiment in detective work. We *need* practice."

"Business is certainly not too brisk," agreed Tommy. "All the same, Tuppence, what you want is to go to the Three Arts Ball and dance! Talk of red herrings."

Tuppence laughed shamelessly.

"Be a sport, Tommy. Try and forget you're thirty-two and have got one grey hair in your left eyebrow."

"I was always weak where women were concerned," murmured her husband. "Have I got to make an ass of myself in fancy dress?"

"Of course, but you can leave that to me. I've got a splendid idea."

Tommy looked at her with some misgiving. He was always profoundly mistrustful of Tuppence's brilliant ideas.

When he returned to the flat on the following evening, Tuppence came flying out of her bedroom to meet him.

"It's come," she announced.

"What's come?"

"The costume. Come and look at it."

Tommy followed her. Spread out on the bed was a complete fireman's kit with shining helmet.

"Good God!" groaned Tommy. "Have I joined the Wembley fire brigade?"

"Guess again," said Tuppence. "You haven't caught the idea yet. Use your little grey cells, *mon ami*. Scintillate, Watson. Be a bull that has been more than ten minutes in the arena."

"Wait a minute," said Tommy. "I begin to see. There

is a dark purpose in this. What are you going to wear, Tuppence?"

"An old suit of your clothes, an American hat and some horn spectacles."

"Crude," said Tommy. "But I catch the idea. McCarty incog. And I am Riordan."

"That's it. I thought we ought to practise American detective methods as well as English ones. Just for once I am going to be the star, and you will be the humble assistant."

"Don't forget," said Tommy warningly, "that it's always an innocent remark by the simple Denny that puts McCarty on the right track."

But Tuppence only laughed. She was in high spirits.

It was a most successful evening. The crowds, the music, the fantastic dresses—everything conspired to make the young couple enjoy themselves. Tommy forgot his role of the bored husband dragged out against his will.

At ten minutes to twelve they drove off in the car to the famous—or infamous—Ace of Spades. As Tuppence had said, it was an underground den, mean and tawdry in appearance, but it was nevertheless crowded with couples in fancy dress. There were closed-in booths round the walls, and Tommy and Tuppence secured one of these. They left the doors purposely a little ajar so that they could see what was going on outside.

"I wonder which they are—our people, I mean," said Tuppence. "What about that Columbine over there with the red Mephistopheles?"

"I fancy the wicked Mandarin and the lady who calls herself a Battleship—more of a fast Cruiser, I should say."

"Isn't he witty?" said Tuppence. "All done on a little

drop of drink! Who's this coming in dressed as the Queen of Hearts—rather a good get-up, that."

The girl in question passed into the booth next to them, accompanied by her escort, who was "the gentleman dressed in newspaper" from *Alice in Wonderland.* They were both wearing masks—it seemed to be rather a common custom at the Ace of Spades.

"I'm sure we're in a real den of iniquity," said Tuppence with a pleased face. "Scandals all round us. What a row everyone makes."

A cry, as of protest, rang out from the booth next door and was covered by a man's loud laugh. Everybody was laughing and singing. The shrill voices of the girls rose above the booming of their male escorts.

"What about that shepherdess?" demanded Tommy. "The one with the comic Frenchman. They might be our little lot."

"Any one might be," confessed Tuppence. "I'm not going to bother. The great thing is that we are enjoying ourselves."

"I could have enjoyed myself better in another costume," grumbled Tommy. "You've no idea of the heat of this one."

"Cheer up," said Tuppence. "You look lovely."

"I'm glad of that," said Tommy. "It's more than you do. You're the funniest little guy I've ever seen."

"Will you keep a civil tongue in your head, Denny, my boy. Hullo, the gentleman in newspaper is leaving his lady alone. Where's he going, do you think?"

"Going to hurry up the drinks, I expect," said Tommy. "I wouldn't mind doing the same thing."

"He's a long time doing it," said Tuppence, when four or

five minutes had passed. "Tommy, would you think me an awful ass—" She paused.

Suddenly she jumped up.

"Call me an ass if you like. I'm going in next door."

"Look here, Tuppence—you can't—"

"I've a feeling there's something wrong. I *know* there is. Don't try and stop me."

She passed quickly out of their own booth, and Tommy followed her. The doors of the one next door were closed. Tuppence pushed them apart and went in, Tommy on her heels.

The girl dressed as the Queen of Hearts sat in the corner leaning up against the wall in a queer huddled position. Her eyes regarded them steadily through her mask, but she did not move. Her dress was carried out in a bold design of red and white, but on the left hand side the pattern seemed to have got mixed. There was more red than there should have been. . . .

With a cry Tuppence hurried forward. At the same time, Tommy saw what she had seen, the hilt of a jewelled dagger just below the heart. Tuppence dropped on her knees by the girl's side.

"Quick, Tommy, she's still alive. Get hold of the manager and make him get a doctor at once."

"Right. Mind you don't touch the handle of that dagger, Tuppence."

"I'll be careful. Go quickly."

Tommy hurried out, pulling the doors to behind him. Tuppence passed her arm round the girl. The latter made a faint gesture, and Tuppence realised that she wanted to get rid of the mask. Tuppence unfastened it gently. She saw a fresh, flower-like face, and wide starry eyes that were full of horror, suffering, and a kind of dazed bewilderment.

"My dear," said Tuppence, very gently. "Can you speak at all? Will you tell me, if you can, who did this?"

She felt the eyes fix themselves on her face. The girl was sighing, the deep palpitating sighs of a failing heart. And still she looked steadily at Tuppence. Then her lips parted.

"Bingo did it—" she said in a strained whisper.

Then her hands relaxed, and she seemed to nestle down on Tuppence's shoulder.

Tommy came in, two men with him. The bigger of the two came forward with an air of authority, the word 'doctor' written all over him.

Tuppence relinquished her burden.

"She's dead, I'm afraid," she said with a catch in her voice.

The doctor made a swift examination.

"Yes," he said. "Nothing to be done. We had better leave things as they are till the police come. How did the thing happen?"

Tuppence explained rather haltingly, slurring over her reasons for entering the booth.

"It's a curious business," said the doctor. "You heard nothing?"

"I heard her give a kind of cry, but then the man laughed. Naturally I didn't think—"

"Naturally not," agreed the doctor. "And the man wore a mask you say. You wouldn't recognise him?"

"I'm afraid not. Would you, Tommy?"

"No. Still there is his costume."

"The first thing will be to identify this poor lady," said the doctor. "After that, well, I suppose the police will get down to things pretty quickly. It ought not to be a difficult case. Ah, here they come."

The Gentleman Dressed in Newspaper

It was after three o'clock when, weary and sick at heart, the husband and wife reached home. Several hours passed before Tuppence could sleep. She lay tossing from side to side, seeing always that flower-like face with the horror-stricken eyes.

The dawn was coming in through the shutters when Tuppence finally dropped off to sleep. After the excitement, she slept heavily and dreamlessly. It was broad daylight when she awoke to find Tommy, up and dressed, standing by the bedside, shaking her gently by the arm.

"Wake up, old thing. Inspector Marriot and another man are here and want to see you."

"What time is it?"

"Just on eleven. I'll get Alice to bring you your tea right away."

"Yes, do. Tell Inspector Marriot I'll be there in ten minutes."

A quarter of an hour later, Tuppence came hurrying into the sitting room. Inspector Marriot, who was sitting looking very straight and solemn, rose to greet her.

"Good morning, Mrs. Beresford. This is Sir Arthur Merivale."

Tuppence shook hands with a tall thin man with haggard eyes and greying hair.

"It's about this sad business last night," said Inspector

Marriot. "I want Sir Arthur to hear from your own lips what you told me—the words the poor lady said before she died. Sir Arthur has been very hard to convince."

"I can't believe," said the other, "and I won't believe, that Bingo Hale ever hurt a hair of Vere's head."

Inspector Marriot went on.

"We've made some progress since last night, Mrs. Beresford," he said. "First of all we managed to identify the lady as Lady Merivale. We communicated with Sir Arthur here. He recognised the body at once, and was horrified beyond words, of course. Then I asked him if he knew anyone called Bingo."

"You must understand, Mrs. Beresford," said Sir Arthur, "that Captain Hale, who is known to all his friends as Bingo, is the dearest pal I have. He practically lives with us. He was staying at my house when they arrested him this morning. I cannot but believe that you have made a mistake—it was not his name that my wife uttered."

"There is no possibility of mistake," said Tuppence gently. "She said, 'Bingo did it—' "

"You see, Sir Arthur," said Marriot.

The unhappy man sank into a chair and covered his face with his hands.

"It's incredible. What earthly motive could there be? Oh, I know your idea, Inspector Marriot. You think Hale was my wife's lover, but even if that were so—which I don't admit for a moment—what motive was there for killing her?"

Inspector Marriot coughed.

"It's not a very pleasant thing to say, sir. But Captain Hale has been paying a lot of attention to a certain young American lady of late—a young lady with a considerable amount of money. If Lady Merivale liked to turn nasty, she could probably stop his marriage."

"This is outrageous, Inspector."

Sir Arthur sprang angrily to his feet. The other calmed him with a soothing gesture.

"I beg your pardon, I'm sure, Sir Arthur. You say that you and Captain Hale both decided to attend this show. Your wife was away on a visit at the time, and you had no idea that she was to be there?"

"Not the least idea."

"Just show him that advertisement you told me about, Mrs. Beresford."

Tuppence complied.

"That seems to me clear enough. It was inserted by Captain Hale to catch your wife's eye. They had already arranged to meet there. But you only made up your mind to go the day before, hence it was necessary to warn her. That is the explanation of the phrase, 'Necessary to finesse the King.' You ordered your costume from a theatrical firm at the last minute, but Captain Hale's was a home-made affair. He went as the Gentleman dressed in Newspaper. Do you know, Sir Arthur, what we found clasped in the dead lady's hand? A fragment torn from a newspaper. My men have orders to take Captain Hale's costume away with them from your house. I shall find it at the Yard when I get back. If there's a tear in it corresponding to the missing piece—well, it'll be the end of the case."

"You won't find it," said Sir Arthur. "I know Bingo Hale."

Apologising to Tuppence for disturbing her, they took their leave.

Late that evening there was a ring at the bell, and somewhat to the astonishment of the young pair Inspector Marriot once more walked in.

"I thought Blunt's Brilliant Detectives would like to hear the latest developments," he said, with a hint of a smile.

"They would," said Tommy. "Have a drink?"

He placed materials hospitably at Inspector Marriot's elbow.

"It's a clear case," said the latter, after a minute or two. "Dagger was the lady's own—the idea was to have made it look like suicide evidently, but thanks to you two being on the spot, that didn't come off. We've found plenty of letters—they'd been carrying on together for some time, that's clear—without Sir Arthur tumbling to it. Then we found the last link—"

"The last what?" said Tuppence sharply.

"The last link in the chain—that fragment of the *Daily Leader.* It was torn from the dress he wore—fits exactly. Oh, yes, it's a perfectly clear case. By the way, I brought round a photograph of those two exhibits—I thought they might interest you. It's very seldom that you get such a perfectly clear case."

"Tommy," said Tuppence, when her husband returned from showing the Scotland Yard man out, "why do you think Inspector Marriot keeps repeating that it's a perfectly clear case?"

"I don't know. Smug satisfaction, I suppose."

"Not a bit of it. He's trying to get us irritated. You know, Tommy, butchers, for instance, know something about meat, don't they?"

"I should say so, but what on earth—"

"And in the same way, greengrocers know all about vegetables, and fishermen about fish. Detectives, professional detectives, must know all about criminals. They know the real thing when they see it—and they know when it isn't the real thing. Marriot's expert knowledge tells him that Captain Hale isn't a criminal—but all the facts are dead against him. As a last resource Marriot is egging us on, hoping against hope that some little detail or other will come back to us—something that happened last night—which will throw a different light on things. Tommy, why shouldn't it be suicide, after all?"

"Remember what she said to you."

"I know—but take that a different way. It was Bingo's doing—his conduct that drove her to kill herself. It's just possible."

"Just. But it doesn't explain that fragment of newspaper."

"Let's have a look at Marriot's photographs. I forgot to ask him what Hale's account of the matter was."

"I asked him that in the hall just now. Hale declared he had never spoken to Lady Merivale at the show. Says somebody shoved a note into his hand which said, "Don't try and speak to me tonight. Arthur suspects." He couldn't produce the piece of paper, though, and it doesn't sound a very likely story. Anyway, you and I *know* he was with her at the Ace of Spades, because we saw him."

Tuppence nodded and pored over the two photographs.

One was a tiny fragment with the legend DAILY LE—and the rest torn off. The other was the front sheet of the *Daily Leader* with the small round tear at the top of it. There was no doubt about it. Those two fitted together perfectly.

"What are all those marks down the side?" asked Tommy.

"Stitches," said Tuppence. "Where it was sewn to the others, you know."

"I thought it might be a new scheme of dots," said Tommy. Then he gave a slight shiver. "My word, Tuppence, how creepy it makes one feel. To think that you and I were discussing dots and puzzling over that advertisement—all as lighthearted as anything."

Tuppence did not answer. Tommy looked at her and was startled to observe that she was staring ahead of her, her mouth slightly open, and a bewildered expression on her face.

"Tuppence," said Tommy gently, shaking her by the arm, "what's the matter with you? Are you just going to have a stroke or something?"

But Tuppence remained motionless. Presently she said in a faraway voice:

"Denis Riordan."

"Eh?" said Tommy, staring.

"It's just as you said. One simple innocent remark! Find me all this week's *Daily Leaders*."

"What are you up to?"

"I'm being McCarty. I've been worrying round, and thanks to you, I've got a notion at last. This is the front sheet of Tuesday's paper. I seem to remember that Tuesday's paper was the one with two dots in the L of LEADER. This has a dot in the D of DAILY—and one in the L too. Get me the papers and let's make sure."

They compared them anxiously. Tuppence had been quite right in her remembrance.

"You see? This fragment wasn't torn from Tuesday's paper."

"But Tuppence, we can't be sure. It may merely be different editions."

"It may—but at any rate it's given me an idea. It can't be coincidence—that's certain. There's only one thing it can be if I'm right in my idea. Ring up Sir Arthur, Tommy. Ask him to come round here at once. Say I've got important news for him. Then get hold of Marriot. Scotland Yard will know his address if he's gone home."

Sir Arthur Merivale, very much intrigued by the summons, arrived at the flat in about half an hour's time. Tuppence came forward to greet him.

"I must apologise for sending for you in such a peremptory fashion," she said. "But my husband and I have discovered something that we think you ought to know at once. Do sit down."

Sir Arthur sat down, and Tuppence went on.

"You are, I know, very anxious to clear your friend."

Sir Arthur shook his head sadly.

"I was, but even I have had to give in to the overwhelming evidence."

"What would you say if I told you that chance has placed in my hands a piece of evidence that will certainly clear him of all complicity?"

"I should be overjoyed to hear it, Mrs. Beresford."

"Supposing," continued Tuppence, "that I had come across a girl who was actually dancing with Captain Hale last night at twelve o'clock—the hour when he was supposed to be at the Ace of Spades."

"Marvellous!" cried Sir Arthur. "I knew there was some mistake. Poor Vere must have killed herself after all."

"Hardly that," said Tuppence. "You forget the other man."

"What other man?"

"The one my husband and I saw leave the booth. You see, Sir Arthur, there must have been a second man dressed in newspaper at the ball. By the way, what was your own costume?"

"Mine? I went as a seventeenth century executioner."

"How very appropriate," said Tuppence softly.

"Appropriate, Mrs. Beresford. What do you mean by appropriate?"

"For the part you played. Shall I tell you my ideas on the subject, Sir Arthur? The newspaper dress is easily put on over that of an executioner. Previously a little note has been slipped into Captain Hale's hand, asking him not to speak to a certain lady. But the lady herself knows nothing of that note. She goes to the Ace of Spades at the appointed time and sees the figure she expects to see. They go into the booth. He takes her in his arms, I think, and kisses her—the kiss of a Judas, and as he kisses he strikes with the dagger. She only utters one faint cry and he covers that with a laugh. Presently he goes away—and to the last, horrified and bewildered, she believes her lover is the man who killed her.

"But she has torn a small fragment from the costume. The murderer notices that—he is a man who pays great attention to detail. To make the case absolutely clear against his victim the fragment must seem to have been torn from Captain Hale's costume. That would present great difficulties unless the two men happened to be living in the same house. Then, of course, the thing would be simplicity itself. He makes an exact duplicate of the tear in Captain Hale's costume—then he burns his own and prepares to play the part of the loyal friend."

Tuppence paused.

"Well, Sir Arthur?"

Sir Arthur rose and made her a bow.

"The rather vivid imagination of a charming lady who reads too much fiction."

"You think so?" said Tommy.

"And a husband who is guided by his wife," said Sir Arthur. "I do not fancy you will find anybody to take the matter seriously."

He laughed out loud, and Tuppence stiffened in her chair.

"I would swear to that laugh anywhere," she said. "I heard it last in the Ace of Spades. And you are under a little misapprehension about us both. Beresford is our real name, but we have another."

She picked up a card from the table and handed it to him. Sir Arthur read it aloud.

"International Detective Agency . . ." He drew his breath sharply. "So that is what you really are! That was why Marriot brought me here this morning. It was a trap—"

He strolled to the window.

"A fine view you have from here," he said. "Right over London."

"Inspector Marriot," cried Tommy sharply.

In a flash the Inspector appeared from the communicating door in the opposite wall.

A little smile of amusement came to Sir Arthur's lips.

"I thought as much," he said. "But you won't get me this time, I'm afraid, Inspector. I prefer to take my own way out."

And putting his hands on the sill, he vaulted clean through the window.

Tuppence shrieked and clapped her hands to her ears to shut out the sound she had already imagined—the sickening thud far beneath. Inspector Marriot uttered an oath.

"We should have thought of the window," he said. "Though, mind you, it would have been a difficult thing to prove. I'll go down and—and—see to things."

"Poor devil," said Tommy slowly. "If he was fond of his wife—"

But the Inspector interrupted him with a snort.

"Fond of her? That's as may be. He was at his wits' end where to turn for money. Lady Merivale had a large fortune of her own, and it all went to him. If she'd bolted with young Hale, he'd never have seen a penny of it."

"That was it, was it?"

"Of course, from the very start, I sensed that Sir Arthur was a bad lot, and that Captain Hale was all right. We know pretty well what's what at the Yard—but it's awkward when you're up against facts. I'll be going down now—I should give your wife a glass of brandy if I were you, Mr. Beresford—it's been upsetting like for her."

"Greengrocers," said Tuppence in a low voice as the door closed behind the imperturbable Inspector, "butchers, fishermen, detectives. I was right, wasn't I? He knew."

Tommy, who had been busy at the sideboard, approached her with a large glass.

"Drink this."

"What is it? Brandy?"

"No, it's a large cocktail—suitable for a triumphant

McCarty. Yes, Marriot's right all round—that was the way of it. A bold finesse for game and rubber."

Tuppence nodded.

"But he finessed the wrong way round."

"And so," said Tommy, "exit the King."

Fruitful Sunday

Well, really, I call this too delightful," said Miss Dorothy Pratt for the fourth time. "How I wish the old cat could see me now. She and her Janes!"

The "old cat" thus scathingly alluded to was Miss Pratt's highly estimable employer, Mrs. Mackenzie Jones, who had strong views upon the Christian names suitable for parlour-maids and had repudiated Dorothy in favour of Miss Pratt's despised second name of Jane.

Miss Pratt's companion did not reply at once—for the best of reasons. When you have just purchased a Baby Austin, fourth hand, for the sum of twenty pounds, and are taking it out for the second time only, your whole attention is necessarily focused on the difficult task of using both hands and feet as the emergencies of the moment dictate.

"Er—ah!" said Mr. Edward Palgrove and negotiated a crisis with a horrible grinding sound that would have set a true motorist's teeth on edge.

"Well, you don't talk to a girl much," complained Dorothy.

Mr. Palgrove was saved from having to respond as at that moment he was roundly and soundly cursed by the driver of a motor omnibus.

"Well, of all the impudence," said Miss Pratt, tossing her head.

"I only wish *he* had this foot brake," said her swain bitterly.

"Is there anything wrong with it?"

"You can put your foot on it till kingdom comes," said Mr. Palgrove. "But nothing happens."

"Oh, well, Ted, you can't expect everything for twenty pounds. After all, here we are, in a real car, on Sunday afternoon going out of town the same as everybody else."

More grinding and crashing sounds.

"Ah," said Ted, flushed with triumph. "That was a better change."

"You do drive something beautiful," said Dorothy admiringly.

Emboldened by feminine appreciation, Mr. Palgrove attempted a dash across Hammersmith Broadway, and was severely spoken to by a policeman.

"Well, I never," said Dorothy, as they proceeded towards Hammersmith Bridge in a chastened fashion. "I don't know what the police are coming to. You'd think they'd be a bit more civil spoken seeing the way they've been shown up lately."

"Anyway, I didn't want to go along this road," said Edward sadly. "I wanted to go down the Great West Road and do a bust."

"And be caught in a trap as likely as not," said Dorothy. "That's what happened to the master the other day. Five pounds and costs."

"The police aren't so dusty after all," said Edward generously. "They pitch into the rich all right. No favour. It makes me mad to think of these swells who can walk into a place and buy a couple of Rolls-Royces without turning a hair. There's no sense in it. I'm as good as they are."

"And the jewellery," said Dorothy, sighing. "Those shops in Bond Street. Diamonds and pearls and I don't know what! And me with a string of Woolworth pearls."

She brooded sadly upon the subject. Edward was able once more to give his full attention to his driving. They managed to get through Richmond without mishap. The altercation with the policeman had shaken Edward's nerve. He now took the line of least resistance, following blindly behind any car in front whenever a choice of thoroughfares presented itself.

In this way he presently found himself following a shady country lane which many an experienced motorist would have given his soul to find.

"Rather clever turning off the way I did," said Edward, taking all the credit to himself.

"Sweetly pretty, I call it," said Miss Pratt. "And I do declare, there's a man with fruit to sell."

Sure enough, at a convenient corner, was a small wicker table with baskets of fruit on it, and the legend EAT MORE FRUIT displayed on a banner.

"How much?" said Edward apprehensively when frenzied pulling of the hand brake had produced the desired result.

"Lovely strawberries," said the man in charge.

He was an unprepossessing-looking individual with a leer.

"Just the thing for the lady. Ripe fruit, fresh picked.

Cherries too. Genuine English. Have a basket of cherries, lady?"

"They do look nice ones," said Dorothy.

"Lovely, that's what they are," said the man hoarsely. "Bring you luck, lady, that basket will." He at last condescended to reply to Edward. "Two shillings, sir, and dirt cheap. You'd say so if you knew what was inside the basket."

"They look awfully nice," said Dorothy.

Edward sighed and paid over two shillings. His mind was obsessed by calculation. Tea later, petrol—this Sunday motoring business wasn't what you'd call *cheap.* That was the worst of taking girls out! They always wanted everything they saw.

"Thank you, sir," said the unprepossessing-looking one. "You've got more than your money's worth in that basket of cherries."

Edward shoved his foot savagely down and the Baby Austin leaped at the cherry vendor after the manner of an infuriated Alsatian.

"Sorry," said Edward. "I forgot she was in gear."

"You ought to be careful, dear," said Dorothy. "You might have hurt him."

Edward did not reply. Another half mile brought them to an ideal spot by the banks of a stream. The Austin was left by the side of the road and Edward and Dorothy sat affectionately upon the river bank and munched cherries. A Sunday paper lay unheeded at their feet.

"What's the news?" said Edward at last, stretching himself flat on his back and tilting his hat to shade his eyes.

Dorothy glanced over the headlines.

"The Woeful Wife. Extraordinary story. Twenty-eight people drowned last week. Reported death of Airman. Startling Jewel Robbery. Ruby Necklace worth fifty thousand pounds missing. Oh, Ted! Fifty thousand pounds. Just fancy!" She went on reading. "The necklace is composed of twenty-one stones set in platinum and was sent by registered post from Paris. On arrival, the packet was found to contain a few pebbles and the jewels were missing."

"Pinched in the post," said Edward. "The posts in France are awful, I believe."

"I'd like to see a necklace like that," said Dorothy. "All glowing like blood—pigeon's blood, that's what they call the colour. I wonder what it would feel like to have a thing like that hanging round your neck."

"Well, *you're* never likely to know, my girl," said Edward facetiously.

Dorothy tossed her head.

"Why not, I should like to know. It's amazing the way girls can get on in the world. I might go on the stage."

"Girls that behave themselves don't get anywhere," said Edward discouragingly.

Dorothy opened her mouth to reply, checked herself, and murmured, "Pass me the cherries.

"I've been eating more than you have," she remarked. "I'll divide up what's left and—why, whatever's this at the bottom of the basket?"

She drew it out as she spoke—a long glittering chain of blood-red stones.

They both stared at it in amazement.

"In the basket, did you say?" said Edward at last.

Dorothy nodded.

"Right at the bottom—under the fruit."

Again they stared at each other.

"How did it get there, do you think?"

"I can't imagine. It's odd, Ted, just after reading that bit in the paper—about the rubies."

Edward laughed.

"You don't imagine you're holding fifty thousand pounds in your hand, do you?"

"I just said it was odd. Rubies set in platinum. Platinum is that sort of dull silvery stuff—like this. Don't they sparkle and aren't they a lovely colour? I wonder how many of them there are?" She counted. "I say, Ted, there are twenty-one exactly."

"No!"

"Yes. The same number as the paper said. Oh, Ted, you don't think—"

"It could be." But he spoke irresolutely. "There's some sort of way you can tell—scratching them on glass."

"That's diamonds. But you know, Ted, that was a very odd-looking man—the man with the fruit—a nasty-looking man. And he was funny about it—said we'd got more than our money's worth in the basket."

"Yes, but look here, Dorothy, what would he want to hand us over fifty thousand pounds for?"

Miss Pratt shook her head, discouraged.

"It doesn't seem to make sense," she admitted. "Unless the police were after him."

"The police?" Edward paled slightly.

"Yes. It goes on to say in the paper—'the police have a clue.'"

Cold shivers ran down Edward's spine.

"I don't like this, Dorothy. Supposing the police get after *us*."

Dorothy stared at him with her mouth open.

"But we haven't done anything, Ted. We found it in the basket."

"And that'll sound a silly sort of story to tell! It isn't likely."

"It isn't very," admitted Dorothy. "Oh, Ted, do you really think it is it? It's like a fairy story!"

"I don't think it sounds like a fairy story," said Edward. "It sounds to me more like the kind of story where the hero goes to Dartmoor unjustly accused for fourteen years."

But Dorothy was not listening. She had clasped the necklace round her neck and was judging the effect in a small mirror taken from her handbag.

"The same as a duchess might wear," she murmured ecstatically.

"I won't believe it," said Edward violently. "They're imitation. They *must* be imitation."

"Yes, dear," said Dorothy, still intent on her reflection in the mirror. "Very likely."

"Anything else would be too much of a—a coincidence."

"Pigeon's blood," murmured Dorothy.

"It's absurd. That's what I say. Absurd. Look here, Dorothy, are you listening to what I say, or are you not?"

Dorothy put away the mirror. She turned to him, one hand on the rubies round her neck.

"How do I look?" she asked.

Edward stared at her, his grievance forgotten. He had never seen Dorothy quite like this. There was a triumph about her, a kind of regal beauty that was completely new to him. The belief that she had jewels round her neck worth fifty thousand pounds had made of Dorothy Pratt a new woman. She looked insolently serene, a kind of Cleopatra and Semiramis and Zenobia rolled into one.

"You look—you look—stunning," said Edward humbly.

Dorothy laughed, and her laugh, too, was entirely different.

"Look here," said Edward. "We've got to do something. We must take them to a police station or something."

"Nonsense," said Dorothy. "You said yourself just now that they wouldn't believe you. You'll probably be sent to prison for stealing them."

"But—but what else can we do?"

"Keep them," said the new Dorothy Pratt.

Edward stared at her.

"Keep them? You're mad."

"We found them, didn't we? Why should we think they're valuable. We'll keep them and I shall wear them."

"And the police will pinch *you*."

Dorothy considered this for a minute or two.

"All right," she said. "We'll sell them. And you can buy a Rolls-Royce, or two Rolls-Royces, and I'll buy a diamond head-thing and some rings."

Still Edward stared. Dorothy showed impatience.

"You've got your chance now—it's up to you to take it. We didn't steal the thing—I wouldn't hold with that. It's come to us and it's probably the only chance we'll ever have of getting all the things we want. Haven't you got any spunk at all, Edward Palgrove?"

Edward found his voice.

"Sell it, you say? That wouldn't be so jolly easy. Any jeweller would want to know where I got the blooming thing."

"You don't take it to a jeweller. Don't you ever read detective stories, Ted? You take it to a 'fence,' of course."

"And how should I know any fences? I've been brought up respectable."

"Men ought to know everything," said Dorothy. "That's what they're for."

He looked at her. She was serene and unyielding.

"I wouldn't have believed it of you," he said weakly.

"I thought you had more spirit."

There was a pause. Then Dorothy rose to her feet.

"Well," she said lightly. "We'd best be getting home."

"Wearing that thing round your neck?"

Dorothy removed the necklace, looked at it reverently and dropped it into her handbag.

"Look here," said Edward. "You give that to me."

"No."

"Yes, you do. I've been brought up honest, my girl."

"Well, you can go on being honest. You need have nothing to do with it."

"Oh, hand it over," said Edward recklessly. "I'll do it. I'll find a fence. As you say, it's the only chance we shall ever have. We came by it honest—bought it for two shillings. It's no more than what gentlemen do in antique shops every day of their life and are proud of it."

"That's it!" said Dorothy. "Oh, Edward, you're splendid!"

She handed over the necklace and he dropped it into his

pocket. He felt worked up, exalted, the very devil of a fellow! In this mood he started the Austin. They were both too excited to remember tea. They drove back to London in silence. Once at a crossroads, a policeman stepped towards the car, and Edward's heart missed a beat. By a miracle, they reached home without mishap.

Edward's last words to Dorothy were imbued with the adventurous spirit.

"We'll go through with this. Fifty thousand pounds! It's worth it!"

He dreamt that night of broad arrows and Dartmoor, and rose early, haggard and unrefreshed. He had to set about finding a fence—and how to do it he had not the remotest idea!

His work at the office was slovenly and brought down upon him two sharp rebukes before lunch.

How did one find a "fence?" Whitechapel, he fancied, was the correct neighbourhood—or was it Stepney?

On his return to the office a call came through for him on the telephone. Dorothy's voice spoke—tragic and tearful.

"Is that you, Ted? I'm using the telephone, but she may come in any minute, and I'll have to stop. Ted, you haven't done anything, have you?"

Edward replied in the negative.

"Well, look here, Ted, you mustn't. I've been lying awake all night. It's been awful. Thinking of how it says in the Bible you mustn't steal. I must have been mad yesterday—I really must. You won't do anything, will you, Ted, dear?"

Did a feeling of relief steal over Mr. Palgrove? Possibly it did—but he wasn't going to admit any such thing.

"When I say I'm going through with a thing, I go through with it," he said in a voice such as might belong to a strong superman with eyes of steel.

"Oh, but, Ted, dear, you mustn't. Oh, Lord, she's coming. Look here, Ted, she's going out to dinner tonight. I can slip out and meet you. Don't do anything till you've seen me. Eight o'clock. Wait for me round the corner." Her voice changed to a seraphic murmur. "Yes, ma'am, I think it was a wrong number. It was Bloomsbury 0234 they wanted."

As Edward left the office at six o'clock, a huge headline caught his eye.

JEWEL ROBBERY. LATEST DEVELOPMENTS

Hurriedly he extended a penny. Safely ensconced in the Tube, having dexterously managed to gain a seat, he eagerly perused the printed sheet. He found what he sought easily enough.

A suppressed whistle escaped him.

"Well—I'm—"

And then another adjacent paragraph caught his eye. He read it through and let the paper slip to the floor unheeded.

Precisely at eight o'clock, he was waiting at the rendezvous. A breathless Dorothy, looking pale but pretty, came hurrying along to join him.

"You haven't done anything, Ted?"

"I haven't done anything." He took the ruby chain from his pocket. "You can put it on."

"But, Ted—"

"The police have got the rubies all right—and the man who pinched them. And now read this!"

He thrust a newspaper paragraph under her nose. Dorothy read:

New Advertising Stunt

> A clever new advertising dodge is being adopted by the All-English Fivepenny Fair who intend to challenge the famous Woolworths. Baskets of fruit were sold yesterday and will be on sale every Sunday. Out of every fifty baskets, one will contain an imitation necklace in different coloured stones. These necklaces are really wonderful value for the money. Great excitement and merriment was caused by them yesterday and EAT MORE FRUIT will have a great vogue next Sunday. We congratulate the Fivepenny Fair on their resource and wish them all good luck in their campaign of Buy British Goods.

"Well—" said Dorothy.

And after a pause: "Well!"

"Yes," said Edward. "I felt the same."

A passing man thrust a paper into his hand.

"Take one, brother," he said.

"The price of a virtuous woman is far above rubies."

"There!" said Edward. "I hope that cheers you up."

"I don't know," said Dorothy doubtfully. "I don't exactly want to *look* like a good woman."

"You don't," said Edward. "That's why the man gave me

that paper. With those rubies round your neck you don't look one little bit like a good woman."

Dorothy laughed.

"You're rather a dear, Ted," she said. "Come on, let's go to the pictures."

Wasps' Nest

Out of the house came John Harrison and stood a moment on the terrace looking out over the garden. He was a big man with a lean, cadaverous face. His aspect was usually somewhat grim but when, as now, the rugged features softened into a smile, there was something very attractive about him.

John Harrison loved his garden, and it had never looked better than it did on this August evening, summery and languorous. The rambler roses were still beautiful; sweet peas scented the air.

A well-known creaking sound made Harrison turn his head sharply. Who was coming in through the garden gate? In another minute, an expression of utter astonishment came over his face, for the dandified figure coming up the path was the last he expected to see in this part of the world.

"By all that's wonderful," cried Harrison. "Monsieur Poirot!"

It was, indeed, the famous Hercule Poirot whose renown as a detective had spread over the whole world.

"Yes," he said, "it is. You said to me once: 'If you are ever in this part of the world, come and see me.' I take you at your word. I arrive."

"And I'm obliged," said Harrison heartily. "Sit down and have a drink."

With a hospitable hand, he indicated a table on the veranda bearing assorted bottles.

"I thank you," said Poirot, sinking down into a basket chair. "You have, I suppose, no *sirop?* No, no. I thought not. A little plain soda water then—no whisky." And he added in a feeling voice as the other placed the glass beside him: "Alas, my moustaches are limp. It is this heat!"

"And what brings you into this quiet spot?" asked Harrison as he dropped into another chair. "Pleasure?"

"No, *mon ami,* business."

"Business? In this out-of-the-way place?"

Poirot nodded gravely. "But yes, my friend, all crimes are not committed in crowds, you know?"

The other laughed. "I suppose that was rather an idiotic remark of mine. But what particular crime are you investigating down here, or is that a thing I mustn't ask?"

"You may ask," said the detective. "Indeed, I would prefer that you asked."

Harrison looked at him curiously. He sensed something a little unusual in the other's manner. "You are investigating a crime, you say?" he advanced rather hesitatingly. "A serious crime?"

"A crime of the most serious there is."

"You mean. . . ."

"Murder."

So gravely did Hercule Poirot say that word that Harrison was quite taken aback. The detective was looking straight at him and again there was something so unusual in his glance that Harrison hardly knew how to proceed. At last, he said: "But I have heard of no murder."

"No," said Poirot, "you would not have heard of it."

"Who has been murdered?"

"As yet," said Hercule Poirot, "nobody."

"What?"

"That is why I said you would not have heard of it. I am investigating a crime that has not yet taken place."

"But look here, that is nonsense."

"Not at all. If one can investigate a murder before it has happened, surely that is very much better than afterwards. One might even—a little idea—prevent it."

Harrison stared at him. "You are not serious, Monsieur Poirot."

"But yes, I am serious."

"You really believe that a murder is going to be committed? Oh, it's absurd!"

Hercule Poirot finished the first part of the sentence without taking any notice of the exclamation.

"Unless we can manage to prevent it. Yes, *mon ami,* that is what I mean."

"We?"

"I said we. I shall need your cooperation."

"Is that why you came down here?"

Again Poirot looked at him, and again an indefinable something made Harrison uneasy.

"I came here, Monsieur Harrison, because I—well—like you."

And then he added in an entirely different voice: "I see, Monsieur Harrison, that you have a wasps' nest there. You should destroy it."

The change of subject made Harrison frown in a puzzled way. He followed Poirot's glance and said in a bewildered voice: "As a matter of fact, I'm going to. Or rather, young Langton is. You remember Claude Langton? He was at that same dinner where I met you. He's coming over this evening to take the nest. Rather fancies himself at the job."

"Ah," said Poirot. "And how is he going to do it?"

"Petrol and the garden syringe. He's bringing his own syringe over; it's a more convenient size than mine."

"There is another way, is there not?" asked Poirot. "With cyanide of potassium?"

Harrison looked a little surprised. "Yes, but that's rather dangerous stuff. Always a risk having it about the place."

Poirot nodded gravely. "Yes, it is deadly poison." He waited a minute and then repeated in a grave voice, "Deadly poison."

"Useful if you want to do away with your mother-in-law, eh?" said Harrison with a laugh.

But Hercule Poirot remained grave. "And you are quite sure, Monsieur Harrison, that it is with petrol that Monsieur Langton is going to destroy your wasps' nest?"

"Quite sure. Why?"

"I wondered. I was at the chemist's in Barchester this afternoon. For one of my purchases I had to sign the poison book. I saw the last entry. It was for cyanide of potassium and it was signed by Claude Langton."

Harrison stared. "That's odd," he said. "Langton told me

the other day that he'd never dream of using the stuff; in fact, he said it oughtn't to be sold for the purpose."

Poirot looked out over the garden. His voice was very quiet as he asked a question. "Do you like Langton?"

The other started. The question somehow seemed to find him quite unprepared. "I—I—well, I mean—of course, I like him. Why shouldn't I?"

"I only wondered," said Poirot placidly, "whether you did."

And as the other did not answer, he went on. "I also wondered if he liked you?"

"What are you getting at, Monsieur Poirot? There's something in your mind I can't fathom."

"I am going to be very frank. You are engaged to be married, Monsieur Harrison. I know Miss Molly Deane. She is a very charming, a very beautiful girl. Before she was engaged to you, she was engaged to Claude Langton. She threw him over for you."

Harrison nodded.

"I do not ask what her reasons were: she may have been justified. But I tell you this, it is not too much to suppose that Langton has not forgotten or forgiven."

"You're wrong, Monsieur Poirot. I swear you're wrong. Langton's been a sportsman; he's taken things like a man. He's been amazingly decent to me—gone out of his way to be friendly."

"And that does not strike you as unusual? You use the word 'amazingly,' but you do not seem to be amazed."

"What do you mean, M. Poirot?"

"I mean," said Poirot, and his voice had a new note in

it, "that a man may conceal his hate till the proper time comes."

"Hate?" Harrison shook his head and laughed.

"The English are very stupid," said Poirot. "They think that they can deceive anyone but that no one can deceive them. The sportsman—the good fellow—never will they believe evil of him. And because they are brave, but stupid, sometimes they die when they need not die."

"You are warning me," said Harrison in a low voice. "I see it now—what has puzzled me all along. You are warning me against Claude Langton. You came here today to warn me. . . ."

Poirot nodded. Harrison sprang up suddenly. "But *you* are mad, Monsieur Poirot. This is England. Things don't happen like that here. Disappointed suitors don't go about stabbing people in the back and poisoning them. And you're wrong about Langton. That chap wouldn't hurt a fly."

"The lives of flies are not my concern," said Poirot placidly. "And although you say Monsieur Langton would not take the life of one, yet you forget that he is even now preparing to take the lives of several thousand wasps."

Harrison did not at once reply. The little detective in his turn sprang to his feet. He advanced to his friend and laid a hand on his shoulder. So agitated was he that he almost shook the big man, and, as he did so, he hissed into his ear: "Rouse yourself, my friend, rouse yourself. And look—look where I am pointing. There on the bank, close by that tree root. See you, the wasps returning home, placid at the end of the day? In a little hour, there will be destruction, and they know it not. There is no one to tell them. They have not, it seems, a Hercule Poirot. I tell you, Monsieur Harrison, I am down here on business. Murder is my business. And it is my business before it has happened as well as afterwards. At what time does Monsieur Langton come to take this wasps' nest?"

"Langton would never. . . ."

"At what time?"

"At nine o'clock. But I tell you, you're all wrong. Langton would never. . . ."

"These English!" cried Poirot in a passion. He caught up his hat and stick and moved down the path, pausing to speak over his shoulder. "I do not stay to argue with you. I should only enrage myself. But you understand, I return at nine o'clock?"

Harrison opened his mouth to speak, but Poirot did not give him the chance. "I know what you would say: 'Langton would never,' et cetera. Ah, Langton would never! But all the same I return at nine o'clock. But, yes, it will amuse me—put it like that—it will amuse me to see the taking of a wasps' nest. Another of your English sports!"

He waited for no reply but passed rapidly down the path and out through the door that creaked. Once outside on the road, his pace slackened. His vivacity died down, his face became grave and troubled. Once he drew his watch from his pocket and consulted it. The hands pointed to ten minutes past eight. "Over three quarters of an hour," he murmured. "I wonder if I should have waited."

His footsteps slackened; he almost seemed on the point of returning. Some vague foreboding seemed to assail him. He shook it off resolutely, however, and continued to walk in the direction of the village. But his face was still troubled, and once or twice he shook his head like a man only partly satisfied.

It was still some minutes off nine when he once more approached the garden door. It was a clear, still evening; hardly a breeze stirred the leaves. There was, perhaps, something a little sinister in the stillness, like the lull before a storm.

Poirot's footsteps quickened ever so slightly. He was suddenly alarmed—and uncertain. He feared he knew not what.

And at that moment the garden door opened and Claude Langton stepped quickly out into the road. He started when he saw Poirot.

"Oh—er—good evening."

"Good evening, Monsieur Langton. You are early."

Langton stared at him. "I don't know what you mean."

"You have taken the wasps' nest?"

"As a matter of fact, I didn't."

"Oh," said Poirot softly. "So you did not take the wasps' nest. What did you do then?"

"Oh, just sat and yarned a bit with old Harrison. I really must hurry along now, Monsieur Poirot. I'd no idea you were remaining in this part of the world."

"I had business here, you see."

"Oh! Well, you'll find Harrison on the terrace. Sorry I can't stop."

He hurried away. Poirot looked after him. A nervous young fellow, good-looking with a weak mouth!

"So I shall find Harrison on the terrace," murmured Poirot. "I wonder." He went in through the garden door and up the path. Harrison was sitting in a chair by the table. He sat motionless and did not even turn his head as Poirot came up to him.

"Ah! *Mon ami,*" said Poirot. "You are all right, eh?"

There was a long pause and then Harrison said in a queer, dazed voice, "What did you say?"

"I said—are you all right?"

"All right? Yes, I'm all right. Why not?"

"You feel no ill effects? That is good."

"Ill effects? From what?"

"Washing soda."

Harrison roused himself suddenly. "Washing soda? What do you mean?"

Poirot made an apologetic gesture. "I infinitely regret the necessity, but I put some in your pocket."

"You put some in my pocket? What on earth for?"

Harrison stared at him. Poirot spoke quietly and impersonally like a lecturer coming down to the level of a small child.

"You see, one of the advantages, or disadvantages, of being a detective is that it brings you into contact with the criminal classes. And the criminal classes, they can teach you some very interesting and curious things. There was a pickpocket once—I interested myself in him because for once in a way he had not done what they say he has done—and so I get him off. And because he is grateful he pays me in the only way he can think of—which is to show me the tricks of his trade.

"And so it happens that I can pick a man's pocket if I choose without his ever suspecting the fact. I lay one hand on his shoulder, I excite myself, and he feels nothing. But all the same I have managed to transfer what is in his pocket to my pocket and leave washing soda in its place.

"You see," continued Poirot dreamily, "if a man wants to get at some poison quickly to put in a glass, unobserved, he positively must keep it in his right-hand coat pocket; there is nowhere else. I knew it would be there."

He dropped his hand into his pocket and brought out a few white, lumpy crystals. "Exceedingly dangerous," he murmured, "to carry it like that—loose."

Calmly and without hurrying himself, he took from another pocket a wide-mouthed bottle. He slipped in the crystals, stepped to the table and filled up the bottle with plain water. Then carefully corking it, he shook it until all the crystals were dissolved. Harrison watched him as though fascinated.

Satisfied with his solution, Poirot stepped across to the nest. He uncorked the bottle, turned his head aside, and poured the solution into the wasps' nest, then stood back a pace or two watching.

Some wasps that were returning alighted, quivered a little and then lay still. Other wasps crawled out of the hole only to die. Poirot watched for a minute or two and then nodded his head and came back to the veranda.

"A quick death," he said. "A very quick death."

Harrison found his voice. "How much do you know?"

Poirot looked straight ahead. "As I told you, I saw Claude Langton's name in the book. What I did not tell you was that almost immediately afterwards, I happened to meet him. He told me he had been buying cyanide of potassium at your request—to take a wasps' nest. That struck me as a little odd, my friend, because I remember that at that dinner of which you spoke, you held forth on the superior merits of petrol and denounced the buying of cyanide as dangerous and unnecessary."

"Go on."

"I knew something else. I had seen Claude Langton and Molly Deane together when they thought no one saw them. I do not know what lovers' quarrel it was that originally parted them and drove her into your arms, but I realized that misunderstandings were over and that Miss Deane was drifting back to her love."

"Go on."

"I knew something more, my friend. I was in Harley Street the other day, and I saw you come out of a certain doctor's house. I know the doctor and for what disease one consults him, and I read the expression on your face. I have seen it only once or twice in my lifetime, but it is not easily mistaken. It was the face of a man under sentence of death. I am right, am I not?"

"Quite right. He gave me two months."

"You did not see me, my friend, for you had other things to think about. I saw something else on your face—the thing that I told you this afternoon men try to conceal. I saw hate there, my friend. You did not trouble to conceal it, because you thought there were none to observe."

"Go on," said Harrison.

"There is not much more to say. I came down here, saw Langton's name by accident in the poison book as I tell you, met him, and came here to you. I laid traps for you. You denied having asked Langton to get cyanide, or rather you expressed surprise at his having done so. You were taken aback at first at my appearance, but presently you saw how well it would fit in and you encouraged my suspicions. I knew from Langton himself that he was coming at half past eight. You told me nine o'clock, thinking I should come and find everything over. And so I knew everything."

"Why did you come?" cried Harrison. "If only you hadn't come!"

Poirot drew himself up. "I told you," he said, "murder is my business."

"Murder? Suicide, you mean."

"No." Poirot's voice rang out sharply and clearly. "I mean murder. Your death was to be quick and easy, but the death you planned for Langton was the worst death any man can die. He bought the poison; he comes to see you, and he is alone with you. You die suddenly, and the cyanide is found in your glass, and Claude Langton hangs. That was your plan."

Again Harrison moaned.

"Why did you come? Why did you come?"

"I have told you, but there is another reason. I liked you. Listen, *mon ami,* you are a dying man; you have lost the girl you loved, but there is one thing that you are not; you are not a murderer. Tell me now: are you glad or sorry that I came?"

There was a moment's pause and Harrison drew himself up. There was a new dignity in his face—the look of a man who has conquered his own baser self. He stretched out his hand across the table.

"Thank goodness you came," he cried. "Oh, thank goodness you came."

The Case of the Caretaker

"Well," demanded Doctor Haydock of his patient. "And how goes it today?"

Miss Marple smiled at him wanly from pillows.

"I suppose, really, that I'm better," she admitted, "but I feel so terribly depressed. I can't help feeling how much better it would have been if I had died. After all, I'm an old woman. Nobody wants me or cares about me."

Doctor Haydock interrupted with his usual brusqueness. "Yes, yes, typical after-reaction of this type of flu. What you need is something to take you out of yourself. A mental tonic."

Miss Marple sighed and shook her head.

"And what's more," continued Doctor Haydock, "I've brought my medicine with me!"

He tossed a long envelope on to the bed.

"Just the thing for you. The kind of puzzle that is right up your street."

"A puzzle?" Miss Marple looked interested.

"Literary effort of mine," said the doctor, blushing a little. "Tried to make a regular story of it. 'He said,' 'she said,' 'the girl thought,' etc. Facts of the story are true."

"But why a puzzle?" asked Miss Marple.

Doctor Haydock grinned. "Because the interpretation is up to you. I want to see if you're as clever as you always make out."

With that Parthian shot he departed.

Miss Marple picked up the manuscript and began to read.

"And where is the bride?" asked Miss Harmon genially.

The village was all agog to see the rich and beautiful young wife that Harry Laxton had brought back from abroad. There was a general indulgent feeling that Harry—wicked young scapegrace—had had all the luck. Everyone had always felt indulgent towards Harry. Even the owners of windows that had suffered from his indiscriminate use of a catapult had found their indignation dissipated by young Harry's abject expression of regret. He had broken windows, robbed orchards, poached rabbits, and later had run into debt, got entangled with the local tobacconist's daughter—been disentangled and sent off to Africa—and the village as represented by various ageing spinsters had murmured indulgently. "Ah, well! Wild oats! He'll settle down!"

And now, sure enough, the prodigal had returned—not in affliction, but in triumph. Harry Laxton had "made good" as the saying goes. He had pulled himself together, worked hard, and had finally met and successfully wooed a young Anglo-French girl who was the possessor of a considerable fortune.

Harry might have lived in London, or purchased an estate in some fashionable hunting county, but he preferred to come back to the part of the world that was home to him. And there, in the most romantic way, he purchased the derelict estate in the dower house of which he had passed his childhood.

Kingsdean House had been unoccupied for nearly seventy years. It had gradually fallen into decay and abandon. An elderly caretaker and his wife lived in the one habitable corner of it. It was a vast, unprepossessing grandiose mansion, the gardens overgrown with rank vegetation and the trees hemming it in like some gloomy enchanter's den.

The dower house was a pleasant, unpretentious house and had been let for a long term of years to Major Laxton, Harry's father. As a boy, Harry had roamed over the Kingsdean estate and knew every inch of the tangled woods, and the old house itself had always fascinated him.

Major Laxton had died some years ago, so it might have been thought that Harry would have had no ties to bring him back—nevertheless it was to the home of his boyhood that Harry brought his bride. The ruined old Kingsdean House was pulled down. An army of builders and contractors swooped down upon the place, and in almost a miraculously short space of time—so marvellously does wealth tell—the new house rose white and gleaming among the trees.

Next came a posse of gardeners and after them a procession of furniture vans.

The house was ready. Servants arrived. Lastly, a costly limousine deposited Harry and Mrs. Harry at the front door.

The village rushed to call, and Mrs. Price, who owned the largest house, and who considered herself to lead society in the place, sent out cards of invitation for a party "to meet the bride."

It was a great event. Several ladies had new frocks for the occasion. Everyone was excited, curious, anxious to see this fabulous creature. They said it was all so like a fairy story!

Miss Harmon, weather-beaten, hearty spinster, threw out her question as she squeezed her way through the crowded drawing room door. Little Miss Brent, a thin, acidulated spinster, fluttered out information.

"Oh, my dear, quite charming. Such pretty manners. And quite young. Really, you know, it makes one feel quite envious to see someone who has everything like that. Good looks and money and breeding—most distinguished, nothing in the least common about her—and dear Harry so devoted!"

"Ah," said Miss Harmon, "it's early days yet!"

Miss Brent's thin nose quivered appreciatively. "Oh, my dear, do you really think—"

"We all know what Harry is," said Miss Harmon.

"We know what he was! But I expect now—"

"Ah," said Miss Harmon, "men are always the same. Once a gay deceiver, always a gay deceiver. I know them."

"Dear, dear. Poor young thing." Miss Brent looked much happier. "Yes, I expect she'll have trouble with him. Someone ought really to warn her. I wonder if she's heard anything of the old story?"

"It seems so very unfair," said Miss Brent, "that she should know nothing. So awkward. Especially with only the one chemist's shop in the village."

For the erstwhile tobacconist's daughter was now married to Mr. Edge, the chemist.

"It would be so much nicer," said Miss Brent, "if Mrs. Laxton were to deal with Boots in Much Benham."

"I dare say," said Miss Harmon, "that Harry Laxton will suggest that himself."

And again a significant look passed between them.

"But I certainly think," said Miss Harmon, "that she ought to know."

"Beasts!" said Clarice Vane indignantly to her uncle, Doctor Haydock. "Absolute beasts some people are."

He looked at her curiously.

She was a tall, dark girl, handsome, warmhearted and impulsive. Her big brown eyes were alight now with indignation as she said, "All these cats—saying things—hinting things."

"About Harry Laxton?"

"Yes, about his affair with the tobacconist's daughter."

"Oh, that!" The doctor shrugged his shoulders. "A great many young men have affairs of that kind."

"Of course they do. And it's all over. So why harp on it? And bring it up years after? It's like ghouls feasting on dead bodies."

"I dare say, my dear, it does seem like that to you. But you see, they have very little to talk about down here, and so I'm afraid they do tend to dwell upon past scandals. But I'm curious to know why it upsets you so much?"

Clarice Vane bit her lip and flushed. She said, in a curiously muffled voice. "They—they look so happy. The Laxtons, I mean. They're young and in love, and it's all so lovely for them. I hate to think of it being spoiled by whispers and hints and innuendoes and general beastliness."

"H'm. I see."

Clarice went on. "He was talking to me just now. He's so happy and eager and excited and—yes, thrilled—at having got his heart's desire and rebuilt Kingsdean. He's like a child about it all. And she—well, I don't suppose anything has ever gone wrong in her whole life. She's always had everything. You've seen her. What did you think of her?"

The doctor did not answer at once. For other people, Louise Laxton might be an object of envy. A spoiled darling of fortune. To him she had brought only the refrain of a popular song heard many years ago, Poor little rich girl—

A small, delicate figure, with flaxen hair curled rather stiffly round her face and big, wistful blue eyes.

Louise was drooping a little. The long stream of congratulations had tired her. She was hoping it might soon be time to go. Perhaps, even now, Harry might say so. She looked at him sideways. So tall and broadshouldered with his eager pleasure in this horrible, dull party.

Poor little rich girl—

"Ooph!" It was a sigh of relief.

Harry turned to look at his wife amusedly. They were driving away from the party.

She said, "Darling, what a frightful party!"

Harry laughed. "Yes, pretty terrible. Never mind, my sweet. It had to be done, you know. All these old pussies knew me when I lived here as a boy. They'd have been terribly disappointed not to have got a look at you close up."

Louise made a grimace. She said, "Shall we have to see a lot of them?"

"What? Oh, no. They'll come and make ceremonious calls with card cases, and you'll return the calls and then you needn't bother anymore. You can have your own friends down or whatever you like."

Louise said, after a minute or two, "Isn't there anyone amusing living down here?"

"Oh, yes. There's the County, you know. Though you may find them a bit dull, too. Mostly interested in bulbs and dogs and horses. You'll ride, of course. You'll enjoy that. There's a horse over at Eglinton I'd like you to see. A beautiful animal, perfectly trained, no vice in him but plenty of spirit."

The car slowed down to take the turn into the gates of Kingsdean. Harry wrenched the wheel and swore as a grotesque figure sprang up in the middle of the road and he only just managed to avoid it. It stood there, shaking a fist and shouting after them.

Louise clutched his arm. "Who's that—that horrible old woman?"

Harry's brow was black. "That's old Murgatroyd. She and her husband were caretakers in the old house. They were there for nearly thirty years."

"Why does she shake her fist at you?"

Harry's face got red. "She—well, she resented the house being pulled down. And she got the sack, of course. Her husband's been dead two years. They say she got a bit queer after he died."

"Is she—she isn't—starving?"

Louise's ideas were vague and somewhat melodramatic. Riches prevented you coming into contact with reality.

Harry was outraged. "Good Lord, Louise, what an idea! I pensioned her off, of course—and handsomely, too! Found her a new cottage and everything."

Louise asked, bewildered, "Then why does she mind?"

Harry was frowning, his brows drawn together. "Oh, how should I know? Craziness! She loved the house."

"But it was a ruin, wasn't it?"

"Of course it was—crumbling to pieces—roof leaking—more

or less unsafe. All the same I suppose it meant something to her. She'd been there a long time. Oh, I don't know! The old devil's cracked, I think."

Louise said uneasily, "She—I think she cursed us. Oh, Harry, I wish she hadn't."

It seemed to Louise that her new home was tainted and poisoned by the malevolent figure of one crazy old woman. When she went out in the car, when she rode, when she walked out with the dogs, there was always the same figure waiting. Crouched down on herself, a battered hat over wisps of iron-grey hair, and the slow muttering of imprecations.

Louise came to believe that Harry was right—the old woman was mad. Nevertheless that did not make things easier. Mrs. Murgatroyd never actually came to the house, nor did she use definite threats, nor offer violence. Her squatting figure remained always just outside the gates. To appeal to the police would have been useless and, in any case, Harry Laxton was averse to that course of action. It would, he said, arouse local sympathy for the old brute. He took the matter more easily than Louise did.

"Don't worry about it, darling. She'll get tired of this silly cursing business. Probably she's only trying it on."

"She isn't, Harry. She—she hates us! I can feel it. She—she's illwishing us."

"She's not a witch, darling, although she may look like one! Don't be morbid about it all."

Louise was silent. Now that the first excitement of settling in was over, she felt curiously lonely and at a loose end. She had been used to life in London and the Riviera. She had no knowledge of or taste for English country life. She was ignorant of gardening, except for the final act of "doing the flowers." She did not really care for dogs. She was bored by such neighbours as she met. She enjoyed riding best, sometimes with Harry, sometimes, when he was busy about the estate, by herself. She hacked through the woods and lanes, enjoying the easy paces of the beautiful horse that Harry had bought for her. Yet even Prince Hal, most sensitive of chestnut steeds, was wont to shy and snort as he carried his mistress past the huddled figure of a malevolent old woman.

One day Louise took her courage in both hands. She was out walking. She had passed Mrs. Murgatroyd, pretending not to notice her, but suddenly she swerved back and went right up to her. She said, a little breathlessly, "What is it? What's the matter? What do you want?"

The old woman blinked at her. She had a cunning, dark gypsy face, with wisps of iron-grey hair, and bleared, suspicious eyes. Louise wondered if she drank.

She spoke in a whining and yet threatening voice. "What do I want, you ask? What, indeed! That which has been took away from me. Who turned me out of Kingsdean House? I'd lived there, girl and woman, for near on forty years. It was a black deed to turn me out and it's black bad luck it'll bring to you and him!"

Louise said, "You've got a very nice cottage and—"

She broke off. The old woman's arms flew up. She screamed, "What's the good of that to me? It's my own place I want and my own fire as I sat beside all them years. And as for you and him, I'm telling you there will be no happiness for you in your new fine house. It's the black sorrow will be upon you! Sorrow and death and my curse. May your fair face rot."

Louise turned away and broke into a little stumbling run.

She thought, I must get away from here! We must sell the house! We must go away.

At the moment, such a solution seemed easy to her. But Harry's utter incomprehension took her back. He exclaimed, "Leave here? Sell the house? Because of a crazy old woman's threats? You must be mad."

"No, I'm not. But she—she frightens me, I know something will happen."

Harry Laxton said grimly, "Leave Mrs. Murgatroyd to me. I'll settle her!"

A friendship had sprung up between Clarice Vane and young Mrs. Laxton. The two girls were much of an age, though dissimilar both in character and in tastes. In Clarice's company, Louise found reassurance. Clarice was so self-reliant, so sure of herself. Louise mentioned the matter of Mrs. Murgatroyd and her threats, but Clarice seemed to regard the matter as more annoying than frightening.

"It's so stupid, that sort of thing," she said. "And really very annoying for you."

"You know, Clarice, I—I feel quite frightened sometimes. My heart gives the most awful jumps."

"Nonsense, you mustn't let a silly thing like that get you down. She'll soon tire of it."

She was silent for a minute or two. Clarice said, "What's the matter?"

Louise paused for a minute, then her answer came with a rush. "I hate this place! I hate being here. The woods and this house, and the awful silence at night, and the queer noise owls make. Oh, and the people and everything."

"The people. What people?"

"The people in the village. Those prying, gossiping old maids."

Clarice said sharply, "What have they been saying?"

"I don't know. Nothing particular. But they've got nasty minds. When you've talked to them you feel you wouldn't trust anybody—not anybody at all."

Clarice said harshly, "Forget them. They've nothing to do but gossip. And most of the muck they talk they just invent."

Louise said, "I wish we'd never come here. But Harry adores it so." Her voice softened.

Clarice thought, How she adores him. *She said abruptly, "I must go now."*

"I'll send you back in the car. Come again soon."

Clarice nodded. Louise felt comforted by her new friend's visit. Harry was pleased to find her more cheerful and from then on urged her to have Clarice often to the house.

Then one day he said, "Good news for you, darling."

"Oh, what?"

"I've fixed the Murgatroyd. She's got a son in America, you know. Well, I've arranged for her to go out and join him. I'll pay her passage."

"Oh, Harry, how wonderful. I believe I might get to like Kingsdean after all."

"Get to like it? Why, it's the most wonderful place in the world!"

Louise gave a little shiver. She could not rid herself of her superstitious fear so easily.

If the ladies of St. Mary Mead had hoped for the pleasure of imparting information about her husband's past to the bride, this pleasure was denied them by Harry Laxton's own prompt action.

Miss Harmon and Clarice Vane were both in Mr. Edge's shop, the one buying mothballs and the other a packet of boracic, when Harry Laxton and his wife came in.

After greeting the two ladies, Harry turned to the counter and was just demanding a toothbrush when he stopped in mid-speech and exclaimed heartily, "Well, well, just see who's here! Bella, I do declare."

Mrs. Edge, who had hurried out from the back parlour to attend to the congestion of business, beamed back cheerfully at him, showing her big white teeth. She had been a dark, handsome girl and was still a reasonably handsome woman, though she had put on weight, and the lines of her face had coarsened; but her large brown eyes were full of warmth as she answered, "Bella, it is, Mr. Harry, and pleased to see you after all these years."

Harry turned to his wife. "Bella's an old flame of mine, Louise," he said. "Head-over-heels in love with her, wasn't I, Bella?"

"That's what you say," said Mrs. Edge.

Louise laughed. She said, "My husband's very happy seeing all his old friends again."

"Ah," said Mrs. Edge, "we haven't forgotten you, Mr. Harry. Seems like a fairy tale to think of you married and building up a new house instead of that ruined old Kingsdean House."

"You look very well and blooming," said Harry, and Mrs. Edge laughed and said there was nothing wrong with her and what about that toothbrush?

Clarice, watching the baffled look on Miss Harmon's face,

said to herself exultantly, Oh, well-done, Harry. You've spiked their guns.

Doctor Haydock said abruptly to his niece, "What's all this nonsense about old Mrs. Murgatroyd hanging about Kingsdean and shaking her fist and cursing the new regime?"

"It isn't nonsense. It's quite true. It's upset Louise a good deal."

"Tell her she needn't worry—when the Murgatroyds were caretakers they never stopped grumbling about the place—they only stayed because Murgatroyd drank and couldn't get another job."

"I'll tell her," said Clarice doubtfully, "but I don't think she'll believe you. The old woman fairly screams with rage."

"Always used to be fond of Harry as a boy. I can't understand it."

Clarice said, "Oh, well—they'll be rid of her soon. Harry's paying her passage to America."

Three days later, Louise was thrown from her horse and killed.

Two men in a baker's van were witnesses of the accident. They saw Louise ride out of the gates, saw the old woman spring up and stand in the road waving her arms and shouting, saw the horse start, swerve, and then bolt madly down the road, flinging Louise Laxton over his head.

One of them stood over the unconscious figure, not knowing what to do, while the other rushed to the house to get help.

Harry Laxton came running out, his face ghastly. They took off a door of the van and carried her on it to the house. She died without regaining consciousness and before the doctor arrived.

(End of Doctor Haydock's manuscript.)

When Doctor Haydock arrived the following day, he was pleased to note that there was a pink flush in Miss Marple's cheek and decidedly more animation in her manner.

"Well," he said, "what's the verdict?"

"What's the problem, Doctor Haydock?" countered Miss Marple.

"Oh, my dear lady, do I have to tell you that?"

"I suppose," said Miss Marple, "that it's the curious conduct of the caretaker. Why did she behave in that very odd way? People do mind being turned out of their old homes. But it wasn't her home. In fact, she used to complain and grumble while she was there. Yes, it certainly looks very fishy. What became of her, by the way?"

"Did a bunk to Liverpool. The accident scared her. Thought she'd wait there for her boat."

"All very convenient for somebody," said Miss Marple. "Yes, I think the 'Problem of the Caretaker's Conduct' can be solved easily enough. Bribery, was it not?"

"That's your solution?"

"Well, if it wasn't natural for her to behave in that way, she must have been 'putting on an act' as people say, and that means that somebody paid her to do what she did."

"And you know who that somebody was?"

"Oh, I think so. Money again, I'm afraid. And I've always noticed that gentlemen always tend to admire the same type."

"Now I'm out of my depth."

"No, no, it all hangs together. Harry Laxton admired Bella Edge, a dark, vivacious type. Your niece Clarice was the same. But the poor little wife was quite a different type—fair-haired and clinging—not his type at all. So he must have married her for her money. And murdered her for her money, too!"

"You use the word 'murder'?"

"Well, he sounds the right type. Attractive to women and quite unscrupulous. I suppose he wanted to keep his wife's money and marry your niece. He may have been seen talking to Mrs. Edge. But I don't fancy he was attached to her anymore. Though I dare say he made the poor woman think he was, for ends of his own. He soon had her well under his thumb, I fancy."

"How exactly did he murder her, do you think?"

Miss Marple stared ahead of her for some minutes with dreamy blue eyes.

"It was very well-timed—with the baker's van as witness. They could see the old woman and, of course, they'd put down the horse's fright to that. But I should imagine, myself, that an air gun, or perhaps a catapult. Yes, just as the horse came through the gates. The horse bolted, of course, and Mrs. Laxton was thrown."

She paused, frowning.

"The fall might have killed her. But he couldn't be sure of that. And he seems the sort of man who would lay his plans carefully and leave nothing to chance. After all, Mrs. Edge could get him something suitable without her husband knowing. Otherwise, why would Harry bother with her? Yes, I think he had some powerful drug handy, that could be administered before you arrived. After all, if a woman is thrown from her horse and has serious injuries and dies without recovering consciousness, well—a doctor wouldn't normally be suspicious, would he? He'd put it down to shock or something."

Doctor Haydock nodded.

"Why did you suspect?" asked Miss Marple.

"It wasn't any particular cleverness on my part," said Doctor Haydock. "It was just the trite, well-known fact that a murderer is so pleased with his cleverness that he doesn't take proper precautions. I was just saying a few consolatory words to the bereaved husband—and feeling damned sorry for the fellow, too—when he flung himself down on the settee to do a bit of playacting and a hypodermic syringe fell out of his pocket.

"He snatched it up and looked so scared that I began to think. Harry Laxton didn't drug; he was in perfect health; what was he doing with a hypodermic syringe? I did the autopsy with a view to certain possibilities. I found strophanthin. The rest was easy. There was strophanthin in Laxton's possession, and Bella Edge, questioned by the police, broke down and admitted to having got it for him. And finally old Mrs. Murgatroyd confessed that it was Harry Laxton who had put her up to the cursing stunt."

"And your niece got over it?"

"Yes, she was attracted by the fellow, but it hadn't gone far."

The doctor picked up his manuscript.

"Full marks to you, Miss Marple—and full marks to me for my prescription. You're looking almost yourself again."

The Man in the Mist

I

Tommy was not pleased with life. Blunt's Brilliant Detectives had met with a reverse, distressing to their pride if not to their pockets. Called in professionally to elucidate the mystery of a stolen pearl necklace at Adlington Hall, Adlington, Blunt's Brilliant Detectives had failed to make good. Whilst Tommy, hard on the track of a gambling Countess, was tracking her in the disguise of a Roman Catholic priest, and Tuppence was "getting off" with the nephew of the house on the golf links, the local Inspector of Police had unemotionally arrested the second footman who proved to be a thief well-known at headquarters, and who admitted his guilt without making any bones about it.

Tommy and Tuppence, therefore, had withdrawn with what dignity they could muster, and were at the present moment solacing themselves with cocktails at the Grand Adlington Hotel. Tommy still wore his clerical disguise.

"Hardly a Father Brown touch, that," he remarked gloomily. "And yet I've got just the right kind of umbrella."

"It wasn't a Father Brown problem," said Tuppence. "One needs a certain atmosphere from the start. One must be doing something quite ordinary, and then bizarre things begin to happen. That's the idea."

"Unfortunately," said Tommy, "we have to return to town. Perhaps something bizarre will happen on the way to the station."

He raised the glass he was holding to his lips, but the liquid in it was suddenly spilled, as a heavy hand smacked him on the shoulder, and a voice to match the hand boomed out words of greeting.

"Upon my soul, it is! Old Tommy! And Mrs. Tommy too. Where did you blow in from? Haven't seen or heard anything of you for years."

"Why, it's Bulger!" said Tommy, setting down what was left of the cocktail, and turning to look at the intruder, a big square-shouldered man of thirty years of age, with a round red beaming face, and dressed in golfing kit. "Good old Bulger!"

"But I say, old chap," said Bulger (whose real name, by the way, was Marvyn Estcourt), "I never knew you'd taken orders. Fancy you a blinking parson."

Tuppence burst out laughing, and Tommy looked embarrassed. And then they suddenly became conscious of a fourth person.

A tall, slender creature, with very golden hair and very round blue eyes, almost impossibly beautiful, with an effect of really expensive black topped by wonderful ermines, and very large pearl earrings. She was smiling. And her smile said many things. It asserted, for instance, that she knew perfectly well that she herself was the thing best worth looking at, certainly in England, and possibly in the whole world. She was not vain about it in any way, but she just knew, with certainty and confidence, that it was so.

Both Tommy and Tuppence recognised her immediately. They had seen her three times in *The Secret of the Heart,* and an equal number of times in that other great success, *Pillars of Fire,* and in innumerable other plays. There was, perhaps, no other actress in England who had so firm a hold on the British public, as Miss Gilda Glen. She was reported to be the most beautiful woman in England. It was also rumoured that she was the stupidest.

"Old friends of mine, Miss Glen," said Estcourt, with a tinge of apology in his voice for having presumed, even for a moment, to forget such a radiant creature. "Tommy and Mrs. Tommy, let me introduce you to Miss Gilda Glen."

The ring of pride in his voice was unmistakable. By merely being seen in his company, Miss Glen had conferred great glory upon him.

The actress was staring with frank interest at Tommy.

"Are you really a priest?" she asked. "A Roman Catholic priest, I mean? Because I thought they didn't have wives."

Estcourt went off in a boom of laughter again.

"That's good," he exploded. "You sly dog, Tommy. Glad he hasn't renounced you, Mrs. Tommy, with all the rest of the pomps and vanities."

Gilda Glen took not the faintest notice of him. She continued to stare at Tommy with puzzled eyes.

"Are you a priest?" she demanded.

"Very few of us are what we seem to be," said Tommy gently. "My profession is not unlike that of a priest. I don't give absolution—but I listen to confessions—I—"

"Don't you listen to him," interrupted Estcourt. "He's pulling your leg."

"If you're not a clergyman, I don't see why you're dressed up like one," she puzzled. "That is, unless—"

"Not a criminal flying from justice," said Tommy. "The other thing."

"Oh!" she frowned, and looked at him with beautiful bewildered eyes.

"I wonder if she'll ever get that," thought Tommy to himself. "Not unless I put it in words of one syllable for her, I should say."

Aloud he said:

"Know anything about the trains back to town, Bulger? We've got to be pushing for home. How far is it to the station?"

"Ten minutes walk. But no hurry. Next train up is the 6:35 and it's only about twenty to six now. You've just missed one."

"Which way is it to the station from here?"

"Sharp to the left when you turn out of the hotel. Then—let me see—down Morgan's Avenue would be the best way, wouldn't it?"

"Morgan's Avenue?" Miss Glen started violently, and stared at him with startled eyes.

"I know what you're thinking of," said Estcourt, laughing. "The Ghost. Morgan's Avenue is bounded by the cemetery on one side, and tradition has it that a policeman who met his death by violence gets up and walks on his old beat, up and down Morgan's Avenue. A spook policeman! Can you beat it? But lots of people swear to having seen him."

"A policeman?" said Miss Glen. She shivered a little. "But there aren't really any ghosts, are there? I mean—there aren't such things?"

She got up, folding her wrap tighter round her.

"Goodbye," she said vaguely.

She had ignored Tuppence completely throughout, and now she did not even glance in her direction. But, over her shoulder, she threw one puzzled questioning glance at Tommy.

Just as she got to the door, she encountered a tall man with grey hair and a puffy face, who uttered an exclamation of surprise. His hand on her arm, he led her through the doorway, talking in an animated fashion.

"Beautiful creature, isn't she?" said Estcourt. "Brains of a rabbit. Rumour has it that she's going to marry Lord Leconbury. That was Leconbury in the doorway."

"He doesn't look a very nice sort of man to marry," remarked Tuppence.

Estcourt shrugged his shoulders.

"A title has a kind of glamour still, I suppose," he said. "And Leconbury is not an impoverished peer by any means. She'll be in clover. Nobody knows where she sprang from. Pretty near the gutter, I dare say. There's something deuced mysterious about her being down here anyway. She's not staying at the hotel. And when I tried to find out where she was staying, she snubbed me—snubbed me quite crudely, in the only way she knows. Blessed if I know what it's all about."

He glanced at his watch and uttered an exclamation.

"I must be off. Jolly glad to have seen you two again. We must have a bust in town together some night. So long."

He hurried away, and as he did so, a page approached with a note on a salver. The note was unaddressed.

"But it's for you, sir," he said to Tommy. "From Miss Gilda Glen."

Tommy tore it open and read it with some curiosity. Inside were a few lines written in a straggling untidy hand.

I'm not sure, but I think you might be able to help me. And you'll be going that way to the station. Could you be at The White House, Morgan's Avenue, at ten minutes past six?

Yours sincerely,

Gilda Glen.

Tommy nodded to the page, who departed, and then handed the note to Tuppence.

"Extraordinary!" said Tuppence. "Is it because she still thinks you're a priest?"

"No," said Tommy thoughtfully. "I should say it's because she's at last taken in that I'm not one. Hullo! what's this?"

"This" was a young man with flaming red hair, a pugnacious jaw, and appallingly shabby clothes. He had walked into the room and was now striding up and down muttering to himself.

"Hell!" said the red-haired man, loudly and forcibly. "That's what I say—Hell!"

He dropped into a chair near the young couple and stared at them moodily.

"Damn all women, that's what I say," said the young man, eyeing Tuppence ferociously. "Oh! all right, kick up a row if you like. Have me turned out of the hotel. It won't be for the first time. Why shouldn't we say what we think? Why should we go about bottling up our feelings, and smirking, and saying things exactly like everyone else. I don't feel pleasant and polite. I feel like getting hold of someone round the throat and gradually choking them to death."

He paused.

"Any particular person?" asked Tuppence. "Or just anybody?"

"One particular person," said the young man grimly.

"This is very interesting," said Tuppence. "Won't you tell us some more?"

"My name's Reilly," said the red-haired man. "James Reilly. You may have heard it. I wrote a little volume of Pacifist poems—good stuff, although I say so."

"Pacifist poems?" said Tuppence.

"Yes—why not?" demanded Mr. Reilly belligerently.

"Oh! nothing," said Tuppence hastily.

"I'm for peace all the time," said Mr. Reilly fiercely. "To Hell with war. And women! Women! Did you see that creature who was trailing around here just now? Gilda Glen, she calls herself. Gilda Glen! God! how I've worshipped that woman. And I'll tell you this—if she's got a heart at all, it's on my side. She cared once for me, and I could make her care again. And if she sells herself to that muck heap, Leconbury—well, God help her. I'd as soon kill her with my own hands."

And on this, suddenly, he rose and rushed from the room.

Tommy raised his eyebrows.

"A somewhat excitable gentleman," he murmured. "Well, Tuppence, shall we start?"

A fine mist was coming up as they emerged from the hotel into the cool outer air. Obeying Estcourt's directions, they turned sharp to the left, and in a few minutes they came to a turning labelled Morgan's Avenue.

The mist had increased. It was soft and white, and hurried past them in little eddying drifts. To their left was the high wall of the cemetery, on their right a row of small houses. Presently these ceased, and a high hedge took their place.

"Tommy," said Tuppence. "I'm beginning to feel jumpy. The mist—and the silence. As though we were miles from anywhere."

"One does feel like that," agreed Tommy. "All alone in the world. It's the effect of the mist, and not being able to see ahead of one."

Tuppence nodded.

"Just our footsteps echoing on the pavement. What's that?"

"What's what?"

"I thought I heard other footsteps behind us."

"You'll be seeing the ghost in a minute if you work yourself up like this," said Tommy kindly. "Don't be so nervy. Are you afraid the spook policeman will lay his hands on your shoulder?"

Tuppence emitted a shrill squeal.

"Don't, Tommy. Now you've put it into my head."

She craned her head back over her shoulder, trying to peer into the white veil that was wrapped all round them.

"There they are again," she whispered. "No, they're in front now. Oh! Tommy, don't say you can't hear them?"

"I do hear something. Yes, it's footsteps behind us. Somebody else walking this way to catch the train. I wonder—"

He stopped suddenly, and stood still, and Tuppence gave a gasp.

For the curtain of mist in front of them suddenly parted in the most artificial manner, and there, not twenty feet away, a gigantic policeman suddenly appeared, as though materialised out of the fog. One minute he was not there, the next minute he was—so at least it seemed to the rather superheated imaginations of the two watchers. Then as the mist rolled back still more, a little scene appeared, as though set on a stage.

The big blue policeman, a scarlet pillar box, and on the right of the road the outlines of a white house.

"Red, white, and blue," said Tommy. "It's damned pictorial. Come on, Tuppence, there's nothing to be afraid of."

For, as he had already seen, the policeman was a real policeman. And, moreover, he was not nearly so gigantic as he had at first seemed looming up out of the mist.

But as they started forward, footsteps came from behind them. A man passed them, hurrying along. He turned in at the gate of the white house, ascended the steps, and beat a deafening tattoo upon the knocker. He was admitted just as they reached the spot where the policeman was standing staring after him.

"There's a gentleman seems to be in a hurry," commented the policeman.

He spoke in a slow reflective voice, as one whose thoughts took some time to mature.

"He's the sort of gentleman always would be in a hurry," remarked Tommy.

The policeman's stare, slow and rather suspicious, came round to rest on his face.

"Friend of yours?" he demanded, and there was distinct suspicion now in his voice.

"No," said Tommy. "He's not a friend of mine, but I happen to know who he is. Name of Reilly."

"Ah!" said the policeman. "Well, I'd better be getting along."

"Can you tell me where the White House is?" asked Tommy.

The constable jerked his head sideways.

"This is it. Mrs. Honeycott's." He paused, and added, evidently with the idea of giving them valuable information, "Nervous party. Always suspecting burglars is around. Always asking me to have a look around the place. Middle-aged women get like that."

"Middle-aged, eh?" said Tommy. "Do you happen to know if there's a young lady staying there?"

"A young lady," said the policeman, ruminating. "A young lady. No, I can't say I know anything about that."

"She mayn't be staying here, Tommy," said Tuppence. "And anyway, she mayn't be here yet. She could only have started just before we did."

"Ah!" said the policeman suddenly. "Now that I call it to mind, a young lady did go in at this gate. I saw her as I was coming up the road. About three or four minutes ago it might be."

"With ermine furs on?" asked Tuppence eagerly.

"She had some kind of white rabbit round her throat," admitted the policeman.

Tuppence smiled. The policeman went on in the direction from which they had just come, and they prepared to enter the gate of the White House.

Suddenly, a faint, muffled cry sounded from inside the house, and almost immediately afterwards the front door opened and James Reilly came rushing down the steps. His face was white and twisted, and his eyes glared in front of him unseeingly. He staggered like a drunken man.

He passed Tommy and Tuppence as though he did not see them, muttering to himself with a kind of dreadful repetition.

"My God! My God! Oh, my God!"

He clutched at the gatepost, as though to steady himself, and then, as though animated by sudden panic, he raced off down the road as hard as he could go in the opposite direction from that taken by the policeman.

II

Tommy and Tuppence stared at each other in bewilderment.

"Well," said Tommy, "something's happened in that house to scare our friend Reilly pretty badly."

Tuppence drew her finger absently across the gatepost.

"He must have put his hand on some wet red paint somewhere," she said idly.

"H'm," said Tommy. "I think we'd better go inside rather quickly. I don't understand this business."

In the doorway of the house a white-capped maidservant was standing, almost speechless with indignation.

"Did you ever see the likes of that now, Father," she burst out, as Tommy ascended the steps. "That fellow comes here, asks for the young lady, rushes upstairs without how or by your leave. She lets out a screech like a wild cat—and what wonder, poor pretty dear, and straightaway he comes rushing down again, with the white face on him, like one who's seen a ghost. What will be the meaning of it all?"

"Who are you talking with at the front door, Ellen?" demanded a sharp voice from the interior of the hall.

"Here's Missus," said Ellen, somewhat unnecessarily.

She drew back, and Tommy found himself confronting a grey-haired, middle-aged woman, with frosty blue eyes imperfectly concealed by pince-nez, and a spare figure clad in black with bugle trimming.

"Mrs. Honeycott?" said Tommy. "I came here to see Miss Glen."

"Mrs. Honeycott gave him a sharp glance, then went on to Tuppence and took in every detail of her appearance.

"Oh, you did, did you?" she said. "Well, you'd better come inside."

She led the way into the hall and along it into a room at the back of the house, facing on the garden. It was a fair-sized room, but looked smaller than it was, owing to the large amount of chairs and tables crowded into it. A big fire burned in the grate, and a chintz-covered sofa stood at one side of it. The wallpaper was a small grey stripe with a festoon of roses round the top. Quantities of engravings and oil paintings covered the walls.

It was a room almost impossible to associate with the expensive personality of Miss Gilda Glen.

"Sit down," said Mrs. Honeycott. "To begin with, you'll excuse me if I say I don't hold with the Roman Catholic religion. Never did I think to see a Roman Catholic priest in my house. But if Gilda's gone over to the Scarlet Woman, it's only what's to be expected in a life like hers—and I dare say it might be worse. She mightn't have any religion at all. I should think more of Roman Catholics if their priests were married—I always speak my mind. And to think of those convents—quantities of beautiful young girls shut up there, and no one knowing what becomes of them—well, it won't bear thinking about."

Mrs. Honeycott came to a full stop, and drew a deep breath.

Without entering upon a defence of the celibacy of the priesthood or the other controversial points touched upon, Tommy went straight to the point.

"I understand, Mrs. Honeycott, that Miss Glen is in this house."

"She is. Mind you, I don't approve. Marriage is marriage and your husband's your husband. As you make your bed, so you must lie on it."

"I don't quite understand—" began Tommy, bewildered.

"I thought as much. That's the reason I brought you in here. You can go up to Gilda after I've spoken my mind. She came to me—after all these years, think of it!—and asked me to help her. Wanted me to see this man and persuade him to agree to a divorce. I told her straight out I'd have nothing whatever to do with it. Divorce is sinful. But I couldn't refuse my own sister shelter in my house, could I now?"

"Your sister?" exclaimed Tommy.

"Yes, Gilda's my sister. Didn't she tell you?"

Tommy stared at her openmouthed. The thing seemed fantastically impossible. Then he remembered that the angelic beauty of Gilda Glen had been in evidence for many years. He had been taken to see her act as quite a small boy. Yes, it was possible after all. But what a piquant contrast. So it was from this lower middle-class respectability that Gilda Glen had sprung. How well she had guarded her secret!

"I am not yet quite clear," he said. "Your sister is married?"

"Ran away to be married as a girl of seventeen," said Mrs. Honeycott succinctly. "Some common fellow far below her in station. And our father a reverend. It was a disgrace. Then she left her husband and went on the stage. Playacting! I've never been inside a theatre in my life. I hold no truck with wickedness. Now, after all these years, she wants to divorce the man. Means to marry some big wig, I suppose. But her husband's standing firm—not to be bullied and not to be bribed—I admire him for it."

"What is his name?" asked Tommy suddenly.

"That's an extraordinary thing now, but I can't remember! It's nearly twenty years ago, you know, since I heard it. My father forbade it to be mentioned. And I've refused to discuss the matter with Gilda. She knows what I think, and that's enough for her."

"It wasn't Reilly, was it?"

"Might have been. I really can't say. It's gone clean out of my head."

"The man I mean was here just now."

"That man! I thought he was an escaped lunatic. I'd been in the kitchen giving orders to Ellen. I'd just got back into this room, and was wondering whether Gilda had come in yet (she has a latchkey), when I heard her. She hesitated a minute or two in the hall and then went straight upstairs. About three minutes later all this tremendous rat-tatting began. I went out into the hall, and just saw a man rushing upstairs. Then there was a sort of cry upstairs, and presently down he came again and rushed out like a madman. Pretty goings on."

Tommy rose.

"Mrs. Honeycott, let us go upstairs at once. I am afraid—"

"What of?"

"Afraid that you have no red wet paint in the house."

Mrs. Honeycott stared at him.

"Of course I haven't."

"That is what I feared," said Tommy gravely. "Please let us go to your sister's room at once."

Momentarily silenced, Mrs. Honeycott led the way. They caught a glimpse of Ellen in the hall, backing hastily into one of the rooms.

Mrs. Honeycott opened the first door at the top of the stairs. Tommy and Tuppence entered close behind her.

Suddenly she gave a gasp and fell back.

A motionless figure in black and ermine lay stretched on the sofa. The face was untouched, a beautiful soulless face like a mature child asleep. The wound was on the side of the head, a heavy blow with some blunt instrument had crushed in the skull. Blood was dripping slowly on to the floor, but the wound itself had long ceased to bleed. . . .

Tommy examined the prostrate figure, his face very white.

"So," he said at last, "he didn't strangle her after all."

"What do you mean? Who?" cried Mrs. Honeycott. "Is she dead?"

"Oh, yes, Mrs. Honeycott, she's dead. Murdered. The question is—by whom? Not that it is much of a question.

Funny—for all his ranting words, I didn't think the fellow had got it in him."

He paused a minute, then turned to Tuppence with decision.

"Will you go out and get a policeman, or ring up the police station from somewhere?"

Tuppence nodded. She too, was very white. Tommy led Mrs. Honeycott downstairs again.

"I don't want there to be any mistake about this," he said. "Do you know exactly what time it was when your sister came in?"

"Yes, I do," said Mrs. Honeycott. "Because I was just setting the clock on five minutes as I have to do every evening. It loses just five minutes a day. It was exactly eight minutes past six by my watch, and that never loses or gains a second."

Tommy nodded. That agreed perfectly with the policeman's story. He had seen the woman with the white furs go in at the gate, probably three minutes had elapsed before he and Tuppence had reached the same spot. He had glanced at his own watch then and had noted that it was just one minute after the time of their appointment.

There was just the faint chance that someone might have been waiting for Gilda Glen in the room upstairs. But if so, he must still be hiding in the house. No one but James Reilly had left it.

He ran upstairs and made a quick but efficient search of the premises. But there was no one concealed anywhere.

Then he spoke to Ellen. After breaking the news to her, and waiting for her first lamentations and invocations to the saints to have exhausted themselves, he asked a few questions.

Had any one else come to the house that afternoon asking for Miss Glen? No one whatsoever. Had she herself been upstairs at all that evening? Yes she'd gone up at six o'clock as usual to draw the curtains—or it might have been a few minutes after six. Anyway it was just before that wild fellow came breaking the knocker down. She'd run downstairs to answer the door. And him a black-hearted murderer all the time.

Tommy let it go at that. But he still felt a curious pity for Reilly, and unwillingness to believe the worst of him. And yet there was no one else who could have murdered Gilda Glen. Mrs. Honeycott and Ellen had been the only two people in the house.

He heard voices in the hall, and went out to find Tuppence and the policeman from the beat outside. The latter had produced a notebook, and a rather blunt pencil, which he licked surreptitiously. He went upstairs and surveyed the victim stolidly, merely remarking that if he was to touch anything the Inspector would give him beans. He listened to all Mrs. Honeycott's hysterical outbursts and confused explanations, and occasionally he wrote something down. His presence was calming and soothing.

Tommy finally got him alone for a minute or two on the steps outside ere he departed to telephone headquarters.

"Look here," said Tommy, "you saw the deceased turning in at the gate, you say. Are you sure she was alone?"

"Oh! she was alone all right. Nobody with her."

"And between that time and when you met us, nobody came out of the gate?"

"Not a soul."

"You'd have seen them if they had?"

"Of course I should. Nobody come out till that wild chap did."

The majesty of the law moved portentously down the steps and paused by the white gatepost, which bore the imprint of a hand in red.

"Kind of amateur he must have been," he said pityingly. "To leave a thing like that."

Then he swung out into the road.

III

It was the day after the crime. Tommy and Tuppence were still at the Grand Hotel, but Tommy had thought it prudent to discard his clerical disguise.

James Reilly had been apprehended, and was in custody. His solicitor, Mr. Marvell, had just finished a lengthy conversation with Tommy on the subject of the crime.

"I never would have believed it of James Reilly," he said simply. "He's always been a man of violent speech, but that's all."

Tommy nodded.

"If you disperse energy in speech, it doesn't leave you too much over for action. What I realise is that I shall be one of the principal witnesses against him. That conversation he had with me just before the crime was particularly damning. And, in spite of everything, I like the man, and if there was anyone else to suspect, I should believe him to be innocent. What's his own story?"

The solicitor pursed up his lips.

"He declares that he found her lying there dead. But that's

impossible, of course. He's using the first lie that comes into his head."

"Because, if he happened to be speaking the truth, it would mean that the garrulous Mrs. Honeycott committed the crime—and that is fantastic. Yes, he must have done it."

"The maid heard her cry out, remember."

"The maid—yes—"

Tommy was silent a moment. Then he said thoughtfully.

"What credulous creatures we are, really. We believe evidence as though it were gospel truth. And what is it really? Only the impression conveyed to the mind by the senses—and suppose they're the wrong impressions?"

The lawyer shrugged his shoulders.

"Oh! we all know that there are unreliable witnesses, witnesses who remember more and more as time goes on, with no real intention to deceive."

"I don't mean only that. I mean all of us—we say things that aren't really so, and never know that we've done so. For instance, both you and I, without doubt, have said some time or other, 'There's the post,' when what we really meant was that we'd heard a double knock and the rattle of the letter-box. Nine times out of ten we'd be right, and it would be the post, but just possibly the tenth time it might be only a little urchin playing a joke on us. See what I mean?"

"Ye-es," said Mr. Marvell slowly. "But I don't see what you're driving at?"

"Don't you? I'm not so sure that I do myself. But I'm beginning to see. It's like the stick, Tuppence. You remember? One end of it pointed one way—but the other end always points the opposite way. It depends whether you get hold of it by the right end. Doors open—but they also shut. People go upstairs, but they also go downstairs. Boxes shut, but they also open."

"What *do* you mean?" demanded Tuppence.

"It's so ridiculously easy, really," said Tommy. "And yet it's only just come to me. How do you know when a person's come into the house. You hear the door open and bang to, and if you're expecting any one to come in, you will be quite sure it is them. But it might just as easily be someone going *out*."

"But Miss Glen didn't go out?"

"No, I know *she* didn't. But some one else did—the murderer."

"But how did she get in, then?"

"She came in whilst Mrs. Honeycott was in the kitchen talking to Ellen. They didn't hear her. Mrs. Honeycott went back to the drawing room, wondered if her sister had come in and began to put the clock right, and then, as she thought, she heard her come in and go upstairs."

"Well, what about that? The footsteps going upstairs?"

"That was Ellen, going up to draw the curtains. You remember, Mrs. Honeycott said her sister paused before going up. That pause was just the time needed for Ellen to come out from the kitchen into the hall. She just missed seeing the murderer."

"But, Tommy," cried Tuppence. "The cry she gave?"

"That was James Reilly. Didn't you notice what a high-pitched voice he has? In moments of great emotion, men often squeal just like a woman."

"But the murderer? We'd have seen him?"

"We *did* see him. We even stood talking to him. Do

you remember the sudden way that policeman appeared? That was because he stepped out of the gate, just after the mist cleared from the road. It made us jump, don't you remember? After all, though we never think of them as that, policemen are men just like any other men. They love and they hate. They marry. . . .

"I think Gilda Glen met her husband suddenly just outside that gate, and took him in with her to thrash the matter out. He hadn't Reilly's relief of violent words, remember. He just saw red—and he had his truncheon handy. . . ."

The Case of the Rich Woman

The name of Mrs. Abner Rymer was brought to Mr. Parker Pyne. He knew the name and he raised his eyebrows.

Presently his client was shown into the room.

Mrs. Rymer was a tall woman, big-boned. Her figure was ungainly and the velvet dress and the heavy fur coat she wore did not disguise the fact. The knuckles of her large hands were pronounced. Her face was big and broad and highly coloured. Her black hair was fashionably dressed, and there were many tips of curled ostrich in her hat.

She plumped herself down on a chair with a nod. "Good morning," she said. Her voice had a rough accent. "If you're any good at all you'll tell me how to spend my money!"

"Most original," murmured Mr. Parker Pyne. "Few ask me that in these days. So you really find it difficult, Mrs. Rymer?"

"Yes, I do," said the lady bluntly. "I've got three fur coats, a lot of Paris dresses and such like. I've got a car and a house in Park Lane. I've had a yacht but I don't like the sea. I've got a lot of those high-class servants that look down their nose at you. I've travelled a bit and seen foreign parts. And I'm blessed if I can think of anything more to buy or do." She looked hopefully at Mr. Payne.

"There are hospitals," he said.

"What? Give it away, you mean? No, that I won't do! That money was worked for, let me tell you, worked for hard. If you think I'm going to hand it out like so much dirt—well, you're mistaken. I want to spend it; spend it and get some good out of it. Now, if you've got any ideas that are worthwhile in that line, you can depend on a good fee."

"Your proposition interests me," said Mr. Pyne. "You do not mention a country house."

"I forgot it, but I've got one. Bores me to death."

"You must tell me more about yourself. Your problem is not easy to solve."

"I'll tell you and willing. I'm not ashamed of what I've come from. Worked in a farmhouse, I did, when I was a girl. Hard work it was too. Then I took up with Abner—he was a workman in the mills near by. He courted me for eight years, and then we got married."

"And you were happy?" asked Mr. Pyne.

"I was. He was a good man to me, Abner. We had a hard struggle of it, though; he was out of a job twice, and children coming along. Four we had, three boys and a girl. And none of them lived to grow up. I daresay it would have been different if they had." Her face softened; looked suddenly younger.

"His chest was weak—Abner's was. They wouldn't take him for the war. He did well at home. He was made foreman. He was a clever fellow, Abner. He worked out a process. They treated him fair, I will say; gave him a good sum for it. He used that money for another idea of his. That brought in money hand over fist. It's still coming in.

"Mind you, it was rare fun at first. Having a house and a tip-top bathroom and servants of one's own. No more cooking and scrubbing and washing to do. Just sit back on your silk cushions in the drawing room and ring the bell for tea—like any countess might! Grand fun it was, and we enjoyed it. And then we came up to London. I went to swell dressmakers for my clothes. We went to Paris and the Riviera. Rare fun it was."

"And then," said Mr. Parker Pyne.

"We got used to it, I suppose," said Mrs. Rymer. "After a bit it didn't seem so much fun. Why, there were days when we didn't even fancy our meals properly—us, with any dish we fancied to choose from! As for baths—well, in the end, one bath a day's enough for anyone. And Abner's health began to worry him. Paid good money to doctors, we did, but they couldn't do anything. They tried this and they tried that. But it was no use. He died." She paused. "He was a young man, only forty-three."

Mr. Pyne nodded sympathetically.

"That was five years ago. Money's still rolling in. It seems wasteful not to be able to do anything with it. But as I tell you, I can't think of anything else to buy that I haven't got already."

"In other words," said Mr. Pyne, "your life is dull. You are not enjoying it."

"I'm sick of it," said Mrs. Rymer gloomily. "I've no friends. The new lot only want subscriptions, and they laugh at me behind my back. The old lot won't have anything to do with me. My rolling up in a car makes them shy. Can you do anything or suggest anything?"

"It is possible that I can," said Mr. Pyne slowly. "It will

be difficult, but I believe there is a chance of success. I think it's possible I can give you back what you have lost—your interest in life."

"How?" demanded Mrs. Rymer curtly.

"That," said Mr. Parker Pyne, "is my professional secret. I never disclose my methods beforehand. The question is, will you take a chance? I do not guarantee success, but I do think there is a reasonable possibility of it.

"I shall have to adopt unusual methods, and therefore it will be expensive. My charges will be one thousand pounds, payable in advance."

"You can open your mouth all right, can't you?" said Mrs. Rymer appreciatively. "Well, I'll risk it. I'm used to paying top price. Only, when I pay for a thing, I take good care that I get it."

"You shall get it," said Mr. Parker Pyne. "Never fear."

"I'll send you the cheque this evening," said Mrs. Rymer, rising. "I'm sure I don't know why I should trust you. Fools and their money are soon parted, they say. I daresay I'm a fool. You've got nerve, to advertise in all the papers that you can make people happy!"

"Those advertisements cost me money," said Mr. Pyne. "If I could not make my words good, that money would be wasted. I *know* what causes unhappiness, and consequently I have a clear idea of how to produce an opposite condition."

Mrs. Rymer shook her head doubtfully and departed, leaving a cloud of expensive mixed essences behind her.

The handsome Claude Luttrell strolled into the office. "Something in my line?"

Mr. Pyne shook his head. "Nothing so simple," he said.

"No, this is a difficult case. We must, I fear, take a few risks. We must attempt the unusual."

"Mrs. Oliver?"

Mr. Pyne smiled at the mention of the world-famous novelist. "Mrs. Oliver," he said, "is really the most conventional of all of us. I have in mind a bold and audacious coup. By the way, you might ring up Dr. Antrobus."

"Antrobus?"

"Yes. His services will be needed."

A week later Mrs. Rymer once more entered Mr. Parker Pyne's office. He rose to receive her.

"This delay, I assure you, has been necessary," he said. "Many things had to be arranged, and I had to secure the services of an unusual man who had to come half-across Europe."

"Oh!" She said it suspiciously. It was constantly present in her mind that she had paid out a cheque for a thousand pounds and the cheque had been cashed.

Mr. Parker Pyne touched a buzzer. A young girl, dark, Oriental looking, but dressed in white nurse's kit, answered it.

"Is everything ready, Nurse de Sara?"

"Yes. Doctor Constantine is waiting."

"What are you going to do?" asked Mrs. Rymer with a touch of uneasiness.

"Introduce you to some Eastern magic, dear lady," said Mr. Parker Pyne.

Mrs. Rymer followed the nurse up to the next floor. Here she was ushered into a room that bore no relation to the rest of the house. Oriental embroideries covered the walls. There were divans with soft cushions and beautiful rugs on the floor. A man was bending over a coffeepot. He straightened as they entered.

"Doctor Constantine," said the nurse.

The doctor was dressed in European clothes, but his face was swarthy and his eyes were dark and oblique with a peculiarly piercing power in their glance.

"So this is my patient?" he said in a low, vibrant voice.

"I'm not a patient," said Mrs. Rymer.

"Your body is not sick," said the doctor, "but your soul is weary. We of the East know how to cure that disease. Sit down and drink a cup of coffee."

Mrs. Rymer sat down and accepted a tiny cup of the fragrant brew. As she sipped it the doctor talked.

"Here in the West, they treat only the body. A mistake. The body is only the instrument. A tune is played upon it. It may be a sad, weary tune. It may be a gay tune full of delight. The last is what we shall give you. You have money. You shall spend it and enjoy. Life shall be worth living again. It is easy—easy—so easy. . . ."

A feeling of languor crept over Mrs. Rymer. The figures of the doctor and the nurse grew hazy. She felt blissfully happy and very sleepy. The doctor's figure grew bigger. The whole world was growing bigger.

The doctor was looking into her eyes. "Sleep," he was saying. "Sleep. Your eyelids are closing. Soon you will sleep. You will sleep. You will sleep. . . ."

Mrs. Rymer's eyelids closed. She floated with a wonderful great big world. . . .

* * *

When her eyes opened it seemed to her that a long time had passed. She remembered several things vaguely—strange, impossible dreams; then a feeling of waking; then further dreams. She remembered something about a car and the dark, beautiful girl in a nurse's uniform bending over her.

Anyway, she was properly awake now, and in her own bed.

At least, was it her own bed? It felt different. It lacked the delicious softness of her own bed. It was vaguely reminiscent of days almost forgotten. She moved, and it creaked. Mrs. Rymer's bed in Park Lane never creaked.

She looked round. Decidedly, this was not Park Lane. Was it a hospital? No, she decided, not a hospital. Nor was it a hotel. It was a bare room, the walls an uncertain shade of lilac. There was a deal washstand with a jug and basin upon it. There was a deal chest of drawers and a tin trunk. There were unfamiliar clothes hanging on pegs. There was the bed covered with a much-mended quilt and there was herself in it.

"Where *am* I?" said Mrs. Rymer.

The door opened and a plump little woman bustled in. She had red cheeks and a good-humoured air. Her sleeves were rolled up and she wore an apron.

"There!" she exclaimed. "She's awake. Come in, doctor."

Mrs. Rymer opened her mouth to say several things—but they remained unsaid, for the man who followed the plump woman into the room was not in the least like the elegant, swarthy Doctor Constantine. He was a bent old man who peered through thick glasses.

"That's better," he said, advancing to the bed and taking up Mrs. Rymer's wrist. "You'll soon be better now, my dear."

"What's been the matter with me?" demanded Mrs. Rymer.

"You had a kind of seizure," said the doctor. "You've been unconscious for a day or two. Nothing to worry about."

"Gave us a fright you did, Hannah," said the plump woman. "You've been raving too, saying the oddest things."

"Yes, yes, Mrs. Gardner," said the doctor repressively. "But we musn't excite the patient. You'll soon be up and about again, my dear."

"But don't you worry about the work, Hannah," said Mrs. Gardner. "Mrs. Roberts has been in to give me a hand and we've got on fine. Just lie still and get well, my dear."

"Why do you call me Hannah?" said Mrs. Rymer.

"Well, it's your name," said Mrs. Gardner, bewildered.

"No, it isn't. My name is Amelia. Amelia Rymer. Mrs. Abner Rymer."

The doctor and Mrs. Gardner exchanged glances.

"Well, just you lie still," said Mrs. Gardner.

"Yes, yes; no worry," said the doctor.

They withdrew. Mrs. Rymer lay puzzling. Why did they call her Hannah, and why had they exchanged that glance of amused incredulity when she had given them her name? Where was she and what had happened?

She slipped out of bed. She felt a little uncertain on her legs, but she walked slowly to the small dormer window and looked out—on a farmyard! Completely mystified, she went back to bed. What was she doing in a farmhouse that she had never seen before?

Mrs. Gardner re-entered the room with a bowl of soup on a tray.

Mrs. Rymer began her questions. "What am I doing in this house?" she demanded. "Who brought me here?"

"Nobody brought you, my dear. It's your home. Leastways, you've lived here for the last five years—and me not suspecting once that you were liable to fits."

"*Lived* here! *Five* years?"

"That's right. Why, Hannah, you don't mean that you still don't remember?"

"I've never lived here! I've never seen you before."

"You see, you've had this illness and you've forgotten."

"I've never lived here."

"But you have, my dear." Suddenly Mrs. Gardner darted across to the chest of drawers and brought to Mrs. Rymer a faded photograph in a frame.

It represented a group of four persons: a bearded man, a plump woman (Mrs. Gardner), a tall, lank man with a pleasantly sheepish grin, and somebody in a print dress and apron—herself!

Stupefied, Mrs. Rymer gazed at the photograph. Mrs. Gardner put the soup down beside her and quietly left the room.

Mrs. Rymer sipped the soup mechanically. It was good soup, strong and hot. All the time her brain was in a whirl. Who was mad? Mrs. Gardner or herself? One of them must be! But there was the doctor too.

"I'm Amelia Rymer," she said firmly to herself. "I know I'm Amelia Rymer and nobody's going to tell me different."

She had finished the soup. She put the bowl back on the tray. A folded newspaper caught her eye and she picked it up and looked at the date on it, October 19. What day had she gone to Mr. Parker Pyne's office? Either the fifteenth or the sixteenth. Then she must have been ill for three days.

"That rascally doctor!" said Mrs. Rymer wrathfully.

All the same, she was a shade relieved. She had heard of cases where people had forgotten who they were for years at a time. She had been afraid some such thing had happened to her.

She began turning the pages of the paper, scanning the columns idly, when suddenly a paragraph caught her eye.

> Mrs. Abner Rymer, widow of Abner Rymer, the "button shank" king, was removed yesterday to a private home for mental cases. For the past two days she has persisted in declaring she was not herself, but a servant girl named Hannah Moorhouse.

"Hannah Moorhouse! So that's it," said Mrs. Rymer. "She's me and I'm her. Kind of double, I suppose. Well, we can soon put *that* right! If that oily hypocrite of a Parker Pyne is up to some game or other—"

But at this minute her eye was caught by the name Constantine staring at her from the printed page. This time it was a headline.

DR. CONSTANTINE'S CLAIM

> At a farewell lecture given last night on the eve of his departure for Japan, Dr. Claudius Constantine advanced some startling theories. He declared that it was possible

> to prove the existence of the soul by transferring a soul from one body to another. In the course of his experiments in the East he had, he claimed, successfully effected a double transfer—the soul of a hypnotized body A being transferred to a hypnotized body B and the soul of body B to the soul of body A. On recovering from the hypnotic sleep, A declared herself to be B, and B thought herself to be A. For the experiment to succeed, it was necessary to find two people with a great bodily resemblance. It was an undoubted fact that two people resembling each other were *en rapport*. This was very noticeable in the case of twins, but two strangers, varying widely in social position, but with a marked similarity of feature, were found to exhibit the same harmony of structure.

Mrs. Rymer cast the paper from her. "The scoundrel!"

She saw the whole thing now! It was a dastardly plot to get hold of her money. This Hannah Moorhouse was Mr. Pyne's tool—possibly an innocent one. He and that devil Constantine had brought off this fantastic coup.

But she'd expose him! She'd show him up! She'd have the law on him! She'd tell everyone—

Abruptly Mrs. Rymer came to a stop in the tide of her indignation. She remembered the first paragraph. Hannah Moorhouse had not been a docile tool. She had protested; had declared her individuality. And what had happened?

"Clapped into a lunatic asylum, poor girl," said Mrs. Rymer.

A chill ran down her spine.

A lunatic asylum. They got you in there and they never

let you get out. The more you said you were sane, the less they'd believe you. There you were and there you stayed. No, Mrs. Rymer wasn't going to run the risk of that.

The door opened and Mrs. Gardner came in.

"Ah, you've drunk your soup, my dear. That's good. You'll soon be better now."

"When was I taken ill?" demanded Mrs. Rymer.

"Let me see. It was three days ago—on Wednesday.

That was the fifteenth. You were took bad about four o'clock."

"Ah!" The ejaculation was fraught with meaning. It had been just about four o'clock when Mrs. Rymer had entered the presence of Doctor Constantine.

"You slipped down in your chair," said Mrs. Gardner. "'Oh!' you says. 'Oh!' just like that. And then: 'I'm falling asleep,' you says in a dreamy voice. 'I'm falling asleep.' And fall asleep you did, and we put you to bed and sent for the doctor, and here you've been ever since."

"I suppose," Mrs. Rymer ventured, "there isn't any way you could know who I am—apart from my face, I mean."

"Well, that's a queer thing to say," said Mrs. Gardner. "What is there to go by better than a person's face, I'd like to know? There's your birthmark, though, if that satisfies you better."

"A birthmark?" said Mrs. Rymer, brightening. She had no such thing.

"Strawberry mark just under the right elbow," said Mrs. Gardner. "Look for yourself, my dear."

"This will prove it," said Mrs. Rymer to herself. She knew that she had no strawberry mark under the right elbow. She turned back the sleeve of her nightdress. The strawberry mark was there.

Mrs. Rymer burst into tears.

Four days later Mrs. Rymer rose from her bed. She had thought out several plans of action and rejected them.

She might show the paragraph in the paper to Mrs. Gardner and explain. Would they believe her? Mrs. Rymer was sure they would not.

She might go to the police. Would they believe her? Again she thought not.

She might go to Mr. Pyne's office. That idea undoubtedly pleased her best. For one thing, she would like to tell that oily scoundrel what she thought of him. She was debarred from putting this plan into operation by a vital obstacle. She was at present in Cornwall (so she had learned), and she had no money for the journey to London. Two and fourpence in a worn purse seemed to represent her financial position.

And so, after four days, Mrs. Rymer made a sporting decision. For the present she would accept things! She was Hannah Moorhouse. Very well, she would be Hannah Moorhouse. For the present she would accept that role, and later, when she had saved sufficient money, she would go to London and beard the swindler in his den.

And having thus decided, Mrs. Rymer accepted her role with perfect good temper, even with a kind of sardonic amusement. History was repeating itself indeed. This life reminded her of her girlhood. How long ago that seemed!

* * *

The work was a bit hard after her years of soft living, but after the first week she found herself slipping into the ways of the farm.

Mrs. Gardner was a good-tempered, kindly woman. Her husband, a big, taciturn man, was kindly also. The lank, shambling man of the photograph had gone; another farmhand came in his stead, a good-humoured giant of forty-five, slow of speech and thought, but with a shy twinkle in his blue eyes.

The weeks went by. At last the day came when Mrs. Rymer had enough money to pay her fare to London. But she did not go. She put it off. Time enough, she thought. She wasn't easy in her mind about asylums yet. That scoundrel, Parker Pyne, was clever. He'd get a doctor to say she was mad and she'd be clapped away out of sight with no one knowing anything about it.

"Besides," said Mrs. Rymer to herself, "a bit of a change does one good."

She rose early and worked hard. Joe Welsh, the new farmhand, was ill that winter, and she and Mrs. Gardner nursed him. The big man was pathetically dependent on them.

Spring came—lambing time; there were wild flowers in the hedges, a treacherous softness in the air. Joe Welsh gave Hannah a hand with her work. Hannah did Joe's mending.

Sometimes, on Sundays, they went for a walk together. Joe was a widower. His wife had died four years before. Since her death he had, he frankly confessed it, taken a drop too much.

He didn't go much to the Crown nowadays. He bought himself some new clothes. Mr. and Mrs. Gardner laughed.

Hannah made fun of Joe. She teased him about his clumsiness. Joe didn't mind. He looked bashful but happy.

After spring came summer—a good summer that year. Everyone worked hard.

Harvest was over. The leaves were red and golden on the trees.

It was October eighth when Hannah looked up one day from a cabbage she was cutting and saw Mr. Parker Pyne leaning over the fence.

"You!" said Hannah, alias Mrs. Rymer. "You. . . ."

It was some time before she got it all out, and when she had said her say, she was out of breath.

Mr. Parker Pyne smiled blandly. "I quite agree with you," he said.

"A cheat and a liar, that's what you are!" said Mrs. Rymer, repeating herself. "You with your Constantines and your hypnotizing, and that poor girl Hannah Moorhouse shut up with—loonies."

"No," said Mr. Parker Pyne, "there you misjudge me. Hannah Moorhouse is not in a lunatic asylum, because Hannah Moorhouse never existed."

"Indeed?" said Mrs. Rymer. "And what about the photograph of her that I saw with my own eyes?"

"Faked," said Mr. Pyne. "Quite a simple thing to manage."

"And the piece in the paper about her?"

"The whole paper was faked so as to include two items in a natural manner which would carry conviction. As it did."

"That rogue, Doctor Constantine!"

"An assumed name—assumed by a friend of mine with a talent for acting."

Mrs. Rymer snorted. "Ho! And I wasn't hypnotized either, I suppose?"

"As a matter of fact, you were not. You drank in your coffee a preparation of Indian hemp. After that, other drugs were administered and you were brought down here by car and allowed to recover consciousness."

"Then Mrs. Gardner has been in it all the time?" said Mrs. Rymer.

Mr. Parker Pyne nodded.

"Bribed by you, I suppose! Or filled up with a lot of lies!"

"Mrs. Gardner trusts me," said Mr. Pyne. "I once saved her only son from penal servitude."

Something in his manner silenced Mrs. Rymer on that tack. "What about the birthmark!" she demanded.

Mr. Pyne smiled. "It is already fading. In another six months it will have disappeared altogether."

"And what's the meaning of all this tomfoolery? Making a fool of me, sticking me down here as a servant—me with all that good money in the bank. But I suppose I needn't ask. You've been helping yourself to it, my fine fellow. That's the meaning of all this."

"It is true," said Mr. Parker Pyne, "that I did obtain from you, while you were under the influence of drugs, a power of attorney and that during your—er—absence, I have assumed control of your financial affairs, but I can assure you, my dear madam, that apart from that original thousand pounds, no money of yours has found its way into my pocket. As a matter of fact, by judicious investments your financial position is actually improved." He beamed at her.

"Then why—?" began Mrs. Rymer.

"I am going to ask you a question, Mrs. Rymer," said Mr. Parker Pyne. "You are an honest woman. You will answer me honestly, I know. I am going to ask you if you are happy."

"Happy! That's a pretty question! Steal a woman's money and ask her if she's happy. I like your impudence!"

"You are still angry," he said. "Most natural. But leave my misdeeds out of it for the moment. Mrs. Rymer, when you came to my office a year ago today, you were an unhappy woman. Will you tell me that you are unhappy now? If so, I apologize, and you are at liberty to take what steps you please against me. Moreover, I will refund the thousand pounds you paid me. Come, Mrs. Rymer, are you an unhappy woman now?"

Mrs. Rymer looked at Mr. Parker Pyne, but she dropped her eyes when she spoke at last.

"No," she said. "I'm not unhappy." A tone of wonder crept into her voice. "You've got me there. I admit it. I've not been as happy as I am now since Abner died. I—I'm going to marry a man who works here—Joe Welsh. Our banns are going up next Sunday; that, is they *were* going up next Sunday."

"But now, of course, everything is different."

Mrs. Rymer's face flamed. She took a step forward.

"What do you mean, different? Do you think that if I had all the money in the world it would make me a lady? I don't want to be a lady, thank you; a helpless good-for-nothing lot they are. Joe's good enough for me and I'm good enough for him. We suit each other and we're going to be happy. As you for, Mr. Nosey Parker, you take yourself off and don't interfere with what doesn't concern you!"

Mr. Parker Pyne took a paper from his pocket and handed it to her. "The power of attorney," he said. "Shall I tear it up? You will assume control of your own fortune now, I take it."

A strange expression came over Mrs. Rymer's face. She thrust back the paper.

"Take it. I've said hard things to you—and some of them you deserved. You're a downy fellow, but all the same I trust you. Seven hundred pounds I'll have in the bank here—that'll buy us a farm we've got our eye on. The rest of it—well, let the hospitals have it."

"You cannot mean to hand over your entire fortune to hospitals?"

"That's just what I do mean. Joe's a dear, good fellow, but he's weak. Give him money and you'd ruin him. I've got him off the drink now, and I'll keep him off it. Thank God, I know my own mind. I'm not going to let money come between me and happiness."

"You are a remarkable woman," said Mr. Pyne slowly. "Only one woman in a thousand would act as you are doing."

"Then only one woman in a thousand's got sense," said Mrs. Rymer.

"I take my hat off to you," said Mr. Parker Pyne, and there was an unusual note in his voice. He raised his hat with solemnity and moved away.

"And Joe's never to know, mind!" Mrs. Rymer called after him.

She stood there with the dying sun behind her, a great blue-green cabbage in her hands, her head thrown back and her shoulders squared. A grand figure of a peasant woman, outlined against the setting sun. . . .

Magnolia Blossom

Vincent Easton was waiting under the clock at Victoria Station. Now and then he glanced up at it uneasily. He thought to himself: "How many other men have waited here for a woman who didn't come?"

A sharp pang shot through him. Supposing that Theo didn't come, that she had changed her mind? Women did that sort of thing. Was he sure of her—had he ever been sure of her? Did he really know anything at all about her? Hadn't she puzzled him from the first? There had seemed to be two women—the lovely, laughing creature who was Richard Darrell's wife, and the other—silent, mysterious, who had walked by his side in the garden of Haymer's Close. Like a magnolia flower—that was how he thought of her—perhaps because it was under the magnolia tree that they had tasted their first rapturous, incredulous kiss. The air had been sweet with the scent of magnolia bloom, and one or two petals, velvety-soft and fragrant, had floated down, resting on that upturned face that was as creamy and as soft and as silent as they. Magnolia blossom—exotic, fragrant, mysterious.

That had been a fortnight ago—the second day he had

met her. And now he was waiting for her to come to him forever. Again incredulity shot through him. She wouldn't come. How could he ever have believed it? It would be giving up so much. The beautiful Mrs. Darrell couldn't do this sort of thing quietly. It was bound to be a nine days' wonder, a far-reaching scandal that would never quite be forgotten. There were better, more expedient ways of doing these things—a discreet divorce, for instance.

But they had never thought of that for a moment—at least he had not. Had she? he wondered. He had never known anything of her thoughts. He had asked her to come away with him almost timorously—for after all, what was he? Nobody in particular—one of a thousand orange growers in the Transvaal. What a life to take her to—after the brilliance of London! And yet, since he wanted her so desperately, he must needs ask.

She had consented very quietly, with no hesitations or protests, as though it were the simplest thing in the world that he was asking her.

"Tomorrow?" he had said, amazed, almost unbelieving.

And she had promised in that soft, broken voice that was so different from the laughing brilliance of her social manner. He had compared her to a diamond when he first saw her—a thing of flashing fire, reflecting light from a hundred facets. But at that first touch, that first kiss, she had changed miraculously to the clouded softness of a pearl—a pearl like a magnolia blossom, creamy pink.

She had promised. And now he was waiting for her to fulfil that promise.

He looked again at the clock. If she did not come soon, they would miss the train.

Sharply a wave of reaction set in. She wouldn't come! Of course she wouldn't come. Fool that he had been ever to expect it! What were promises? He would find a letter when he got back to his rooms—explaining, protesting, saying all the things that women do when they are excusing themselves for lack of courage.

He felt anger—anger and the bitterness of frustration.

Then he saw her coming towards him down the platform, a faint smile on her face. She walked slowly, without haste or fluster, as one who had all eternity before her. She was in black—soft black that clung, with a little black hat that framed the wonderful creamy pallor of her face.

He found himself grasping her hand, muttering stupidly: "So you've come—you have come. After all!"

"Of course."

How calm her voice sounded! How calm!

"I thought you wouldn't," he said, releasing her hand and breathing hard.

Her eyes opened—wide, beautiful eyes. There was wonder in them, the simple wonder of a child.

"Why?"

He didn't answer. Instead he turned aside and requisitioned a passing porter. They had not much time. The next few minutes were all bustle and confusion. Then they were sitting in their reserved compartment and the drab houses of southern London were drifting by them.

* * *

Theodora Darrell was sitting opposite him. At last she was his. And he knew now how incredulous, up to the very last minute, he had been. He had not dared to let himself believe. That magical, elusive quality about her had frightened him. It had seemed impossible that she should ever belong to him.

Now the suspense was over. The irrevocable step was taken. He looked across at her. She lay back in the corner, quite still. The faint smile lingered on her lips, her eyes were cast down, the long, black lashes swept the creamy curve of her cheek.

He thought: "What's in her mind now? What is she thinking of? Me? Her husband? What does she think about him anyway? Did she care for him once? Or did she never care? Does she hate him, or is she indifferent to him?" And with a pang the thought swept through him: "I don't know. I never shall know. I love her, and I don't know anything about her—what she thinks or what she feels."

His mind circled round the thought of Theodora Darrell's husband. He had known plenty of married women who were only too ready to talk about their husbands—of how they were misunderstood by them, of how their finer feelings were ignored. Vincent Easton reflected cynically that it was one of the best-known opening gambits.

But except casually, Theo had never spoken of Richard Darrell. Easton knew of him what everybody knew. He was a popular man, handsome, with an engaging, carefree manner. Everybody liked Darrell. His wife always seemed on excellent terms with him. But that proved nothing,

Vincent reflected. Theo was well-bred—she would not air her grievances in public.

And between them, no word had passed. From that second evening of their meeting, when they had walked together in the garden, silent, their shoulders touching, and he had felt the faint tremor that shook her at his touch, there had been no explainings, no defining of the position. She had returned his kisses, a dumb, trembling creature, shorn of all that hard brilliance which, together with her cream-and-rose beauty, had made her famous. Never once had she spoken of her husband. Vincent had been thankful for that at the time. He had been glad to be spared the arguments of a woman who wished to assure herself and her lover that they were justified in yielding to their love.

Yet now the tacit conspiracy of silence worried him. He had again that panic-stricken sense of knowing nothing about this strange creature who was willingly linking her life to his. He was afraid.

In the impulse to reassure himself, he bent forward and laid a hand on the black-clad knee opposite him. He felt once again the faint tremor that shook her, and he reached up for her hand. Bending forward, he kissed the palm, a long, lingering kiss. He felt the response of her fingers on his and, looking up, met her eyes, and was content.

He leaned back in his seat. For the moment, he wanted no more. They were together. She was his. And presently he said in a light, almost bantering tone:

"You're very silent?"

"Am I?"

"Yes." He waited a minute, then said in a graver tone: "You're sure you don't—regret?"

Her eyes opened wide at that. "Oh, no!"

He did not doubt the reply. There was an assurance of sincerity behind it.

"What are you thinking about? I want to know."

In a low voice she answered: "I think I'm afraid."

"Afraid?"

"Of happiness."

He moved over beside her then, held her to him and kissed the softness of her face and neck.

"I love you," he said. "I love you—love you."

Her answer was in the clinging of her body, the abandon of her lips.

Then he moved back to his own corner. He picked up a magazine and so did she. Every now and then, over the top of the magazines, their eyes met. Then they smiled.

They arrived at Dover just after five. They were to spend the night there, and cross to the Continent on the following day. Theo entered their sitting room in the hotel with Vincent close behind her. He had a couple of evening papers in his hand which he threw down on the table. Two of the hotel servants brought in the luggage and withdrew.

Theo turned from the window where she had been standing looking out. In another minute they were in each other's arms.

There was a discreet tap on the door and they drew apart again.

"Damn it all," said Vincent, "it doesn't seem as though we were ever going to be alone."

Theo smiled. "It doesn't look like it," she said softly. Sitting down on the sofa, she picked up one of the papers.

The knock proved to be a waiter bearing tea. He laid it on the table, drawing the latter up to the sofa on which Theo was sitting, cast a deft glance round, inquired if there were anything further, and withdrew.

Vincent, who had gone into the adjoining room, came back into the sitting room.

"Now for tea," he said cheerily, but stopped suddenly in the middle of the room. "Anything wrong?" he asked.

Theo was sitting bolt upright on the sofa. She was staring in front of her with dazed eyes, and her face had gone deathly white.

Vincent took a quick step towards her.

"What is it, sweetheart?"

For answer she held out the paper to him, her finger pointing to the headline.

Vincent took the paper from her. "FAILURE OF HOBSON, JEKYLL AND LUCAS," he read. The name of the big city firm conveyed nothing to him at the moment, though he had an irritating conviction in the back of his mind that it ought to do so. He looked inquiringly at Theo.

"Richard is Hobson, Jekyll and Lucas," she explained.

"Your husband?"

"Yes."

Vincent returned to the paper and read the bald information it conveyed carefully. Phrases such as "sudden crash," "serious revelations to follow," "other houses affected" struck him disagreeably.

Roused by a movement, he looked up. Theo was adjusting her little black hat in front of the mirror. She turned at the movement he made. Her eyes looked steadily into his.

"Vincent—I must go to Richard."

He sprang up.

"Theo—don't be absurd."

She repeated mechanically:

"I must go to Richard."

"But, my dear—"

She made a gesture towards the paper on the floor.

"That means ruin—bankruptcy. I can't choose this day of all others to leave him."

"You had left him before you heard of this. Be reasonable!"

She shook her head mournfully.

"You don't understand. I must go to Richard."

And from that he could not move her. Strange that a creature so soft, so pliant, could be so unyielding. After the first, she did not argue. She let him say what he had to say unhindered. He held her in his arms, seeking to break her will by enslaving her senses, but though her soft mouth returned his kisses, he felt in her something aloof and invincible that withstood all his pleadings.

He let her go at last, sick and weary of the vain endeavour. From pleading he had turned to bitterness, reproaching her with never having loved him. That, too, she took in silence, without protest, her face, dumb and pitiful, giving the lie to his words. Rage mastered him in the end; he hurled at her every cruel word he could think of, seeking only to bruise and batter her to her knees.

At last the words gave out; there was nothing more to say. He sat, his head in his hands, staring down at the red pile carpet. By the door, Theodora stood, a black shadow with a white face.

It was all over.

She said quietly: "Goodbye, Vincent."

He did not answer.

The door opened—and shut again.

The Darrells lived in a house in Chelsea—an intriguing, old-world house, standing in a little garden of its own. Up the front of the house grew a magnolia tree, smutty, dirty, begrimed, but still a magnolia.

Theo looked up at it, as she stood on the doorstep some three hours later. A sudden smile twisted her mouth in pain.

She went straight to the study at the back of the house. A man was pacing up and down in the room—a young man, with a handsome face and a haggard expression.

He gave an ejaculation of relief as she came in.

"Thank God you've turned up, Theo. They said you'd taken your luggage with you and gone off out of town somewhere."

"I heard the news and came back."

Richard Darrell put an arm about her and drew her to the couch. They sat down upon it side by side. Theo drew herself free of the encircling arm in what seemed a perfectly natural manner.

"How bad is it, Richard?" she asked quietly.

"Just as bad as it can be—and that's saying a lot."

"Tell me!"

He began to walk up and down again as he talked. Theo sat and watched him. He was not to know that every now and then the room went dim, and his voice faded from her hearing, while another room in a hotel at Dover came clearly before her eyes.

Nevertheless she managed to listen intelligently enough. He came back and sat down on the couch by her.

"Fortunately," he ended, "they can't touch your marriage settlement. The house is yours also."

Theo nodded thoughtfully.

"We shall have that at any rate," she said. "Then things will not be too bad? It means a fresh start, that is all."

"Oh! Quite so. Yes."

But his voice did not ring true, and Theo thought suddenly: "There's something else. He hasn't told me everything."

"There's nothing more, Richard?" she said gently. "Nothing worse?"

He hesitated for just half a second, then: "Worse? What should there be?"

"I don't know," said Theo.

"It'll be all right," said Richard, speaking more as though to reassure himself than Theo. "Of course, it'll be all right."

He flung an arm about her suddenly.

"I'm glad you're here," he said. "It'll be all right now that you're here. Whatever else happens, I've got you, haven't I?"

She said gently: "Yes, you've got me." And this time she left his arm round her.

He kissed her and held her close to him, as though in some strange way he derived comfort from her nearness.

"I've got you, Theo," he said again presently, and she answered as before: "Yes, Richard."

He slipped from the couch to the floor at her feet.

"I'm tired out," he said fretfully. "My God, it's been a

day. Awful! I don't know what I should do if you weren't here. After all, one's wife is one's wife, isn't she?"

She did not speak, only bowed her head in assent.

He laid his head on her lap. The sigh he gave was like that of a tired child.

Theo thought again: "There's something he hasn't told me. What is it?"

Mechanically her hand dropped to his smooth, dark head, and she stroked it gently, as a mother might comfort a child.

Richard murmured vaguely:

"It'll be all right now you're here. You won't let me down."

His breathing grew slow and even. He slept. Her hand still smoothed his head.

But her eyes looked steadily into the darkness in front of her, seeing nothing.

"Don't you think, Richard," said Theodora, "that you'd better tell me everything?"

It was three days later. They were in the drawing room before dinner.

Richard started, and flushed.

"I don't know what you mean," he parried.

"Don't you?"

He shot a quick glance at her.

"Of course there are—well—details."

"I ought to know everything, don't you think, if I am to help?"

He looked at her strangely.

"What makes you think I want you to help?"

She was a little astonished.

"My dear Richard, I'm your wife."

He smiled suddenly, the old, attractive, carefree smile.

"So you are, Theo. And a very good-looking wife, too. I never could stand ugly women."

He began walking up and down the room, as was his custom when something was worrying him.

"I won't deny you're right in a way," he said presently. "There is something."

He broke off.

"Yes?"

"It's so damned hard to explain things of this kind to women. They get hold of the wrong end of the stick—fancy a thing is—well, what it isn't."

Theo said nothing.

"You see," went on Richard, "the law's one thing, and right and wrong are quite another. I may do a thing that's perfectly right and honest, but the law wouldn't take the same view of it. Nine times out of ten, everything pans out all right, and the tenth time you—well, hit a snag."

Theo began to understand. She thought to herself: "Why am I not surprised? Did I always know, deep down, that he wasn't straight?"

Richard went on talking. He explained himself at unnecessary lengths. Theo was content for him to cloak the actual details of the affair in this mantle of verbosity. The matter concerned a large tract of South African property. Exactly what Richard had done, she was not concerned to know. Morally, he assured her, everything was fair and aboveboard; legally—well, there it was; no getting away from the fact, he had rendered himself liable to criminal prosecution.

He kept shooting quick glances at his wife as he talked. He was nervous and uncomfortable. And still he excused himself and tried to explain away that which a child might have seen in its naked truth. Then finally in a burst of justification, he broke down. Perhaps Theo's eyes, momentarily scornful, had something to do with it. He sank down in a chair by the fireplace, his head in his hands.

"There it is, Theo," he said brokenly. "What are you going to do about it?"

She came over to him with scarcely a moment's pause and, kneeling down by the chair, put her face against his.

"What can be done, Richard? What can we do?"

He caught her to him.

"You mean it? You'll stick to me?"

"Of course. My dear, of course."

He said, moved to sincerity in spite of himself: "I'm a thief, Theo. That's what it means, shorn of fine language—just a thief."

"Then I'm a thief's wife, Richard. We'll sink or swim together."

They were silent for a little while. Presently Richard recovered something of his jaunty manner.

"You know, Theo, I've got a plan, but we'll talk of that later. It's just on dinnertime. We must go and change. Put on that creamy thingummybob of yours, you know—the Caillot model."

Theo raised her eyebrows quizzically.

"For an evening at home?"

"Yes, yes, I know. But I like it. Put it on, there's a good girl. It cheers me up to see you looking your best."

Theo came down to dinner in the Caillot. It was a creation in creamy brocade, with a faint pattern of gold running through it and an undernote of pale pink to give warmth to the cream. It was cut daringly low in the back, and nothing could have been better designed to show off the dazzling whiteness of Theo's neck and shoulders. She was truly now a magnolia flower.

Richard's eye rested upon her in warm approval. "Good girl. You know, you look simply stunning in that dress."

They went in to dinner. Throughout the evening Richard was nervous and unlike himself, joking and laughing about nothing at all, as if in a vain attempt to shake off his cares. Several times Theo tried to lead him back to the subject they had been discussing before, but he edged away from it.

Then suddenly, as she rose to go to bed, he came to the point.

"No, don't go yet. I've got something to say. You know, about this miserable business."

She sat down again.

He began talking rapidly. With a bit of luck, the whole thing could be hushed up. He had covered his tracks fairly well. So long as certain papers didn't get into the receiver's hands—

He stopped significantly.

"Papers?" asked Theo perplexedly. "You mean you will destroy them?"

Richard made a grimace.

"I'd destroy them fast enough if I could get hold of them. That's the devil of it all!"

"Who has them, then?"

"A man we both know—Vincent Easton."

A very faint exclamation escaped Theo. She forced it back, but Richard had noticed it.

"I've suspected he knew something of the business all along. That's why I've asked him here a good bit. You may remember that I asked you to be nice to him?"

"I remember," said Theo.

"Somehow I never seem to have got on really friendly terms with him. Don't know why. But he likes you. I should say he likes you a good deal."

Theo said in a very clear voice: "He does."

"Ah!" said Richard appreciatively. "That's good. Now you see what I'm driving at. I'm convinced that if you went to Vincent Easton and asked him to give you those papers, he wouldn't refuse. Pretty woman, you know—all that sort of thing."

"I can't do that," said Theo quickly.

"Nonsense."

"It's out of the question."

The red came slowly out in blotches on Richard's face. She saw that he was angry.

"My dear girl, I don't think you quite realize the position. If this comes out, I'm liable to go to prison. It's ruin—disgrace."

"Vincent Easton will not use those papers against you. I am sure of that."

"That's not quite the point. He mayn't realize that they

incriminate me. It's only taken in conjunction with—with my affairs—with the figures they're bound to find. Oh! I can't go into details. He'll ruin me without knowing what he's doing unless somebody puts the position before him."

"You can do that yourself, surely. Write to him."

"A fat lot of good that would be! No, Theo, we've only got one hope. You're the trump card. You're my wife. You must help me. Go to Easton tonight—"

A cry broke from Theo.

"Not tonight. Tomorrow perhaps."

"My God, Theo, can't you realize things? Tomorrow may be too late. If you could go now—at once—to Easton's rooms." He saw her flinch, and tried to reassure her. "I know, my dear girl, I know. It's a beastly thing to do. But it's life or death. Theo, you won't fail me? You said you'd do anything to help me—"

Theo heard herself speaking in a hard, dry voice. "Not this thing. There are reasons."

"It's life or death, Theo. I mean it. See here."

He snapped open a drawer of the desk and took out a revolver. If there was something theatrical about that action, it escaped her notice.

"It's that or shooting myself. I can't face the racket. If you won't do as I ask you, I'll be a dead man before morning. I swear to you solemnly that that's the truth."

Theo gave a low cry. "No, Richard, not that!"

"Then help me."

He flung the revolver down on the table and knelt by her side. "Theo my darling—if you love me—if you've ever loved me—do this for me. You're my wife, Theo, I've no one else to turn to."

On and on his voice went, murmuring, pleading. And at last Theo heard her own voice saying: "Very well—yes."

Richard took her to the door and put her into a taxi.

"Theo!"

Vincent Easton sprang up in incredulous delight. She stood in the doorway. Her wrap of white ermine was hanging from her shoulders. Never, Easton thought, had she looked so beautiful.

"You've come after all."

She put out a hand to stop him as he came towards her.

"No, Vincent, this isn't what you think."

She spoke in a low, hurried voice.

"I'm here from my husband. He thinks there are some papers which may—do him harm. I have come to ask you to give them to me."

Vincent stood very still, looking at her. Then he gave a short laugh.

"So that's it, is it? I thought Hobson, Jekyll and Lucas sounded familiar the other day, but I couldn't place them at the minute. Didn't know your husband was connected with the firm. Things have been going wrong there for some time. I was commissioned to look into the matter. I suspected some underling. Never thought of the man at the top."

Theo said nothing. Vincent looked at her curiously.

"It makes no difference to you, this?" he asked. "That—well, to put it plainly, that your husband's a swindler?"

She shook her head.

"It beats me," said Vincent. Then he added quietly: "Will you wait a minute or two? I will get the papers."

Theo sat down in a chair. He went into the other room. Presently he returned and delivered a small package into her hand.

"Thank you," said Theo. "Have you a match?"

Taking the matchbox he proffered, she knelt down by the fireplace. When the papers were reduced to a pile of ashes, she stood up.

"Thank you," she said again.

"Not at all," he answered formally. "Let me get you a taxi."

He put her into it, saw her drive away. A strange, formal little interview. After the first, they had not even dared look at each other. Well, that was that, the end. He would go away, abroad, try and forget.

Theo leaned her head out of the window and spoke to the taxi driver. She could not go back at once to the house in Chelsea. She must have a breathing space. Seeing Vincent again had shaken her horribly. If only—if only. But she pulled herself up. Love for her husband she had none—but she owed him loyalty. He was down, she must stick by him. Whatever else he might have done, he loved her; his offence had been committed against society, not against her.

The taxi meandered on through the wide streets of Hampstead. They came out on the heath, and a breath of cool, invigorating air fanned Theo's cheeks. She had herself in hand again now. The taxi sped back towards Chelsea.

Richard came out to meet her in the hall.

"Well," he demanded, "you've been a long time."

"Have I?"

"Yes—a very long time. Is it—all right?"

He followed her, a cunning look in his eyes. His hands were shaking.

"It's—it's all right, eh?" he said again.

"I burnt them myself."

"Oh!"

She went on into the study, sinking into a big armchair. Her face was dead white and her whole body drooped with fatigue. She thought to herself: "If only I could go to sleep now and never, never wake up again!"

Richard was watching her. His glance, shy, furtive, kept coming and going. She noticed nothing. She was beyond noticing.

"It went off quite all right, eh?"

"I've told you so."

"You're sure they were the right papers? Did you look?"

"No."

"But then—"

"I'm sure, I tell you. Don't bother me, Richard. I can't bear any more tonight."

Richard shifted nervously.

"No, no. I see."

He fidgeted about the room. Presently he came over to her, laid a hand on her shoulder. She shook it off.

"Don't touch me." She tried to laugh. "I'm sorry, Richard. My nerves are on edge. I feel I can't bear to be touched."

"I know. I understand."

Again he wandered up and down.

"Theo," he burst out suddenly. "I'm damned sorry."

"What?" She looked up, vaguely startled.

"I oughtn't to have let you go there at this time of night. I never dreamed that you'd be subjected to any—unpleasantness."

"Unpleasantness?" She laughed. The word seemed to amuse her. "You don't know! Oh, Richard, you don't know!"

"I don't know what?"

She said very gravely, looking straight in front of her: "What this night has cost me."

"My God! Theo! I never meant—You—you did that, for me? The swine! Theo—Theo—I couldn't have known. I couldn't have guessed. My God!"

He was kneeling by her now stammering, his arms round her, and she turned and looked at him with faint surprise, as though his words had at last really penetrated to her attention.

"I—I never meant—"

"You never meant what, Richard?"

Her voice startled him.

"Tell me. What was it that you never meant?"

"Theo, don't let us speak of it. I don't want to know. I want never to think of it."

She was staring at him, wide awake now, with every faculty alert. Her words came clear and distinct:

"You never meant—What do you think happened?"

"It didn't happen, Theo. Let's say it didn't happen."

And still she stared, till the truth began to come to her.

"You think that—"

"I don't want—"

She interrupted him: "You think that Vincent Easton asked a price for those letters? You think that I—paid him?"

Richard said weakly and unconvincingly: "I—I never dreamed he was that kind of man."

"Didn't you?" She looked at him searchingly. His eyes fell before hers. "Why did you ask me to put on this dress this evening? Why did you send me there alone at this time of night? You guessed he—cared for me. You wanted to save your skin—save it at any cost—even at the cost of my honour." She got up.

"I see now. You meant that from the beginning—or at least you saw it as a possibility, and it didn't deter you."

"Theo—"

"You can't deny it. Richard, I thought I knew all there was to know about you years ago. I've known almost from the first that you weren't straight as regards the world. But I thought you were straight with me."

"Theo—"

"Can you deny what I've just been saying?"

He was silent, in spite of himself.

"Listen, Richard. There is something I must tell you. Three days ago when this blow fell on you, the servants told you I was away—gone to the country. That was only partly true. I had gone away with Vincent Easton—"

Richard made an inarticulate sound. She held out a hand to stop him.

"Wait. We were at Dover. I saw a paper—I realized what had happened. Then, as you know, I came back."

She paused.

Richard caught her by the wrist. His eyes burnt into hers.

"You came back—in time?"

Theo gave a short, bitter laugh.

"Yes, I came back, as you say, 'in time,' Richard."

Her husband relinquished his hold on her arm. He stood by the mantelpiece, his head thrown back. He looked handsome and rather noble.

"In that case," he said, "I can forgive."

"I cannot."

The two words came crisply. They had the semblance and the effect of a bomb in the quiet room. Richard started forward, staring, his jaw dropped with an almost ludicrous effect.

"You—er—what did you say, Theo?"

"I said I cannot forgive! In leaving you for another man. I sinned—not technically, perhaps, but in intention, which is the same thing. But if I sinned, I sinned through love. You, too, have not been faithful to me since our marriage. Oh, yes, I know. That I forgave, because I really believed in your love for me. But the thing you have done tonight is different. It is an ugly thing, Richard—a thing no woman should forgive. You sold me, your own wife, to purchase safety!"

She picked up her wrap and turned towards the door.

"Theo," he stammered out, "where are you going?"

She looked back over her shoulder at him.

"We all have to pay in this life, Richard. For my sin I must pay in loneliness. For yours—well, you gambled with the thing you love, and you have lost it!"

"You are going?"

She drew a long breath.

"To freedom. There is nothing to bind me here."

He heard the door shut. Ages passed, or was it a few minutes? Something fluttered down outside the window—the last of the magnolia petals, soft, fragrant.

The Love Detectives

Little Mr. Satterthwaite looked thoughtfully across at his host. The friendship between these two men was an odd one. The colonel was a simple country gentleman whose passion in life was sport. The few weeks that he spent perforce in London, he spent unwillingly. Mr. Satterthwaite, on the other hand, was a town bird. He was an authority on French cooking, on ladies' dress, and on all the latest scandals. His passion was observing human nature, and he was an expert in his own special line—that of an onlooker at life.

It would seem, therefore, that he and Colonel Melrose would have little in common, for the colonel had no interest in his neighbours' affairs and a horror of any kind of emotion. The two men were friends mainly because their fathers before them had been friends. Also they knew the same people and had reactionary views about *nouveaux riches.*

It was about half past seven. The two men were sitting in the colonel's comfortable study, and Melrose was describing a run of the previous winter with a keen hunting man's enthusiasm. Mr. Satterthwaite, whose knowledge of horses consisted chiefly of the time-honoured Sunday morning visit to the stables which still obtains in old-fashioned country houses, listened with his invariable politeness.

The sharp ringing of the telephone interrupted Melrose. He crossed to the table and took up the receiver.

"Hello, yes—Colonel Melrose speaking. What's that?" His whole demeanour altered—became stiff and official. It was the magistrate speaking now, not the sportsman.

He listened for some moments, then said laconically, "Right, Curtis. I'll be over at once." He replaced the receiver and turned to his guest. "Sir James Dwighton has been found in his library—murdered."

"What?"

Mr. Satterthwaite was startled—thrilled.

"I must go over to Alderway at once. Care to come with me?"

Mr. Satterthwaite remembered that the colonel was chief constable of the country.

"If I shan't be in the way—" He hesitated.

"Not at all. That was Inspector Curtis telephoning. Good, honest fellow, but no brains. I'd be glad if you would come with me, Satterthwaite. I've got an idea this is going to turn out a nasty business."

"Have they got the fellow who did it?"

"No," replied Melrose shortly.

Mr. Satterthwaite's trained ear detected a nuance of reserve behind the curt negative. He began to go over in his mind all that he knew of the Dwightons.

A pompous old fellow, the late Sir James, brusque in his

manner. A man that might easily make enemies. Veering on sixty, with grizzled hair and a florid face. Reputed to be tightfisted in the extreme.

His mind went on to Lady Dwighton. Her image floated before him, young, auburn-haired, slender. He remembered various rumours, hints, odd bits of gossip. So that was it—that was why Melrose looked so glum. Then he pulled himself up—his imagination was running away with him.

Five minutes later Mr. Satterthwaite took his place beside his host in the latter's little two-seater, and they drove off together into the night.

The colonel was a taciturn man. They had gone quite a mile and a half before he spoke. Then he jerked out abruptly. "You know 'em, I suppose?"

"The Dwightons? I know all about them, of course." Who was there Mr. Satterthwaite didn't know all about? "I've met him once, I think, and her rather oftener."

"Pretty woman," said Melrose.

"Beautiful!" declared Mr. Satterthwaite.

"Think so?"

"A pure Renaissance type," declared Mr. Satterthwaite, warming up to his theme. "She acted in those theatricals—the charity matinee, you know, last spring. I was very much struck. Nothing modern about her—a pure survival. One can imagine her in the doge's palace, or as Lucrezia Borgia."

The colonel let the car swerve slightly, and Mr. Satterthwaite came to an abrupt stop. He wondered what fatality had brought the name of Lucrezia Borgia to his tongue. Under the circumstances—

"Dwighton was not poisoned, was he?" he asked abruptly.

Melrose looked at him sideways, somewhat curiously. "Why do you ask that, I wonder?" he said.

"Oh, I—I don't know." Mr. Satterthwaite was flustered. "I—It just occurred to me."

"Well, he wasn't," said Melrose gloomily. "If you want to know, he was crashed on the head."

"With a blunt instrument," murmured Mr. Satterthwaite, nodding his head sagely.

"Don't talk like a damned detective story, Satterthwaite. He was hit on the head with a bronze figure."

"Oh," said Satterthwaite, and relapsed into silence.

"Know anything of a chap called Paul Delangua?" asked Melrose after a minute or two.

"Yes. Good-looking young fellow."

"I daresay women would call him so," growled the colonel.

"You don't like him?"

"No, I don't."

"I should have thought you would have. He rides very well."

"Like a foreigner at the horse show. Full of monkey tricks."

Mr. Satterthwaite suppressed a smile. Poor old Melrose was so very British in his outlook. Agreeably conscious himself of a cosmopolitan point of view, Mr. Satterthwaite was able to deplore the insular attitude toward life.

"Has he been down in this part of the world?" he asked.

"He's been staying at Alderway with the Dwightons. The rumour goes that Sir James kicked him out a week ago."

"Why?"

"Found him making love to his wife, I suppose. What the hell—"

There was a violent swerve, and a jarring impact.

"Most dangerous crossroads in England," said Melrose. "All the same, the other fellow should have sounded his horn. We're on the main road. I fancy we've damaged him rather more than he has damaged us."

He sprang out. A figure alighted from the other car and joined him. Fragments of speech reached Satterthwaite.

"Entirely my fault, I'm afraid," the stranger was saying. "But I do not know this part of the country very well, and there's absolutely no sign of any kind to show you're coming onto the main road."

The colonel, mollified, rejoined suitably. The two men bent together over the stranger's car, which a chauffeur was already examining. The conversation became highly technical.

"A matter of half an hour, I'm afraid," said the stranger. "But don't let me detain you. I'm glad your car escaped injury as well as it did."

"As a matter of fact—" the colonel was beginning, but he was interrupted.

Mr. Satterthwaite, seething with excitement, hopped out of the car with a birdlike action, and seized the stranger warmly by the hand.

"It *is!* I thought I recognized the voice," he declared excitedly. "What an extraordinary thing. What a very extraordinary thing."

"Eh?" said Colonel Melrose.

"Mr. Harley Quin. Melrose, I'm sure you've heard me speak many times of Mr. Quin?"

Colonel Melrose did not seem to remember the fact, but he assisted politely at the scene while Mr. Satterthwaite was chirruping gaily on. "I haven't seen you—let me see—"

"Since the night at the Bells and Motley," said the other quietly.

"The Bells and Motley, eh?" said the colonel.

"An inn," explained Mr. Satterthwaite.

"What an odd name for an inn."

"Only an old one," said Mr. Quin. "There was a time, remember, when bells and motley were more common in England than they are nowadays."

"I suppose so, yes, no doubt you are right," said Melrose vaguely. He blinked. By a curious effect of light—the headlights of one car and the red taillight of the other—Mr. Quin seemed for a moment to be dressed in motley himself. But it was only the light.

"We can't leave you here stranded on the road," continued Mr. Satterthwaite. "You must come along with us. There's plenty of room for three, isn't there, Melrose?"

"Oh rather." But the colonel's voice was a little doubtful. "The only thing is," he remarked, "the job we're on. Eh, Satterthwaite?"

Mr. Satterthwaite stood stock-still. Ideas leaped and flashed over him. He positively shook with excitement.

"No," he cried. "No, I should have known better! There is no chance where you are concerned, Mr. Quin. It was not an accident that we all met tonight at the crossroads."

Colonel Melrose stared at his friend in astonishment. Mr. Satterthwaite took him by the arm.

"You remember what I told you—about our friend

Derek Capel? The motive for his suicide, which no one could guess? It was Mr. Quin who solved that problem—and there have been others since. He shows you things that are there all the time, but which you haven't seen. He's marvellous."

"My dear Satterthwaite, you are making me blush," said Mr. Quin, smiling. "As far as I can remember, these discoveries were all made by you, not by me."

"They were made because you were there," said Mr. Satterthwaite with intense conviction.

"Well," said Colonel Melrose, clearing his throat uncomfortably. "We mustn't waste any more time. Let's get on."

He climbed into the driver's seat. He was not too well pleased at having the stranger foisted upon him through Mr. Satterthwaite's enthusiasm, but he had no valid objection to offer, and he was anxious to get on to Alderway as fast as possible.

Mr. Satterthwaite urged Mr. Quin in next, and himself took the outside seat. The car was a roomy one and took three without undue squeezing.

"So you are interested in crime, Mr. Quin?" said the colonel, doing his best to be genial.

"No, not exactly in crime."

"What, then?"

Mr. Quin smiled. "Let us ask Mr. Satterthwaite. He is a very shrewd observer."

"I think," said Satterthwaite slowly, "I may be wrong, but I think—that Mr. Quin is interested in—lovers."

He blushed as he said the last word, which is one no Englishman can pronounce without self-consciousness.

Mr. Satterthwaite brought it out apologetically, and with an effect of inverted commas.

"By gad!" said the colonel, startled and silenced.

He reflected inwardly that this seemed to be a very rum friend of Satterthwaite's. He glanced at him sideways. The fellow looked all right—quite a normal young chap. Rather dark, but not at all foreign-looking.

"And now," said Satterthwaite importantly, "I must tell you all about the case."

He talked for some ten minutes. Sitting there in the darkness, rushing through the night, he had an intoxicating feeling of power. What did it matter if he were only a looker-on at life? He had words at his command, he was master of them, he could string them to a pattern—a strange Renaissance pattern composed of the beauty of Laura Dwighton, with her white arms and red hair—and the shadowy dark figure of Paul Delangua, whom women found handsome.

Set that against the background of Alderway—Alderway that had stood since the days of Henry VII and, some said, before that. Alderway that was English to the core, with its clipped yew and its old beak barn and the fishpond, where monks had kept their carp for Fridays.

In a few deft strokes he had etched in Sir James, a Dwighton who was a true descendant of the old De Wittons, who long ago had wrung money out of the land and locked it fast in coffers, so that whoever else had fallen on evil days, the masters of Alderway had never become impoverished.

At last Mr. Satterthwaite ceased. He was sure, had been

sure all along, of the sympathy of his audience. He waited now the word of praise which was his due. It came.

"You are an artist, Mr. Satterthwaite."

"I—I do my best." The little man was suddenly humble.

They had turned in at the lodge gates some minutes ago. Now the car drew up in front of the doorway, and a police constable came hurriedly down the steps to meet them.

"Good evening, sir. Inspector Curtis is in the library."

"Right."

Melrose ran up the steps followed by the other two. As the three of them passed across the wide hall, an elderly butler peered from a doorway apprehensively. Melrose nodded to him.

"Evening, Miles. This is a sad business."

"It is indeed," the other quavered. "I can hardly believe it, sir; indeed I can't. To think that anyone should strike down the master."

"Yes, yes," said Melrose, cutting him short. "I'll have a talk with you presently."

He strode on to the library. There a big, soldierly-looking inspector greeted him with respect.

"Nasty business, sir. I have not disturbed things. No fingerprints on the weapon. Whoever did it knew his business."

Mr. Satterthwaite looked at the bowed figure sitting at the big writing table, and looked hurriedly away again. The man had been struck down from behind, a smashing blow that had crashed in the skull. The sight was not a pretty one.

The weapon lay on the floor—a bronze figure about two feet high, the base of it stained and wet. Mr. Satterthwaite bent over it curiously.

"A Venus," he said softly. "So he was struck down by Venus."

He found food for poetic meditation in the thought.

"The windows," said the inspector, "were all closed and bolted on the inside."

He paused significantly.

"Making an inside job of it," said the chief constable reluctantly. "Well—well, we'll see."

The murdered man was dressed in golf clothes, and a bag of golf clubs had been flung untidily across a big leather couch.

"Just come in from the links," explained the inspector, following the chief constable's glance. "At five fifteen, that was. Had tea brought here by the butler. Later he rang for his valet to bring him down a pair of soft slippers. As far as we can tell, the valet was the last person to see him alive."

Melrose nodded, and turned his attention once more to the writing table.

A good many of the ornaments had been overturned and broken. Prominent among these was a big dark enamel clock, which lay on its side in the very centre of the table.

The inspector cleared his throat.

"That's what you might call a piece of luck, sir," he said. "As you see, it's stopped. *At half past six.* That gives us the time of the crime. Very convenient."

The colonel was staring at the clock.

"As you say," he remarked. "Very convenient." He paused a minute, and then added, "Too damned convenient! I don't like it, Inspector."

He looked around at the other two. His eye sought Mr. Quin's with a look of appeal in it.

"Damn it all," he said. "It's too neat. You know what I mean. Things don't happen like that."

"You mean," murmured Mr. Quin, "that clocks don't fall like that?"

Melrose stared at him for a moment, then back at the clock, which had that pathetic and innocent look familiar to objects which have been suddenly bereft of their dignity. Very carefully Colonel Melrose replaced it on its legs again. He struck the table a violent blow. The clock rocked, but it did not fall. Melrose repeated the action, and very slowly, with a kind of unwillingness, the clock fell over on its back.

"What time was the crime discovered?" demanded Melrose sharply.

"Just about seven o'clock, sir."

"Who discovered it?"

"The butler."

"Fetch him in," said the chief constable. "I'll see him now. Where is Lady Dwighton, by the way?"

"Lying down, sir. Her maid says that she's prostrated and can't see anyone."

Melrose nodded, and Inspector Curtis went in search of the butler. Mr. Quin was looking thoughtfully into the fireplace. Mr. Satterthwaite followed his example. He blinked at the smouldering logs for a minute or two, and then something bright lying in the gratc caught his eye. He stooped and picked up a little sliver of curved glass.

"You wanted me, sir?"

It was the butler's voice, still quavering and uncertain. Mr. Satterthwaite slipped the fragment of glass into his waistcoat pocket and turned around.

The old man was standing in the doorway.

"Sit down," said the chief constable kindly. "You're shaking all over. It's been a shock to you, I expect."

"It has indeed, sir."

"Well, I shan't keep you long. Your master came in just after five, I believe?"

"Yes, sir. He ordered tea to be brought to him here. Afterward, when I came to take it away, he asked for Jennings to be sent to him—that's his valet, sir."

"What time was that?"

"About ten minutes past six, sir."

"Yes—well?"

"I sent word to Jennings, sir. And it wasn't till I came in here to shut the windows and draw the curtains at seven o'clock that I saw—"

Melrose cut him short. "Yes, yes, you needn't go into all that. You didn't touch the body, or disturb anything, did you?"

"Oh! No indeed, sir! I went as fast as I could go to the telephone to ring up the police."

"And then?"

"I told Jane—her ladyship's maid, sir—to break the news to her ladyship."

"You haven't seen your mistress at all this evening?"

Colonel Melrose put the question casually enough, but Mr. Satterthwaite's keen ears caught anxiety behind the words.

"Not to speak to, sir. Her ladyship has remained in her own apartments since the tragedy."

"Did you see her before?"

The question came sharply, and everyone in the room noted the hesitation before the butler replied.

"I—I just caught a glimpse of her, sir, descending the staircase."

"Did she come in here?"

Mr. Satterthwaite held his breath.

"I—I think so, sir."

"What time was that?"

You might have heard a pin drop. Did the old man know, Mr. Satterthwaite wondered, what hung on his answer?

"It was just upon half past six, sir."

Colonel Melrose drew a deep breath. "That will do, thank you. Just send Jennings, the valet, to me, will you?"

Jennings answered the summons with promptitude. A narrow-faced man with a catlike tread. Something sly and secretive about him.

A man, thought Mr. Satterthwaite, *who would easily murder his master if he could be sure of not being found out.*

He listened eagerly to the man's answers to Colonel Melrose's questions. But his story seemed straightforward enough. He had brought his master down some soft hide slippers and removed the brogues.

"What did you do after that, Jennings?"

"I went back to the stewards' room, sir."

"At what time did you leave your master?"

"It must have been just after a quarter past six, sir."

"Where were you at half past six, Jennings?"

"In the stewards' room, sir."

Colonel Melrose dismissed the man with a nod. He looked across at Curtis inquiringly.

"Quite correct, sir, I checked that up. He was in the stewards' room from about six twenty until seven o'clock."

"Then that lets him out," said the chief constable a trifle regretfully. "Besides, there's no motive."

They looked at each other.

There was a tap at the door.

"Come in," said the colonel.

A scared-looking lady's maid appeared.

"If you please, her ladyship has heard that Colonel Melrose is here and she would like to see him."

"Certainly," said Melrose. "I'll come at once. Will you show me the way?"

But a hand pushed the girl aside. A very different figure now stood in the doorway. Laura Dwighton looked like a visitor from another world.

She was dressed in a clinging medieval tea gown of dull blue brocade. Her auburn hair was parted in the middle and brought down over her ears. Conscious of the fact she had a style of her own, Lady Dwighton had never had her hair cut. It was drawn back into a simple knot on the nape of her neck. Her arms were bare.

One of them was outstretched to steady herself against the frame of the doorway, the other hung down by her side, clasping a book. *She looks,* Mr. Satterthwaite thought, *like a Madonna from an early Italian canvas.*

She stood there, swaying slightly from side to side. Colonel Melrose sprang toward her.

"I've come to tell you—to tell you—"

Her voice was low and rich. Mr. Satterthwaite was so entranced with the dramatic value of the scene that he had forgotten its reality.

"Please, Lady Dwighton—" Melrose had an arm round

her, supporting her. He took her across the hall into a small anteroom, its walls hung with faded silk. Quin and Satterthwaite followed. She sank down on the low settee, her head resting back on a rust-coloured cushion, her eyelids closed. The three men watched her. Suddenly she opened her eyes and sat up. She spoke very quietly.

"I killed him," she said. "That's what I came to tell you. *I killed him!*"

There was a moment's agonized silence. Mr. Satterthwaite's heart missed a beat.

"Lady Dwighton," said Melrose. "You've had a great shock—you're unstrung. I don't think you quite know what you're saying."

Would she draw back now—while there was yet time?

"I know perfectly what I'm saying. It was I who shot him."

Two of the men in the room gasped, the other made no sound. Laura Dwighton leaned still farther forward.

"Don't you understand? I came down and shot him. I admit it."

The book she had been holding in her hand clattered to the floor. There was a paper cutter in it, a thing shaped like a dagger with a jewelled hilt. Mr. Satterthwaite picked it up mechanically and placed it on the table. As he did so he thought, *That's a dangerous toy. You could kill a man with that.*

"Well—" Laura Dwighton's voice was impatient. "—what are you going to do about it? Arrest me? Take me away?"

Colonel Melrose found his voice with difficulty.

"What you have told me is very serious, Lady Dwighton.

I must ask you to go to your room till I have—er—made arrangements."

She nodded and rose to her feet. She was quite composed now, grave and cold.

As she turned toward the door, Mr. Quin spoke. "What did you do with the revolver, Lady Dwighton?"

A flicker of uncertainty passed across her face. "I—I dropped it there on the floor. No, I think I threw it out of the window—oh! I can't remember now. What does it matter? I hardly knew what I was doing. It doesn't matter, does it?"

"No," said Mr. Quin. "I hardly think it matters."

She looked at him in perplexity with a shade of something that might have been alarm. Then she flung back her head and went imperiously out of the room. Mr. Satterthwaite hastened after her. She might, he felt, collapse at any minute. But she was already halfway up the staircase, displaying no sign of her earlier weakness. The scared-looking maid was standing at the foot of the stairway, and Mr. Satterthwaite spoke to her authoritatively.

"Look after your mistress," he said.

"Yes, sir." The girl prepared to ascend after the blue-robed figure. "Oh, please, sir, they don't suspect him, do they?"

"Suspect whom?"

"Jennings, sir. Oh! Indeed, sir, he wouldn't hurt a fly."

"Jennings? No, of course not. Go and look after your mistress."

"Yes, sir."

The girl ran quickly up the staircase. Mr. Satterthwaite returned to the room he had just vacated.

Colonel Melrose was saying heavily, "Well, I'm jiggered. There's more in this than meets the eye. It—it's like those dashed silly things heroines do in many novels."

"It's unreal," agreed Mr. Satterthwaite. "It's like something on the stage."

Mr. Quin nodded. "Yes, you admire the drama, do you not? You are a man who appreciates good acting when you see it."

Mr. Satterthwaite looked hard at him.

In the silence that followed a far-off sound came to their ears.

"Sounds like a shot," said Colonel Melrose. "One of the keepers, I daresay. That's probably what she heard. Perhaps she went down to see. She wouldn't go close or examine the body. She'd leap at once to the conclusion—"

"Mr. Delangua, sir." It was the old butler who spoke, standing apologetically in the doorway.

"Eh?" said Melrose. "What's that?"

"Mr. Delangua is here, sir, and would like to speak to you if he may."

Colonel Melrose leaned back in his chair. "Show him in," he said grimly.

A moment later Paul Delangua stood in the doorway. As Colonel Melrose had hinted, there was something un-English about him—the easy grace of his movements, the dark, handsome face, the eyes set a little too near together. There hung about him the air of the Renaissance. He and Laura Dwighton suggested the same atmosphere.

"Good evening, gentlemen," said Delangua. He made a little theatrical bow.

"I don't know what your business may be, Mr. Delangua," said Colonel Melrose sharply, "but if it is nothing to do with the matter at hand—"

Delangua interrupted him with a laugh. "On the contrary," he said, "it has everything to do with it."

"What do you mean?"

"I mean," said Delangua quietly, "that I have come to give myself up for the murder of Sir James Dwighton."

"You know what you are saying?" said Melrose gravely.

"Perfectly."

The young man's eyes were riveted to the table.

"I don't understand—"

"Why I give myself up? Call it remorse—call it anything you please. I stabbed him, right enough—you may be quite sure of that." He nodded toward the table. "You've got the weapon there, I see. A very handy little tool. Lady Dwighton unfortunately left it lying around in a book, and I happened to snatch it up."

"One minute," said Colonel Melrose. "Am I to understand that you admit stabbing Sir James with this?" He held the dagger aloft.

"Quite right. I stole in through the window, you know. He had his back to me. It was quite easy. I left the same way."

"Through the window?"

"Through the window, of course."

"And what time was this?"

Delangua hesitated. "Let me see—I was talking to the keeper fellow—that was at a quarter past six. I heard the church tower chime. It must have been—well, say somewhere about half past."

A grim smile came to the colonel's lips.

"Quite right, young man," he said. "Half past six was the time. Perhaps you've heard that already? But this is altogether a most peculiar murder!"

"Why?"

"So many people confess to it," said Colonel Melrose.

They heard the sharp intake of the other's breath.

"Who else has confessed to it?" he asked in a voice that he vainly strove to render steady.

"Lady Dwighton."

Delangua threw back his head and laughed in rather a forced manner. "Lady Dwighton is apt to be hysterical," he said lightly. "I shouldn't pay any attention to what she says if I were you."

"I don't think I shall," said Melrose. "But there's another odd thing about this murder."

"What's that?"

"Well," said Melrose, "Lady Dwighton has confessed to having shot Sir James, and you have confessed to having stabbed him. But luckily for both of you, he wasn't shot or stabbed, you see. His skull was smashed in."

"My God!" cried Delangua. "But a woman couldn't possibly do that—"

He stopped, biting his lip. Melrose nodded with the ghost of a smile.

"Often read of it," he volunteered. "Never seen it happen."

"What?"

"Couple of young idiots each accusing themselves because they thought the other had done it," said Melrose. "Now we've got to begin at the beginning."

"The valet," cried Mr. Satterthwaite. "That girl just now—I wasn't paying any attention at the time." He paused, striving for coherence. "She was afraid of our suspecting him. There must be some motive that he had and which we don't know, but she does."

Colonel Melrose frowned, then he rang the bell. When it was answered, he said, "Please ask Lady Dwighton if she will be good enough to come down again."

They waited in silence until she came. At sight of Delangua she started and stretched out a hand to save herself from falling. Colonel Melrose came quickly to the rescue.

"It's quite all right, Lady Dwighton. Please don't be alarmed."

"I don't understand. What is Mr. Delangua doing here?"

Delangua came over to her, "Laura—Laura—why did you do it?"

"Do it?"

"I know. It was for me—because you thought that—After all, it was natural, I suppose. But, oh! You angel!"

Colonel Melrose cleared his throat. He was a man who disliked emotion and had a horror of anything approaching a "scene."

"If you'll allow me to say so, Lady Dwighton, both you and Mr. Delangua have had a lucky escape. He had just arrived in his turn to 'confess' to the murder—oh, it's quite all right, he didn't do it! But what we want to know is the truth. No more shillyshallying. The butler says you went into the library at half past six—is that so?"

Laura looked at Delangua. He nodded.

"The truth, Laura," he said. "That is what we want now."

She breathed a deep sigh. "I will tell you."

She sank down on a chair that Mr. Satterthwaite had hurriedly pushed forward.

"I did come down. I opened the library door and I saw—"

She stopped and swallowed. Mr. Satterthwaite leaned forward and patted her hand encouragingly.

"Yes," he said. "Yes. You saw?"

"My husband was lying across the writing table. I saw his head—the blood—oh!"

She put her hands to her face. The chief constable leaned forward.

"Excuse me, Lady Dwighton. You thought Mr. Delangua had shot him?"

She nodded. "Forgive me, Paul," she pleaded. "But you said—you said—"

"That I'd shoot him like a dog," said Delangua grimly. "I remember. That was the day I discovered he'd been ill-treating you."

The chief constable kept sternly to the matter in hand.

"Then I am to understand, Lady Dwighton, that you went upstairs again and—er—said nothing. We needn't go into your reason. You didn't touch the body or go near the writing table?"

She shuddered.

"No, no. I ran straight out of the room."

"I see, I see. And what time was this exactly? Do you know?"

"It was just half past six when I got back to my bedroom."

"Then at—say five and twenty past six, Sir James was already dead." The chief constable looked at the others.

"That clock—it was faked, eh? We suspected that all along. Nothing easier than to move the hands to whatever time you wished, but they made a mistake to lay it down on its side like that. Well, that seems to narrow it down to the butler or the valet, and I can't believe it's the butler. Tell me, Lady Dwighton, did this man Jennings have any grudge against your husband?"

Laura lifted her face from her hands. "Not exactly a grudge, but—well, James told me only this morning that he'd dismissed him. He'd found him pilfering."

"Ah! Now we're getting at it. Jennings would have been dismissed without a character. A serious matter for him."

"You said something about a clock," said Laura Dwighton. "There's just a chance—if you want to fix the time—James would have been sure to have his little golf watch on him. Mightn't that have been smashed, too, when he fell forward?"

"It's an idea," said the colonel slowly. "But I'm afraid—Curtis!"

The inspector nodded in quick comprehension and left the room. He returned a minute later. On the palm of his hand was a silver watch marked like a golf ball, the kind that are sold for golfers to carry loose in a pocket with balls.

"Here it is, sir," he said, "but I doubt if it will be any good. They're tough, these watches."

The colonel took it from him and held it to his ear.

"It seems to have stopped, anyway," he observed.

He pressed with his thumb, and the lid of the watch flew open. Inside the glass was cracked across.

"Ah!" he said exultantly.

The hand pointed to exactly a quarter past six.

"A very good glass of port, Colonel Melrose," said Mr. Quin.

It was half past nine, and the three men had just finished a belated dinner at Colonel Melrose's house. Mr. Satterthwaite was particularly jubilant.

"I was quite right," he chuckled. "You can't deny it, Mr. Quin. You turned up tonight to save two absurd young people who were both bent on putting their heads into a noose."

"Did I?" said Mr. Quin. "Surely not. I did nothing at all."

"As it turned out, it was not necessary," agreed Mr. Satterthwaite. "But it might have been. It was touch and go, you know. I shall never forget the moment when Lady Dwighton said, 'I killed him.' I've never seen anything on the stage half as dramatic."

"I'm inclined to agree with you," said Mr. Quin.

"Wouldn't have believed such a thing could happen outside a novel," declared the colonel, for perhaps the twentieth time that night.

"Does it?" asked Mr. Quin.

The colonel stared at him, "Damn it, it happened tonight."

"Mind you," interposed Mr. Satterthwaite, leaning back and sipping his port, "Lady Dwighton was magnificent, quite magnificent, but she made one mistake. She shouldn't have leaped to the conclusion that her husband had been shot. In the same way Delangua was a fool to assume that he had been stabbed just because the dagger happened to be lying on the table in front of us. It was a mere coincidence that Lady Dwighton should have brought it down with her."

"Was it?" asked Mr. Quin.

"Now if they'd only confined themselves to saying that they'd killed Sir James, without particularizing how" —went on Mr. Satterthwaite—"what would have been the result?"

"They might have been believed," said Mr. Quin with an odd smile.

"The whole thing was exactly like a novel," said the colonel.

"That's where they got the idea from, I daresay," said Mr. Quin.

"Possibly," agreed Mr. Satterthwaite. "Things one has read do come back to one in the oddest way." He looked across at Mr. Quin. "Of course," he said, "the clock really looked suspicious from the first. One ought never to forget how easy it is to put the hands of a clock or watch forward or back."

Mr. Quin nodded and repeated the words. "Forward," he said, and paused. "Or back."

There was something encouraging in his voice. His bright, dark eyes were fixed on Mr. Satterthwaite.

"The hands of the clock were put forward," said Mr. Satterthwaite. "We know that."

"Were they?" asked Mr. Quin.

Mr. Satterthwaite stared at him. "Do you mean," he said slowly, "that it was the watch which was put back? But that doesn't make sense. It's impossible."

"Not impossible," murmured Mr. Quin.

"Well—absurd. To whose advantage could that be?"

"Only, I suppose, to someone who had an *alibi* for that time."

"By gad!" cried the colonel. "That's the time young Delangua said he was talking to the keeper."

"He told us that very particularly," said Mr. Satterthwaite.

They looked at each other. They had an uneasy feeling as of solid ground failing beneath their feet. Facts went spinning round, turning new and unexpected faces. And in the centre of the kaleidoscope was the dark, smiling face of Mr. Quin.

"But in that case"—began Melrose—"in that case—"

Mr. Satterthwaite, nimble-witted, finished his sentence for him. "It's all the other way round. A plant just the same—but a plant against the valet. Oh, but it can't be! It's impossible. Why each of them accused themselves of the crime."

"Yes," said Mr. Quin. "Up till then you suspected them, didn't you?" His voice went on, placid and dreamy. "Just like something out of a book, you said, colonel. They got the idea there. It's what the innocent hero and heroine do. Of course it made you think them innocent—there was the force of tradition behind them. Mr. Satterthwaite has been saying all along it was like something on the stage. You were both right. It wasn't real. You've been saying so all along without knowing what you were saying. They'd have told a much better story than that if they'd wanted to be believed."

The two men looked at him helplessly.

"It would be clever," said Mr. Satterthwaite slowly. "It would be diabolically clever. And I've thought of something else. The butler said he went in at seven to shut the windows—so he must have expected them to be open."

"That's the way Delangua came in," said Mr. Quin. "He killed Sir James with one blow, and he and she together did what they had to do—"

He looked at Mr. Satterthwaite, encouraging him to reconstruct the scene. He did so, hesitatingly.

"They smashed the clock and put it on its side. Yes. They altered the watch and smashed it. Then he went out of the window, and she fastened it after him. But there's one thing I don't see. Why bother with the watch at all? Why not simply put back the hands of the clock?"

"The clock was always a little obvious," said Mr. Quin. "Anyone might have seen through a rather transparent device like that."

"But surely the watch was too far-fetched. Why, it was pure chance that we ever thought of the watch."

"Oh, no," said Mr. Quin. "It was the lady's suggestion, remember."

Mr. Satterthwaite stared at him, fascinated.

"And yet, you know," said Mr. Quin dreamily, "the one person who wouldn't be likely to overlook the watch would be the valet. Valets know better than anyone what their masters carry in their pockets. If he altered the clock, the valet would have altered the watch, too. They don't understand human nature, those two. They are not like Mr. Satterthwaite."

Mr. Satterthwaite shook his head.

"I was all wrong," he murmured humbly. "I thought that you had come to save them."

"So I did," said Mr. Quin. "Oh! Not those two—the

others. Perhaps you didn't notice the lady's maid? She wasn't wearing blue brocade, or acting a dramatic part. But she's really a very pretty girl, and I think she loves that man Jennings very much. I think that between you you'll be able to save her man from getting hanged."

"We've no proof of any kind," said Colonel Melrose heavily.

Mr. Quin smiled. "Mr. Satterthwaite has."

"I?" Mr. Satterthwaite was astonished.

Mr. Quin went on. "You've got a proof that that watch wasn't smashed in Sir James's pocket. You can't smash a watch like that without opening the case. Just try it and see. Someone took the watch out and opened it, set back the hands, smashed the glass, and then shut it and put it back. They never noticed that a fragment of glass was missing."

"Oh!" cried Mr. Satterthwaite. His hand flew to his waistcoat pocket. He drew out a fragment of curved glass.

It was his moment.

"With this," said Mr. Satterthwaite importantly, "I shall save a man from death."

Affairs of the Heart

Agatha's Early Courtships

By Agatha Christie

I had two near escapes from getting married. I call them near escapes because, looking back now, I realise with certainty that either of them would have been a disaster.

The first one was what you might call "a young girl's high romance." I was staying with the Ralston Patricks. Constance and I drove to a cold and windy meet, and a man mounted on a nice chestnut rode up to speak to Constance and was introduced to me. Charles was, I suppose, about thirty-five, a major in the 17th Lancers, and he came every year to Warwickshire to hunt. I met him again that evening when there was a fancy dress dance, to which I went dressed as Elaine. A pretty costume: I still have it (and wonder how I could ever have got into it). . . . I met Charles several times during my visit, and when I went back home we both expressed polite wishes that we should meet again some time. He mentioned that he might be down in Devonshire later.

Three or four days after getting home I received a parcel.

In it was a small silver-gilt box. Inside the lid was written: "The Asps," a date, and "To Elaine" below it. The Asps was where the meet had taken place, and the date was the date I had met him. I also got a letter from him saying that he hoped to come to see us the following week when he would be in Devon.

That was the beginning of a lightning courtship. Boxes of flowers arrived, occasional books, enormous boxes of exotic chocolates. Nothing was said that could not have been properly said to a young girl, but I was thrilled. He paid us two more visits, and on the third asked me to marry him. He had, he said, fallen in love with me the first moment he saw me. If one was arranging proposals in order of merit, this one would easily go to the top of my list. I was fascinated and partly carried off my feet by his technique. He was a man with a good deal of experience of women, and able to produce most of the reactions he wanted. I was ready for the first time to consider that here was my Fate, my Mr Right. And yet—yes, there it was—and *yet*. . . . When Charles was there, telling me how wonderful I was, how he loved me, what a perfect Elaine, what an exquisite creature I was, how he would spend his whole life making me happy, and so on, his hands trembling and his voice shaking—oh yes, I was charmed like a bird off a tree. And yet—yet, when he was gone away, when I thought of him in absence, there was nothing there. I did not yearn to see him again. I just felt he was—very nice. The alteration between the two moods puzzled me. How can you tell if you are in love with a person? If in absence they mean nothing to you, and in presence they sweep you off your feet, what is your *real* reaction?

* * *

Charles and I had absolutely nothing to talk about except the fact that he was in love with me. Since he was holding himself back on that subject, there was a great deal of embarrassed silence between us. Then he would go away, and I would sit and wonder. What *did* I want to do? Did I want to marry him? Then I would get a letter from him. He wrote, there was no doubt about it, the most glorious love letters, the kind of love letters that any woman would long to get. I pored over them, re-read them, kept them, decided that this was love at last. Then Charles would come back, and I would be excited, carried off my feet—and yet at the same time had a cold feeling at the back of my mind that it was all wrong. In the end my mother suggested that we should not see each other for six months, and that then I should decide definitely. That was adhered to, and during that period there were no letters—which was probably just as well, because I should have fallen for those letters in the end.

When the six months were up I received a telegram. "Cannot stand this indecision any longer. Will you marry me, yes or no." I was in bed with a slight feverish attack at the time. My mother brought me the telegram. I looked at it and at the reply-paid form. I took a pencil and wrote the word No. Immediately I felt an enormous relief: I had decided something. I should not have to go through any more of this uncomfortable up-and-down feeling.

* * *

Life was rather gloomy during the next four or five months. For the first time everything I did bored me, and I began to feel that I had made a great mistake. Then Wilfred Pirie came back into my life.

Martin and Lilian Pirie [were] my father's great friends, whom we met again abroad, in Dinard. We had continued to meet, though I had not again seen the boys. Harold had been at Eton and Wilfred had been a midshipman in the Navy. Now Wilfred was a fully-fledged sub-lieutenant R.N. He was in a submarine, I think, at that time, and often came in with that portion of the Fleet which visited Torquay. He became an immense friend at once, one of the people in my life I have been fondest of. Within a couple of months we were unofficially engaged.

Wilfred was such a relief after Charles. With him there was no excitement, no doubt, no misery. Here was just a dear friend, somebody I knew well. We read books, discussed them, we had always something to talk about. I was completely at home with him. The fact that I was treating him and considering him exactly like a brother did not occur to me. . . . It seemed a perfect marriage from everyone's point of view. Wilfred had a good career ahead of him in the Navy; our fathers had been the closest friends, and our mothers liked each other; mother liked Wilfred, Mrs. Pirie liked me. I still feel I was a monster of ingratitude not to have married him.

My life was now settled for me. In a year or two, when it was suitable (young subalterns and young sub-lieutenants were not encouraged to marry too soon) we would be married. I liked the idea of marrying a sailor. I should live in lodgings at Southsea, Plymouth, or somewhere like that, and when Wilfred was away on foreign stations I could come home to Ashfield and spend my time with mother. Really, nothing in the world could have been so right.

I suppose there is a horrible kink in one's disposition that tends always to kick against anything that is too right or too perfect. I wouldn't admit it for a long time, but the prospect of marrying Wilfred induced in me a depressing feeling of boredom. I liked him, I would have been happy living in the same house with him, but somehow there wasn't any excitement about it; no excitement at all!

* * *

Then one day Wilfred rang up from Portsmouth and said a wonderful chance had come his way. There was a party being assembled to look for treasure trove in South America. Some leave was due to him and he would be able to go off on this expedition. Would I think it terrible of him if he went? It was the sort of exciting chance that might never happen again. . . . Did I think it awful of him, when he could have spent a good part of his leave with me?

I found myself having not the slightest hesitation. I behaved with splendid unselfishness. I said to him I thought it a wonderful opportunity, that of course he must go. . . . Wilfred said I was wonderful; absolutely wonderful; not a girl in a thousand would behave like that. He rang off, sent me a loving letter, and departed.

But I was not a girl in a thousand; I was just a girl who had found out the truth about herself and was rather ashamed about it. I woke up the day after he had actually sailed with the feeling that an enormous load had slipped off my mind. . . .

"What are you looking so cheerful about?" mother asked suspiciously.

"Listen, mother," I said. "I know it's awful, but I am really cheerful because Wilfred has gone away."

The poor darling. Her face fell. I have never felt so mean, so ungrateful as I did then. She had been so happy about Wilfred and me coming together. For one misguided moment I almost felt that I must go through with it, just for the sake of making her happy. Fortunately, I was not quite so sunk in sentimentality as that.

* * *

I had a letter waiting for him when he came back. I told him how sorry I was, how fond of him I was, but I didn't think that there was really the proper kind of feeling between us to engage each other for life. He didn't agree with me, of course, but he took the decision seriously. He said he didn't think he could bear to see me often, but that we would always remain friendly towards each other. I wonder now if he was relieved as well. I don't think so, but on the other hand I do not think it cut him to the heart. *I* think he was lucky. He would have made me a good husband, and would always have been fond of me, and I think I should have made him quite happy in a quiet way, but he could do better for himself—and about three months later he did. He fell violently in love with another girl, and she fell as violently in love with him. They were married in due course, and had six children. Nothing could have been more satisfactory.

As for Charles, about three years later he married a beautiful girl of eighteen.

Really, what a benefactress I was to those two men.

BIBLIOGRAPHY

Agatha Christie's short stories typically appeared first in magazines and then in her short-story books, which tended to be different collections in the UK and the US. This list attempts to catalogue the first publication of each, and gives alternative story titles when used.

The King of Clubs

First published by *The Sketch* in March 1923 in the UK. *The Blue Book Magazine* published the story in the US in in November 1923. In 1951, the story was published as part of the anthology *The Under Dog and Other Stories* in the US. In the UK, the story was published as part of *Poirot's Early Cases* in 1974.

The Face of Helen

First published as "The Magic of Mr. Quin No. 5" in *The Storyteller* in April 1927. It was then published in the collection *The Mysterious Mr. Quin*, in the UK on April 14, 1930, and in the US later in the same year.

Death on the Nile

First published in the US in April 1933 by *Cosmopolitan*. In the UK it was first published by the *Pall Mall Magazine* in July 1933. It was later included in the collection *Parker Pyne Investigates*, published in 1934 in the UK. The collection published in the same year in the US under the title *Mr. Parker Pyne, Detective*.

Death by Drowning

First published in the UK by the *Pall Mall Magazine* in November 1931. In 1932, the story was published as the last short story in the collection *The Thirteen Problems* in the UK in 1932. The collection was published in the US in 1933 under the title *The Tuesday Club Murders*.

The Double Clue

First published by *The Sketch* in December 1923 in the UK. The story was published in the US in *The Blue Book Magazine* in August 1925. It was included in the anthology *Double Sin and Other Stories* published in 1961 in the US. In the UK the story was not anthologized until 1974 when it was included in *Poirot's Early Cases*. This story is the first appearance of the recurrent character Countess Vera Rossakoff.

Finessing the King / The Gentleman Dressed in Newspaper

First published by *The Sketch* in the UK in October 1924. It was then compiled as part of the collection *Partners in Crime* which came out in both the UK and the US in 1929. The stories in the story arc are resequenced in the collection. "Finessing the King" was the original title in magazines. When the story was split into two for compilation, the second chapter was given the title "The Gentleman Dressed in Newspaper."

Fruitful Sunday

First published in the UK by the *Daily Mail* on August 11, 1928. In the UK the story was published as part of the anthology *The Listerdale Mystery* in 1934. In the US the story was not published until 1971 when it was included in *The Golden Ball and Other Stories.*

Wasps' Nest

First published by the *Daily Mail* on November 20, 1928, in the UK and by *Detective Story Magazine* on March 9, 1929. It was included in the anthology *Double Sin and Other Stories* in 1961 in the US. In the UK, the story was not anthologized until 1974 when it was included in *Poirot's Early Cases.*

The Case of the Caretaker

First published in January 1942 in *Strand* magazine. It was later published in the short-story collections *Three Blind Mice and Other Stories* in the US in 1950 and *Miss Marple's Final Cases and Two Other Stories* in the UK in 1978.

The Man in the Mist

First published on Dec 3, 1924, in *The Sketch*. It was later published in the collection *Partners in Crime* in the US and the UK in 1929.

The Case of the Rich Woman

First published in the US by *Cosmopolitan* in August 1932. It was later included in the collection *Parker Pyne Investigates*, published in 1934 in the UK. The collection published in the same year in the US under the title *Mr. Parker Pyne, Detective.*

Magnolia Blossom

First published in issue 329 of the *Royal Magazine* in March 1926 in the UK. The story was later included in the 1982 story collection *The Agatha Christie Hour* to tie in with a television series of the same name. In the US, it was included in *The Golden Ball and Other Stories* in 1971.

The Love Detectives

First published by *Flynn's Weekly* in 1926 under the title "At the Crossroads." The story was later published in the collection *Three Blind Mice and Other Stories* in the US in 1950. The UK later included it in the collection *Problem at Pollensa Bay* in 1991.

Affairs of the Heart: Agatha's Early Courtships

Excerpted from *An Autobiography* (1975).

ABOUT THE AUTHOR

Agatha Christie is the most widely published author of all time, outsold only by the Bible and Shakespeare. Her books have sold more than a billion copies in English and another billion in a hundred foreign languages. She died in 1976, after a prolific career spanning six decades.